The PMS Outlaws

By Sharyn McCrumb

THE ELIZABETH MACPHERSON NOVELS
Sick of Shadows
Lovely in Her Bones
Highland Laddie Gone
Paying the Piper
The Windsor Knot
Missing Susan
MacPherson's Lament
If I'd Killed Him When I Met Him . . .
The PMS Outlaws

If Ever I Return, Pretty Peggy-O
The Hangman's Beautiful Daughter
She Walks These Hills
The Rosewood Casket
The Ballad of Frankie Silver
Bimbos of the Death Sun
Zombies of the Gene Pool

An Elizabeth MacPherson Novel

The
PMS
Outlaws

SHARYN McCRUMB

BALLANTINE BOOKS

NEW YORK

A Ballantine Book
The Ballantine Publishing Group

Copyright © 2000 by Sharyn McCrumb

www.randomhouse.com/BB/

LIBRARY OF CONGRESS CATALOGING-IN-PUBLICATION DATA
McCrumb, Sharyn, 1948–
The pms outlaws : an Elizabeth MacPherson novel / Sharyn McCrumb.—
1st ed.
p. cm.
ISBN 0-345-38231-5
1. MacPherson, Elizabeth (Fictitious character)—Fiction. 2. Women
forensic anthropologists—Fiction.
3. Forensic anthropology—Fiction. I. Title.

PS3563.C3527 P58 2000
813'.54—dc21
00-040374

Text design by Ann Gold

Manufactured in the United States of America

First Edition: September 2000

10 9 8 7 6 5 4 3 2 1

The PMS Outlaws

Chapter 1

If he stayed chained naked to this post much longer, there just wouldn't be any afterward to the foreplay.

Randy Templeton shivered in the soft darkness, wondering whether the girls would think him ungrateful if he called out to hurry them along. It was damp and nearly dark in the basement of the Lonesome Rose Bar, but mostly it was cold. People could say what they wanted to about extra body fat; the spare tire around his middle wasn't doing a thing to keep him warm. He hated to think what shape he'd be in without it.

Whoever had air-conditioned the roadhouse had made a pitiful job of it, too. The barroom itself was hotter than a hubcap in August, while down here beneath, it felt like penguin heaven. If it weren't so dark, he could probably see his breath. He wondered if the girls would mind the cold. He could suggest someplace more comfortable, but he didn't want to ruin the spontaneity of the occasion. Besides, he wasn't sure that motels in his price range took postdated checks.

Randy hoped there weren't any rats around. He had seen a horror movie once where a guy was chained in a dungeon someplace, and rats had come out and started gnawing on his toes. Just thinking about it made him shiver even more than he already had been. He'd never hear rats over the thump of the jukebox from above. At least he had kept his boots on. He wriggled his wrists in the handcuffs, thinking they must be trick cuffs from a store that specialized in magic items and practical jokes, but the steel bands remained firmly shut, yielding no hidden catch. His fingers were beginning to feel numb. Real handcuffs . . . his mind shied away from any more speculation on this point. What with the cold and all, he was having a hard enough time maintaining the mood without going into philosophical suppositions about sexy and gorgeous chicks who carried regulation handcuffs.

Where were those two girls, anyhow? They said they'd gone off to slip into something leather and scanty, but he didn't hear any giggles around the corner. The jukebox again, probably. Its base notes were rolling across the floor above him in a tidal wave of noise. What were those girls' names again? He couldn't quite remember. Maybe he should just stick to calling them "Honey" and "Darlin' "—women were so touchy about things like proper names. He didn't want to spoil the evening, which was the most exciting thing that had happened to him since he'd got one of the lucky bottle caps in the drink machine at the plant and won a hundred bucks just in time to make a car payment.

He couldn't believe his luck this time. He'd stopped in at

the roadhouse after work for a quick one (by which he meant a drink), and before he could say "Colorado Kool-Aid" (by which he meant Coors), two good-looking women in jean shorts and halter tops had come up to him, one on each side, smiling up at him, until he began to wonder who they had mistaken him for. People did say he looked a little like Randy Travis in the right light—if he sucked in his gut and combed his hair forward over his bald spot.

He thought the game would be up when he told them his name. He said, "I'm Randy . . ." and for a few seconds he thought about saying, ". . . Travis," but nervousness impaired his fluency in lying, and he had blurted out "Templeton," the only word in his otherwise empty brain. They just kept smiling, as if they weren't disappointed at all. Then they started making small talk, only instead of yelling loud enough to be heard over the music, they had whispered up close in his ear, until their tongues almost touched his earlobes. It warmed him up just thinking about it. He had made a few gallant remarks about how the two of them were prettier than . . . something or other. . . . He couldn't quite remember what he had said, but it must have been good, because they had smiled knowingly at him and edged in even closer.

But there were two of them. One part of his mind kept waiting for them to ask him if he had a friend, while his remaining brain cells tried to choose which one he wanted and then decide how to get her away from her companion. One of them was a wiry-looking blonde who looked like she played softball or rode horses—a real tomboy; the other one was a top-heavy Miss America type, just shy of being plump, but with the few extra pounds distributed in some wonderful places. What were

---

their names? They were pretty all right, but they weren't the usual sort of girl that you saw in the Lonesome Rose. They talked like schoolteachers, now that he thought about it: all carefully pronounced words, with proper English as far as he could tell, and not much drawl in their voices. Maybe they were schoolteachers. Maybe those X-rated skin flicks he checked out from the Video Mart & Tanning Parlor, with titles like *Lessons in Lust* and *Sex Ed at Honey High*, were documentaries.

At that point in the conversation, Randy had been thinking that he could star in a skin flick called *Horny Zombie in Deep Shock*, when those two gorgeous creatures made it clear that he didn't have to choose between them. He could have them both. They worked as a team, they said. Well, hot damn.

He had allowed himself to be led to the basement by these two whispering playmates, and his brain had pretty much been in neutral, while the rest of him was going into overdrive. While he was still speechless with astonishment, "Honey" and "Dar-lin' " had whispered intoxicating promises in his ear, and working in tandem they divested him of his clothes before he even had time to think about it.

"If you'll put on these handcuffs, Sugar, we can have a real party," said the wiry blonde.

"Like nothing you ever felt before," cooed the plump Miss America.

Speechless with lust and anticipation, he had made a gurgling sound in his throat and held up his wrists, eager for the games to begin.

That had been . . . oh . . . fifteen minutes ago. The chill of the darkened basement and the fear of creepy-crawly things he could not see had taken the edge off his eagerness for erotic

games, but he was sure that the reappearance of those two lus-
cious beauties would revive him again. Where were they, anyhow? He gave a tug on his handcuffs, but they held as tightly
as ever.

"Hello, darlin'?" he called out tentatively into the darkness. Then he tried to cover his nervousness by making a joke of
it. "That wasn't a Conway Twitty imitation," he said. "But it has
been a long time. Are y'all about ready?"

There was no answer. The rumble of the jukebox continued uninterrupted above him.

"Sweet thangs?" he called out, a little louder now. "Are
you coming? I'm handcuffed naked to this post here."

A few minutes later, the silence had so unnerved him that
he knelt down and picked up a discarded curtain rod to try to
reach for his clothes. He distinctly remembered seeing one of
the girls fold his clothes neatly and place them in the corner. After many minutes of futile prodding with the curtain rod in the
dark corner, he had to face the unpleasant fact that his clothes
and his wallet were gone.

Upstairs on the jukebox, the thunder of drumbeats had
subsided, and, as if in mockery of his predicament, Randy distinctly heard Hank Williams's voice crooning "I'm Walking the
Floor over You."

*"Twenty-five years ago, being
crazy meant something. Now
everybody's crazy."*
—Charles Manson

Chapter 2

"I'm in the living room of our house in Scotland, right? Edinburgh, near the Firth of Forth, which I couldn't bear to look at any more. That cruel stretch of gray water . . ." The soft voice in the darkness faltered.

"Skip that part," said the woman in the circle of lamplight.

"Okay." A sharp intake of breath. "I'm okay now. Living room. The curtains are drawn. And I'm sitting on the sofa, reading a magazine, I think. I'm not too clear on that. I was alone, of course. I might have been watching television, but I doubt it. I don't remember a television program. I was probably reading."

"Go on, please."

"So, anyway, in the silence I hear the front door open and close, and I practically jump out of my skin because I'm so star-

----

tled. I'm thinking that an intruder has got into the house, and I'm wondering whether to run or to pick up the poker from the fireplace and go down fighting."

"You think the person who has come in is an intruder?"

"A burglar, maybe. Someone who didn't belong there, any-how. And I'm wavering between fight or flight."

"Which option did you choose?"

"Well, neither of them, really. It all happens too fast. I get up from the sofa, and I take a few steps toward the front hall to see who's there, and then I start to scream."

"In terror?"

"No. Shock. I'm rooted to the spot, waiting to see who it is. And then I'm laughing and crying at the same time, because there in the hall, dripping wet in his old mackintosh and muddy boots is my husband, Cameron Dawson. He went away on an expedition in the North Sea weeks and weeks ago, in a tiny, dilapidated boat, and no one had heard from him since. The boat is missing. He's gone. So, of course, I've been just out of my mind with grief and fear. We had been married only a couple of years, and I had just about given up on him. Then, without a word of warning, the door just opens and in he walks, with a scruffy beard and a sheepish grin, like 'Hi, honey! I'm back,' as if he had only been gone for the afternoon. And I'm too stunned to yell at him for scaring me half to death. I throw myself into his arms, still scream-ing for joy."

"And then what?"

Elizabeth MacPherson's voice quavered. "And then . . . I wake up."

Cherry Hill Psychiatric Hospital
Thursday. Or not.

Dear Bill,

I am as well as can be expected, I suppose. After weeks and weeks of being unutterably weary, and unwilling to stir from my bed, I finally got tired of all the collective nagging from family and friends, and I took myself back to see Dr. Freya. We had been talking about Cameron for weeks already, so she knew about his disappearance, and all my emotional problems resulting from it. But suddenly the fact that he was gone just hit me so hard. I told her about the dream. Over and over, I dream that he comes walking back through the door of our house in Edinburgh. I told her that whenever I tried to read, I'd find myself skimming the same page over and over and I couldn't remember what I'd read.

"Anything else?" she said in that brisk tone of hers, as if she were a mechanic checking out a carburetor.

"Well . . . There's the fact that I can't seem to stop crying," I said.

"I see."

"It's been weeks since it happened, but I'm worse now than I was when Cameron first disappeared," I told her.

"Yes. It happens like that," Dr. Freya said.

I shredded the sodden tissue I'd kept balled in my fist. "I guess I'm losing my faith."

She shook her head. "It isn't a bad sign. Perhaps you are . . . accepting. No longer in denial."

Well, at that I started to cry again, because I realized that nobody thought Cameron was coming back. I had been subconsciously hoping that Dr. Freya would say something about teaching me deep breathing and meditation exercises to keep me calm until Cameron's rescue, but she was treating me like a bereavement case. As if I were a—a widow. I cried even louder. Said I didn't want to live any more.

She sat there in silence for maybe a minute—it seemed like a month—while I groped for more tissues and tried to get a grip on myself, and then she said, "I think you should go someplace for a rest."

Very ominous remark, that, coming from your shrink. Between sobs I said, "A rest? Where?"

"Cherry Hill," she said.

When I took a sudden gulp of air and started to laugh, Dr. Freya sighed and began to make little notes on her legal pad, but I assured her I wasn't becoming hysterical. It really was funny.

"You heard of it?" she asked me.

"Heard of it?" I hooted. "Cherry Hill is my family's Club Med. Our vacation spot of choice. My delusional cousin Eileen was in there for ages, and I think her brother, Charles, went in once for a couple of weeks to see if they could talk him out of wanting to be a physicist, and then Aunt Amanda went in for her drinking problem. Mother took some counseling sessions there after the divorce to figure out why she wasn't attracted to women. . . . They were no help, though. Mel Gibson still makes her drool. Why, Cherry Hill is like a second home to our family. We ought to hold the reunions there."

Dr. Freya ignored me. She always does when I babble. "It's a fine treatment center, particularly for depression," she said briskly. "I'd like you to check yourself in as a voluntary patient. As you move from denial into the other stages of loss, you will need to receive more intensive therapy for grief and depression. At such a time you should not be alone."

"I'm not alone!" I said indignantly. "I have my family. . . ." Daddy with his new girlfriend, and Mother busy finding herself, you in a law practice a couple of states away, and Cameron's family in Scotland—and not really connected to me any more, except by bad memories. "I'll go home and pack," I mumbled.

So here I am at Cherry Hill. I don't remember if you've been here or not. As a visitor, I mean. I'd certainly recall if you had been a patient. Did we visit Cousin Eileen here when we were teenagers? I don't think so. Aunt Amanda was very much in denial about Eileen's mental condition, as I recall. I believe she was referring to Cherry Hill as a finishing school in those days. How very appropriate in my case. I am here because something in my life needs to be finished, and I hope they can teach me how to manage it.

Bill MacPherson set down the letter from his younger sister, Elizabeth. "She's checked herself into Cherry Hill Hospital," he murmured. "Voluntary commitment for depression. Poor kid. I wonder if I should go down there?"

His law partner shrugged. "Maybe later. Just now I don't think you'd be much help. Men never are with other people's troubles. Your sister has lost her husband, and she's getting professional help, which is very sensible of her. Unless she asks you to visit, I think you ought to leave her alone to get on with it."

Bill MacPherson looked relieved. "I probably wouldn't be any use," he admitted.

"Probably not. Send her flowers if it makes you feel any better."

A. P. Hill balanced her coffee mug on the edge of the table and sat down in the plastic chair next to Bill's desk. She looked with distavor at her partner's shabby office, with its Bargain Barn metal office furniture, dusty plastic plant, and a crisp, white William & Mary law degree on the dingy beige wall. "Somebody ought to send me flowers," she muttered. "I have to work in the black hole of Calcutta. If that isn't depressing, I don't know what is."

"What's depressing?"

A. P. Hill waved her hand to indicate the general squalor of Bill's office. "Look at this place."

"I'm not cleaning it," said Bill warily, trying to edge between his partner and her view of his cluttered desk.

"No. Cleaning it wouldn't help. At least the dust is organic." She pointed at the plastic plant and shuddered. "I mean, look how small this place is. And how shabby. My office isn't any better. Except that I don't have a stuffed groundhog in a dress on the top of my filing cabinet." She turned her head to look at the offending object and shuddered again. "This whole building is a disaster. Sometimes I think the best way for us to drum up business for a criminal practice would be to loiter outside in the halls."

"Yes," said Bill, "you'd certainly meet people who need lawyers out there, but they probably couldn't afford us. Unless you'd take a pillowcase full of silverware for a retainer. Still, when we graduated from law school, you said you wanted to set up your own practice. You didn't want to go into a law firm full of—what did you call them?"

"Silverbacks," she muttered.

"Right. I knew it was a term for male gorillas. A law firm full of silverbacks, where large, aging males would call the shots, and you would be the most junior member of the firm. People would try to call you Amy. You said that, as a beginner in a big law firm you'd never get to do anything but scut work, and that you'd probably choke to death on your own rage."

A. P. Hill nodded. "I know. I still feel that way."

"Better to reign in hell than to serve in heaven, you said."

She looked around the shabby office and scowled. "I didn't mean it quite so literally."

"Well, one thing you can say for this place: it doesn't intimidate the clients."

"No. It probably makes the prospect of prison seem less awful, too."

"Unpretentious. That's us."

"I wish we had something to be pretentious about! Bill, we have to get out of here. I know that this place was all we could afford when we graduated, but we're doing better now, and we ought to be representing a better class of clients. We'll never get them if we stay here. I think it's time we looked for more suitable quarters."

"Sure. Fine. Whatever," Bill said cheerfully. "Just find the place, and tell me when to start packing. I can be ready on a day's notice. Less, even. I kept the cardboard box in the coat closet."

"That's just it. I don't have time to look for property. I'm in court in Richmond beginning this week, remember? I'm always up to my neck in case work. I thought maybe you could go."

Bill turned to stare at his partner. "You want me to buy a building? Me? Didn't I find this place?"

"Well . . . talk to a Realtor. See what's out there."

"What did you have in mind?"

"Tara." Edith Creech, their legal secretary, stood in the doorway, cordless phone in hand. "If you want pretentious, you ought to buy one of those run-down old mansions and fix it up. It would look great to clients. It would give them the impression of an old, established firm."

"Sounds expensive," said Bill.

"Well, if you get a big enough place, you could convert the upstairs rooms into apartments for yourselves. That way you could channel your rent money into an investment in the business. It would probably be cheaper anyway."

A. P. Hill nodded. "That might work. We'd pay more for office rent, but we'd save money on housing. It would be nice to have a kitchen on the premises. We could save a fortune on lunches. And an exercise room! We'd have to look into the tax implications, of course. . . ."

Bill looked at Edith with interest. "Are you holding the telephone for any particular reason?"

She gasped. "Lord, I completely forgot! Long-distance call for A. P. Hill. Someone called Purdue."

A. P. Hill looked puzzled and held out her hand for the phone. "It can't be her. What can she want? I'll be in my office," she murmured and hurried away.

Edith looked at Bill. "She doesn't usually get flustered. What was that about?"

Bill sighed. "Voice from the past." He reached for his jacket. "An old friend from law school. At least I think they were friends. It's hard to tell. They had a rivalry going that gave the rest of us headaches."

"A school rivalry, huh? Who won?"

"Too close to call. They both graduated in the top five. A guy named Anthony Chan finished ahead of them, but they didn't seem to care about that. They were out to beat each other. It was personal. If Purdue is calling to say that she's been elected governor of Tennessee or something, it could get dicey around here. Things may start bouncing off walls. And if she's coming to visit ..." He looked around the office, picturing a visitor's reaction to their less-than-luxurious premises. "We have to impress her, or life won't be worth living in Powell's vicinity. I think it's Realtor time."

"Realtor? Already?" Edith blinked. Normally Bill took longer than that to decide which doughnut he wanted. "Don't you want to read the newspaper ads? Shouldn't there be more discussion about what sort of place you're looking for?"

"Powell may be a while on the phone. And I know what

she's like after a session with Purdue. I think I'll get out of here. Tell her where I've gone."

"Right. You're going to buy an office."

"I guess. I'm going to do some serious looking, anyhow. See what's available. Do you really think we ought to get a big house for an office and live in the upstairs?"

Edith shrugged. "That's what the Queen of England does."

A. P. Hill sat down in her leather desk chair and closed her eyes, wondering when she had lost control of the day. It could be some other Purdue, though. Yeah. Sure. Maybe she'd heard about the rats' nest office and was calling to sneer. Mustering calm, she said, "Powell Hill speaking."

"So it is," cackled the voice on the other end of the line. "Pollyanna of the Virginia Bar. How's it going, kiddo? Still practicing law in Mayberry with your St. Bernard puppy?"

"Bill and I are doing fine, Purdue," said A. P. Hill evenly. "Thank you so much for asking." She knew that the other high fliers in law school had regarded her partnership with Bill MacPherson as an act of charity, but she wouldn't stand to have him criticized. He might lack ambition—or ruthlessness—but he had his good points, too. He was honest, loyal, hardworking, and kind. Maybe he trusted people more than was wise, but A. P. Hill thought that she might be bitter and cynical enough for both of them. After a lifetime of driving ambition, being partners with Bill MacPherson was . . . peaceful. She could have done worse.

P. J. Purdue had been one of the brightest students in their class, but she had a wild streak that boded ill for the sober profession of law. She could be recklessly brilliant, but she hated the methodical, painstaking preparation and research required for the practice of law. Still, Purdue's grades had been two-hundredths of a point higher than A. P. Hill's. She was surprised to find that after all this time the fact still rankled. "How are you, Purdue?" she said, trying to sound briskly cheerful. "Still in criminal law?"

The laugh again. "You could say that. Are you being tactful, or what? Tell me: How many of our old buddies have called you lately to talk about me?"

"Called about you?" A. P. Hill couldn't keep the bewilderment out of her voice. "P. J., I haven't heard from you—or about you—in ages. What's going on?"

A pause. "You mean you really don't know?"

"Know what?"

The voice on the other end of the line chuckled softly. "Stay tuned. News may travel slowly in Virginia, but I'm sure it'll filter through the time warp eventually. We may even make a television news channel. Stay tuned."

"P. J., what—"

"I just wanted to tell you this, kiddo. This is more fun than practicing law. Y'hear? A lot more fun."

"What—" But before she could frame a question, A. P. Hill heard the click of a telephone receiver being replaced. P. J. Purdue had vanished again.

She was still sitting there with the phone in her hand when Edith came in to see if she had finished talking.

"Runs the batteries down if you leave it off the hook too long," Edith said, taking the cordless phone back to her desk.

"Is anything the matter? You look like somebody hit you over the head with a parking meter."

A. P. Hill nodded slowly. "Purdue does that to people."

"Yeah, I heard she was an old friend of yours."

"Something like that. I wonder why she called me?"

Edith's eyebrows rose. "Well . . . didn't she tell you?"

A. P. Hill shrugged. "Oh, no. Purdue never does things the easy way. She's going to make me find out."

The realty company was located in a large old house, which had evidently been a private home, until rezoning and urban sprawl had changed the neighborhood to a collection of car lots and fast-food places. The house still sat in its oak-shaded lawn, but the backyard was now a parking lot, and the interior of the house had been carved up into a dozen tiny offices.

Although the parking lot was nearly empty, Bill MacPherson still had trouble deciding where to put his car. All the spots seemed to be allocated for the Realtors themselves: Diamond Realtor of the Year, Agent of the Month, Gold Key Lister (whatever that was), and Top Seller—Commercial. He didn't see any spaces marked CUSTOMER, so he parked against the split-rail fence at the far end of the gravel lot and walked twenty yards or so to the door.

Bill had hoped the walk would give him time to formulate some sort of opening speech about what he was looking for, but nothing sprang readily to mind, so when the door was opened by a pretty young woman in a red blazer, he blurted out, "I'm looking for a house. Are you a Realtor? Have you ever seen *Gone With the Wind*?"

The woman hesitated for less than a heartbeat, long enough to size up the nice-looking young man in the well-cut jacket and the power tie. Then she said, "I'll get the keys. We can talk on the way."

It's like being back in college, thought Elizabeth Mac-Pherson as she lugged her suitcase down the tiled hallway, following the white-coated attendant who would lead her to room 305, her home for the next month. She took a deep breath and studied her surroundings. Just like college. Same dorm smell, same lighting, same feeling of apprehension. Only here, instead of encountering fellow students, you were going to meet crazy people. That turned out to be true of college, too, of course. At least here they were up front about it.

Elizabeth was pleased to find that she was nervous—the sensation of feeling something was a novelty after weeks of numbness. Then she remembered why she had come: an image of Cameron filled her mind, and she pushed it away again. She closed her eyes and took a deep breath. The feelings were gone. All of them.

"You shouldn't have any trouble settling in," the attendant told her. He was a jovial-looking fellow with a round face and lively eyes. "You'll be in a two-person room, but you're the only occupant at the moment. Your hallmates can show you the ropes, though. Laundry procedure, where the drink machine is, stuff like that."

"I don't feel like socializing," said Elizabeth. "I'd rather be left alone."

He nodded cheerfully. "Dr. Freya thought you might. She

said to tell you: 'No way.' You'll be getting a roommate in a day or so."

"But I'm a voluntary patient. I'm here for depression."

"Okay." His tone suggested that it was all the same to him. He would believe anything a patient cared to tell him. If she had said she was a Martian exchange student, his response would have been the same.

"You're not going to put me in with a crazy person, are you?"

There was a long pause in which Elizabeth could imagine sarcastic answers being framed and then discarded. Finally he said, "We don't have dangerous patients here. That we know of, anyhow. Just nonviolent types. You'll be fine."

Elizabeth thought about arguing the point. She could call Dr. Freya and plead her case for privacy, but all that would take energy, and an amount of interest in her own immediate future that she could not quite muster. That's why she was here, wasn't it?

Her escort pushed open the door. "Nobody here yet. Your neighbors are probably in the TV lounge. Well, make yourself at home. If you need anything, there's always folks around."

Elizabeth nodded and trudged inside, slinging her suitcase on the twin bed nearest the door. She gave the attendant a half-hearted wave as the door swung shut behind him. She inspected the room and found that, instead of the prisonlike surroundings she was expecting, which would have suited her mood of despair, she was trapped in one of those back-in-college dreams that always end with a panic attack as you try to take the final exam in a course you had never attended. In Elizabeth's panic dream the quiz was always in trigonometry. She wondered if real trigonometry exams looked anything like the one in her dreams. If she actually took a course in trig some day, would the nightmare go away, or would the exam simply change to . . . say . . . Sanskrit?

The room was the standard setting for the back-to-college nightmare. There was the tile floor, matching twin beds with identical brown cotton bedspreads, chests of drawers built into the wall, sliding-door closets, two wooden study desks with an old straight-backed chair drawn up to each one, and one long window in a beige cinder-block wall. The view was of green lawn and shade trees. Just like college. Only this time she was majoring in grief.

At least she would have a few minutes of solitude before more medical personnel appeared. She opened her suitcase to put her clothes away. It was filled with casual clothes in muted browns and navy (what did a newly widowed woman pack when she was being committed?), and there on the top of the pile, in a leather case the size of a playing card, was a picture of Cameron Dawson on the deck of the boat, smiling into the camera, with his back to the sea and beyond it the cliffs of Scotland. Elizabeth picked up the photograph and looked at it for only a moment before she stuffed it into the top drawer under a pile of underwear. Why did the photo have to show the sea? She couldn't bear to look at it. No use dwelling on it, she told herself. What was the point of trying to come to terms with bereavement if you were just going to wallow in memories. Best to put it away.

Elizabeth MacPherson sat down on the bed and wondered what she was going to do with the rest of her life.

The house-hunting expedition had moved at such a pace that Bill MacPherson had forgotten to be nervous. The pretty young real estate agent, whose name was Holly Milton, had bundled him into her car before he'd had a chance to say much more than his name, and now they were speeding through downtown Danville, apparently en route to Tara. Given a chance to study her as she drove, Bill decided that she was one of those society types who was doing real estate more or less as a hobby. He always had the feeling when he spoke to members of the southern aristocracy that they were communicating in some sort of code. On first meeting him, society types would be all gush and grins, but then after no more than ten minutes' conversation, a marked civility would creep into their manner, the subtlest shading of distance that said, "You're nice, but you're not one of us, are you?" The difference in attitude was so slight that he would be hard-pressed to describe it to anyone for fear of being laughed to scorn, but he knew it when he saw it. It had just happened again. Bill wished he knew what the password was—not that he wanted to be "one of them," but just so he didn't have to wonder about it any more. Anyhow, Holly was being perfectly friendly, and if she realized that he could think of nothing to say to her, she gave no sign.

Holly seemed to know half the lawyers in town, although she had a unique way of classifying them: not as criminal or corporate, or prosecution vs. defense, but town house or subdivision, farm or condo.

"Now I wouldn't have picked you as a Tara type," she was saying as she sailed through the second yellow stoplight in a row. "You know—antiques, gardening, five-year subscription to *Colonial Homes*. Chinese import porcelain in a

stripped French pine cabinet. I wouldn't have guessed that
at all."

Bill's idea of gardening was picking the dead leaves off
his Christmas poinsettia until around Groundhog Day, when it
finally succumbed to neglect. The only thing he owned that
might be considered antique was unfortunately organic and lay
forgotten in a plastic container in his refrigerator. He decided
not to share these facts with the Realtor for fear of discovering
what sort of house she would envision for him.

"You're right," he said. "I'm not into colonial anything or
gardening techniques. I couldn't decorate a shoe box. It's my
partner, really. My law partner," he amended, correctly inter-
preting the look on the young woman's face. "She thinks it
would be good for our . . . our corporate image to have a pic-
turesque old mansion for the law practice. And we thought
we could live upstairs. A good investment, you know. Probably
loads of tax benefits."

"Mmm," said Holly Milton, peering at him over the top of
her sunglasses. "So this was your partner's idea, but she sent
you out to look at houses?"

"She's in court this week. She stays busy, and I have some
free time for the next day or so, so she thought that I could go out
and see what's on the market. I can make recommendations. Well,
anyhow, I can take photocopies of property ads back to her."

Holly Milton smiled. "You certainly picked the right day
to go house hunting! A purchase agreement fell through, which
put a great house back on the market as of this morning. I'll
make it easy for you. This is the perfect house. It's just what you
need for a law practice. You'll have to see it to believe it. It's just
outside the city limits, so you'll save a bit on property taxes, and

it is just beautiful. Or it will be—with some restoration work. Let me tell you about it. . . ." Holly Milton spent the rest of the drive reeling off statistics of square footage, number of bathrooms, fireplace locations, and other amenities calculated to make prospective buyers salivate.

"And you could have note cards printed up with an artist's rendering of the house on the front. That would set such a tone for your firm. And corporate Christmas cards! A photo of the house with snow in the yard and Christmas decorations on the windows. Perfect!"

"I'll mention it," Bill promised, silently resolving to have nothing to do with such schemes. "How old is the house? Is it historic?"

"I'll tell you all about it when you see it," the Realtor promised. "We're coming up on it now, and I want you to focus on that all-important first impression."

She swung into a long paved driveway leading into a grove of pines and sprawling maple trees that shielded the house from view. As the car emerged from the canopy of leaves, Holly stopped just in the curve where the house would be framed in the car's windshield. "There!" she whispered in theatrical tones. "Isn't it heaven?"

Bill nodded slowly. It was. But, he thought, if you had to paint it or mow the lawn, it would be unearthly.

The word *house* did not do justice to the splendor of this building. Most people would call it a mansion. It looked like the photo on a postcard that would have "Hello from Virginia" emblazoned at the top, or perhaps like a movie set for an antebellum southern drama. Bill could picture Jane Seymour in sausage curls and hoop skirts sashaying gracefully down the wide front steps. It was a Georgian-style house of mellow rose-colored brick with a curved portico supported by four ornate and massive white columns. He received the impression of the place in one overwhelming burst, so that if he had been asked later to draw a picture of it, he would have simply drawn a large dollar sign between two lollipop-shaped trees. They couldn't possibly afford it, he thought sadly, but there was no denying that it was a beauty.

"I suppose it's exactly what she wants." He sighed.

Holly gave him a pitying smile. "Well, I guess it is exactly what she wants!" she declared. "It's exactly what all of us want. It's every little girl's dollhouse, life-size. A woman might not kill to get this house, but I'll bet you serious money that she'd commit matrimony to get it."

Bill did not find this declaration as reassuring as it was intended to be. Besides, he couldn't picture A. P. Hill as the kind of little girl who had ever played with dollhouses. She once claimed to have swapped her collection of Barbies for a Daisy Air Rifle. Still, she was the descendant and namesake of a Confederate general, so perhaps the desire to own a white-columned mansion was hardwired into her DNA. Bill tried to think of an appropriate question to ask the Realtor. Since they hadn't even seen the inside of the place, "How much?" seemed a bit too precipitate. Finally he said, "Is it as old as it looks?"

Holly Milton laughed. "No, but that can be your little secret. Actually it was built around 1948 by a local gentleman who had suddenly become wealthy in . . . er . . . manufacturing."

Bill nodded. Danville was famous for tobacco and textile mills. "Cigarettes or fabric?" he asked.

"Um . . . something like that. I think he got into some trouble at one time in his career."

"Oh." Bill digested this information. "Trouble?" He laughed nervously. "You're not trying to tell me there are bodies in the basement, are you?"

"No, no. I think it was some sort of financial trouble. Taxes, perhaps. Anyhow, the old fellow was a shrewd investor, and despite his problems, he prospered. Apparently he put his profits from the business into the stock market, real estate, and blue chip stocks. I think he wanted to build an empire to leave to his children. Unfortunately, they didn't inherit his business sense, which is why the house has to be sold."

"They went broke?"

"Not entirely, but they put up the house as collateral in another business venture, and when it went sour, the other party forced the sale to recoup the money. I don't suppose the children minded. They didn't live here."

"What a shame," said Bill, still staring at the magnificent house. "It's probably just as well that the old man didn't live to see what happened to his house."

"Actually, he did," said Holly Milton. "But we'll talk about that later."

Chapter 3

Elizabeth MacPherson wondered what there was to do for a whole month in a psychiatric facility. The obvious answer—brood about her bereavement—was certainly not the activity that Dr. Freya had been aiming for. Elizabeth felt sure of that. She wished she had thought to bring some books along, but in her present state of sleepwalking through life, that much forethought had been impossible. She felt that given her present condition the fact that she remembered to bring clean underwear and a toothbrush should count as a triumph of will. I wonder if this is what the nursing home will be like someday, she thought. Maybe this month will be a preview of old age. I'll get out again, and I'll still be young, but I'll know what's in store for me at the end of the road. This thought depressed her so much that she sank down on the bed, feeling the tears well up again. She had also forgotten to bring tissues, she thought, rubbing

---

her eyes with the back of her hand. She wondered if she could call anyone and ask them to bring her things she'd forgotten. Were visitors allowed? Were there guards to search incoming packages, or did that sort of thing happen only in prisons?

Was this a prison? The room seemed more bare and cell-like than before, and she wondered if she'd be ready to claw her way out of it before the end of the month. If so, perhaps that would be a good sign. In her present state of depression, Elizabeth didn't feel that she could summon the energy to dodge a runaway truck, much less object to restricted activity and minimalist room decor.

As she brooded about her present circumstances, Elizabeth sat on the bed facing the window so that she did not see the door open slowly behind her. "Nobody important," said a voice from the hall.

Elizabeth spun around, forgetting her grief in the clutch of panic. A heavyset young woman with bangs and black-frame glasses stood in the doorway, inspecting her as if she were a new exhibit of sculpture. The woman was obviously a patient. No member of the nursing staff would come to work in a stained green shift and pistachio-colored flip-flop sandals.

"I beg your pardon?" said Elizabeth, wondering if she were being summoned for mealtime or some other group activity.

"I was talking to Lisa Lynn. She's lurking out there in the hall. She's shy." The woman turned back toward the door and called out, "The new patient is nobody important, L. L. Go back to your room now."

"What do you mean I'm nobody important?" Elizabeth demanded. "Is that any way to talk to a patient?"

The woman shrugged. "I wouldn't know. But let me tell

you, kiddo, from one patient to another: it's the best part of being sick. You get to tell the truth." She shambled into the room and sat down on the other twin bed. "You're a new fish, so you haven't figured out the social order yet. It's a brave new world in here."

"Who are you?"

"Name's Kudan. Emma Owens Kudan, which is a mouthful. In here they call me Emma O. That's what I answer to, anyhow. We were hoping you'd turn out to be a movie star or a country singer having a nervous breakdown, but I see you're not. Too bad. We could use a little novelty." She examined Elizabeth with the air of one doing a patient evaluation. "I see you're not anorectic."

"No. But if it's contagious, I'd like to catch it."

Emma O. shook her head. "Anorexia isn't a disease. It's a career move. At least, that's what I tell Sarah. So . . . what are you in for?"

Elizabeth decided that sharing her emotional problems with this creature in green slippers was the most unappealing offer she'd had in ages. She smiled sweetly. "My voices tell me to go and save France."

Her visitor shrugged. "I doubt that. The presence of delusional impersonators in mental institutions is highly overrated. I don't think we have anybody famous at all—certainly not Napoléon, despite all the loony-bin jokes to the contrary. Oh, wait, we did have Jesus in here a while back. He had a few people convinced, autographed a few Bibles, but beyond that He didn't cause much of a stir. If He can't turn that sludge in the dayroom into decent coffee, what good is He? Still, if you

want to be Joan of Arc, kiddo, there are a couple of arson com-
pulsives in the other wing who would dearly love to light your
fire."

"I'm not delusional," snapped Elizabeth. "I just don't feel
like discussing my case with another patient."

Emma O. gave her a condescending smile. "So group therapy
will be news to you, huh?"

"I don't intend to go to group therapy. I am here for
depression."

"Getting it or giving it?"

"My husband died!"

The young woman looked mildly interested. "Did he? I
had a hamster once that died. It crawled under the cushion of
the sofa and my brother sat on it."

"That's hardly the same thing."

"What, death? I imagine it is, if you're the one experienc-
ing it. Still, I see what you mean. I don't suppose your husband
was smothered by a sofa cushion. Pretty careless of him if he
was."

Elizabeth was so stunned at this lack of sympathy for her
widowed state that she was momentarily speechless. *My husband died.* Those three magic words had served her well for
many weeks, gaining her privacy when she wanted it, special attention when she didn't. People had been tiptoeing around her
life, making no demands at all on her patience or her fortitude.
It was unsettling to meet someone who was not cowed by the
enormity of her loss. This madwoman seemed to think the statement was simply an interesting bit of trivia. Elizabeth didn't
know whether to be outraged or intrigued. She was still trying

to decide how to take it when the madwoman said, "Can they give you pills for grief?"

"Not indefinitely. Sooner or later you have to learn to manage on your own."

Emma O. considered this. "Okay," she said. "Who brought you on the hall today? Thibodeaux?"

"I think so. Tall, blond guy in a white uniform."

"Yeah, that's Tibby."

"He didn't seem very friendly."

"He's all right." Emma O. smiled again. "I told you that this was a different world. In here you have no currency of any value to him, that's all."

Elizabeth blinked. "Was I supposed to tip him?"

"No. I mean social currency. For instance, you may be smart—are you?"

"I have a Ph.D. in forensic anthropology," said Elizabeth with a touch of pride.

"Okay. We'll give you the benefit of the doubt. Say you're smart, but: you're a psychiatric patient, which nullifies your claim to mental superiority. There's obviously something wrong with your mind or you wouldn't be here. Besides, anybody could say they had a Ph.D. in forensic anthropology."

"I could tell a lot from looking at the suture closures in your bare skull," said Elizabeth, in tones suggesting that she would enjoy it.

"Remarks like that will get you sedated to four rungs down the food chain," said Emma O. "Any hint of violence makes the powers-that-be uneasy. They like things to stay peaceful. Where was I? Oh, yes. Currency. Money isn't a factor in here, either, beyond having enough change for the snack machines, so no-body cares if you're rich or not on the outside. You can't spend it in here. And fame or family prestige don't count for much, ei-ther, because there's always a chance that you're lying about who you are. Remember that guy in here who claimed to be Je-sus. Nobody was impressed. Not even the people who believed him. He couldn't—or wouldn't—turn the Salisbury steak into anything else, so we lost interest."

Elizabeth considered all this. "There must be some sort of hierarchy," she said at last. "It's human nature to form a social order. We like to know who we're better than."

"When you get right down to it, there is only one universal currency."

"And that is?"

"Beauty. Beauty is the one status symbol that cannot be taken away. If you're beautiful, you can be set down any-where in the world, without your I.D. or your credit cards, and people will treat you well. Cleverness won't help you if you wind up in a place where they don't speak your language, or if your wisdom is not recognized, but beauty is the universal wealth."

"There are different standards of beauty. . ." Elizabeth be-gan, thinking of foot binding and neck rings.

"Not so much any more. Hollywood tells the world what pretty is these days. And I think people just know instinctively who the pretty people are regardless of differences in culture. It's like radar. Maybe they emit rays or something. Anyhow, pretty people matter. The rest of us don't."

Elizabeth stared at the heavyset young woman, owl-eyed

and scowling behind her glasses. "What are you in here for?" she asked.

Emma O. shrugged. "Well, I have Asperger's syndrome, but that's not treatable. It's just the way I am. They don't put you away for that."

Elizabeth had never heard of Asperger's syndrome, but she thought it might be impolite to ask about someone's illness. She made a mental note to broach the subject with some knowledgeable third party, perhaps Dr. Freya herself, at their next session of therapy. Given the present drift of conversation, Elizabeth thought that this patient could be more useful to therapists outside the institution, drumming up business by making homely women even more depressed.

"I suppose," Emma O. was saying, "I'm in here for the same reason as practically every other female in residence. I'm in here for not being beautiful."

Elizabeth nodded. "Depression."

"Well, depression comes later, I think. First society teaches you a good hard lesson about not being pretty, and then you get depressed about it, which means that you understood the lesson. But depression has its good points, you know. It sharpens perception. Did you know that?"

Elizabeth shook her head.

"Absolutely true. Psychologists have done studies of people with depression versus so-called normal people, and you know what? Depressed people have a much more accurate view of the world."

"What do you mean . . . accurate?"

"The researchers asked both groups to rate themselves

on how smart they thought they were, how good-looking, how well liked, and so on. The normal people *over*estimated themselves in every category. They always gave themselves higher scores for looks and brains and popularity than other people gave them. That's the old rosy view of the world for you—sheer self-delusion."

"The depressed people underrated themselves?" asked Elizabeth.

"No. The depressed patients were right on the money. Their self-scores tallied with the researchers' objective assessment of them every time. So—depressed people may be sadder than normal, but they are the only ones who can look reality dead in the eye. If you want Truth with a capital T and no Pollyanna bullshit—get depressed. It's funny, isn't it? Normal people try to cheer you up by telling you things aren't as bad as you think, and it turns out that you're right and they're wrong."

Elizabeth sighed. She had been on the receiving end of a lot of well-meaning optimism in recent weeks. "I think I'd rather have the rose-colored glasses, thank you."

"Suit yourself. I prefer to take reality straight up, without the sugar coating."

"So why are you here then?"

Emma O. held out her arms so that Elizabeth could see the crisscrossing of thick, white scars encircling both wrists. "I guess you could say I overdosed on the truth."

Bill MacPherson was standing awkwardly in the mansion's two-story marbled entrance hall, peering intently up at the blazing brilliance of the five-tier chandelier, dutifully contemplating the sprawling carved oak staircase that led to a landing with a stained-glass window—and he knew that some sort of reaction was expected of him, but he just didn't get it.

"Oh, you men are hopeless when it comes to houses!" said Holly Milton in some exasperation. She could see that her new client the young lawyer was trying his best to be polite about the magnificent house, but he was hopeless. He felt none of the visceral lust for possession, the rush of instant status that would have hit any woman fifty yards from the front door.

"Bill," sighed the Realtor. "Just pretend it's a sports car, okay?"

He nodded slowly. "So . . . What you mean is that this is an ego thing. Extension of one's self. I own the house, therefore I am the house. Hmmm. Am I not supposed to think about practical things like heating costs and the condition of the roof?"

"Eventually, yes, we can talk about those things. You can even get a second opinion from an independent real estate appraiser before you make an offer. First, though, you must feel the magic of this place. You are the house. That's exactly what I want you to imagine. Think what this house says about the people who live here!"

Bill thought it over. "It says that they have spent a lot of money on a really big house, and now they will spend even more money to keep it from falling slowly to bits. It says that they probably want to brag about owning the house to a lot of people they don't like very much, so that those people will envy them and feel bad that their own houses are not so grand. This house could generate a lot of bad feelings. Sort of haunted, only it's doing the haunting."

Holly sighed, wishing for the hundredth time that the other partner in MacPherson & Hill had come instead. A woman wouldn't have to think about the house at all. She'd fall under its spell in a nanosecond. Men were so hopeless. They acted as if houses were just places to sleep and keep the rain off your clothes.

Summoning a perkiness bordering on cheerleader, the Realtor said, "Come on, then. I'll show you around." Her voice echoed in the cavernous hall. "The rooms are empty—well, most of them. Each one has a fireplace, and all the mantels are different. The one in the front room here is marble. If you look closely at the leaf carvings you can make out little faces— nymphs and satyrs. I think this mantel was imported from Italy just after World War Two. A lot of old castles were in ruins because of the war, and since many of them could not be restored, wonderful things could be bought from the salvagers." She tapped the wall. "This paneling is oak, also imported from an estate in Europe."

Bill, whose interest in architectural details was minimal, had wandered over to the windows and was staring out at the side lawn.

"We'll do the garden later," said Holly. "It has a pleached walk. I'll tell you what that is later, too. Would you like to take notes? No? Well, I think it's all written down in a brochure, anyhow. Now, come back and look at this floor. Solid oak, can you believe it? And this gilt-bronze dolphin light fixture came from a chateau in France. It would cost a fortune to build this house with new materials today."

Bill nodded. "It probably would have cost a fortune in 1948, too, but apparently the builder didn't use new materials.

Didn't you tell me that he just used bits from damaged houses in Europe after the war? Hopefully with the knowledge and permission of the former owners." He scanned the walls. "I don't suppose there are any Van Goghs on display here?"

Holly decided not to know what he was talking about. The conversation was veering dangerously close to the forbidden topics of politics and religion, neither of which had any part in a sales presentation. Smiling, she pushed open the door to the next room. "You know, this paneled dining room is a gem, and it could double as a conference room for your law firm!"

She led him through the dining room and into a small, shabby kitchen. "This will have to be remodeled, of course," she announced briskly, with the generous profligacy of one who knows the changes will not involve her money. "I'd just gut it and start over, if I were you. With some granite countertops, fluorescent lighting, and custom appliances, this kitchen would be wonderful."

Bill stared at the battered white refrigerator. It was shorter than he was and its contours were rounded, in this case an indication of great age for a refrigerator. Its door was dented, and the white finish had chipped away in spots, leaving a smudge of gray and suggesting that its presence in the kitchen was a remnant of an earlier, unlamented era, rather than a sentimental gesture of preservation. The thing looked at least forty years old, and along with the rest of the kitchen, it was sadly out of sync with the magnificence of the mansion. Antique was definitely not a desirable condition in kitchen appliances, Bill decided. When on impulse he opened the refrigerator to see if it still worked, he found himself peering in at an array of blue and silver aluminum cans on one shelf and cellophane wrapped packages on the other. They felt reassuringly cold to the touch, and they were obviously of recent vintage. "Pepsis and Twinkies?" he said.

"The breakfast of champions," said a hoarse voice from the doorway.

They turned to see an ancient old man in a tattered bathrobe standing in the doorway that led to the sunporch. He seemed to be composed entirely of blue veins and wrinkles, but the two bright eyes that peered out from among the folds of skin were as sharp as ever.

"Mr. Dolan!" said Holly in a squeal of delight intended to conceal her horror at finding him on the premises. "How wonderful to see you! I've brought somebody by to look at this marvelous house of yours." She took the old man by the sleeve of his brown bathrobe and propelled him toward Bill's outstretched hand. "Say hello to Bill MacPherson. He's one of Danville's up-and-coming young lawyers. Bill, this is Mr. Jack Dolan, the original owner of this incredible place."

Bill opened his mouth to say "But I thought the original owner was dead," then thought better of it. This old gentleman looked dead. He was ninety if he was a day. The spotted pink skin of his face hung down in a cascade of furrows, giving his eyes a hooded look, reminiscent of a species of lizard. Bill couldn't recall which species of lizard, but he was sure it looked better—and maybe more human—than the tottering specter of wheezing parchment standing before him. "How do you do?" he said faintly. He shook the old man's hand gently, so as not to make it fall off.

Over the old man's shoulder, Holly was mouthing the word "later" to indicate that she did indeed have a good explanation for this apparition, and that Bill would hear about it as soon as they could speak together in private. Bill turned back to the old man. "You still live here, then?" he asked gently.

"Just back there," Mr. Jack jerked his head in the direction of the back of the house where a doorway led from the kitchen into a sunny room with glass walls and a linoleum floor. Bill walked to the threshold. He took in the glass windows, the faded linoleum floor, the unmade sofa bed, and the small space heater standing a few feet from the mattress. "But this is a sunporch. You own the house, but you live on the sunporch?"

The old man favored Bill with a gummy smile. "Don't own the house. Built it. Don't own it."

"Mr. Jack's son-in-law owned the house until two years ago," Holly put in quickly. "He used the house as collateral in a strip-mall development deal, and unfortunately the company went bankrupt, and he lost the house to his creditors."

"But his father-in-law still lived here?"

The old man, who had been following this exchange with rapt attention, nodded happily.

"Well . . . ," said Holly. "Truthfully, the family had been trying to get Mr. Jack into a nursing home for years, haven't they?"

The old man smirked at her and nodded. "I like the sunporch. It's warm."

"He refuses to have live-in help. When his wife died back in the mid-eighties, he sold everything out of the house in a tag sale and retreated to this one room here adjoining the kitchen."

"Less work," Mr. Jack pointed out.

"Umm," said Bill. He thought cholera would have a hard time surviving in the grime and clutter of the sunporch.

"Anyhow, he refused to move. Perhaps his family thought they could force him out when the house changed hands. According to the foreclosure agreement, Mr. Jack was given one year's grace period to occupy the house before eviction could proceed."

"This was two years ago, you said?"

The old man's cackle turned into a wheeze. "They give me one year of grace. Nobody said which year. I'm staying put."

The Realtor sighed. "You see how it is. The new owners—Sunshine Properties—couldn't forcibly move him. Well, they could have, but it would have been a public relations nightmare. So the year's grace period came and went, but Mr. Jack stayed right here. The company didn't feel able to do the structural renovations with him in residence. They'd wanted to turn the place into an apartment building, I believe. Or perhaps a clubhouse for an upscale development on the adjoining land. But that land was recently ruled a protected wetland, so it can't be built upon—not even a parking lot for apartments. That leaves this house virtually useless to them. Keeping it on the company's books is costing them money like the proverbial white elephant. Now Sunshine Properties has decided to cut their losses, sell the house cheap, and let somebody else worry about it." She gave Bill a meaningful look and enunciated slowly, "Very cheap."

Bill shook his head. "So it's a bargain. Yes, I see that. And my investment portfolio has done really well in the last couple of years, so I probably can afford the house if I want it, but, look here, you can't expect me to buy this place out from under that poor old man. I mean, really! Take an elderly man's house away from him. What will become of him then?"

Holly Milton smiled. "We've thought of that. The present owners have offered to provide Mr. Jack with a free apartment or small rental home, if he should agree to go—which they rather doubt, but they hope he will reconsider. Anyhow, failing that, they have set forth a very interesting proposition that you might want to consider."

Mr. Jack beamed up at the prospective new owner. "Care for a Twinkie?"

"Love," P. J. Purdue used to say, "is like flushing yourself down the toilet. A nice cool ride and a lot of crap at the end." That pretty much summed up her opinion of relationships, and I couldn't imagine her ever changing her mind. I wonder if she ever did.

In college we were all terrified of her. She was small, blonde, and vicious. She stalked the halls of the dorm like a drill sergeant's impersonation of Drew Barrymore: black turtleneck, black nail polish, permanent scowl, sneering at the fraternity honeys and at the aerobic princesses on our hall, or perhaps at the whole idea of their pursuit of happiness in the form of another human being. "You're in love?" she would drawl. "How quaint."

In the sexual revolution, P. J. Purdue was the I.R.A. Many a rapturous discussion of rose-petal-pink

----

bridesmaids' dresses ended in a strained silence when Purdue entered the room with a permanent leer that put one in mind of a peckish shark.

A. P. Hill closed the cover of her journal, wondering what had led her to record her memories of a college acquaintance after all this time, instead of her usual log entries of case work and a to-do list. It was probably this morning's cryptic phone call, she thought. She was waiting for the other shoe to drop, so to speak. Something was up.

She yawned and stretched. It was nearly ten o'clock. Time for her evening run. Perhaps that would clear the cobwebs out of her brain, she thought. She would do her customary run in the cool night air, and then she'd be back to her usual untroubled self. Introspection was not a habit that A. P. Hill indulged in. When she had problems, she chose to outrun them, and if she had to keep running until she was too tired to think—well, that worked just as well.

After the phone call, thoughts about P. J. Purdue had drifted in and out of Powell Hill's mind for the rest of the day, as P. J. herself had once drifted in and out of dorm rooms, uninvited and often unwelcome, but oblivious to the havoc she caused, and always a commanding presence that could not be banished for long.

Visions of Purdue's little chicken-hawk face under a Beatle haircut had haunted A. P. Hill in court all day, and in late afternoon as she drove home, she found herself scanning the faces of people in passing cars, as if she expected Purdue to appear grinning alongside her. It was a disturbing thought.

The feeling of uneasiness was still there in the back of A. P. Hill's mind hours later as she laced up her running shoes and sprinted down the steps of her apartment building. She always ran in the evening, but when anything worried her, she ran faster and longer. Tonight was shaping up to be a solo marathon, she thought.

But how could she outrun P. J. Purdue? In law school it had been all she could do to keep up with her.

There was something about the careless brilliance of Purdue that was both fascinating and annoying. A. P. Hill had known that despite their nearly identical grade point averages, Purdue was the smarter of the two. She had resented that fact, perhaps. It still annoyed her to admit it, even to herself, because it didn't seem fair that she'd had to work so hard for her success, while Purdue breezed through with considerably less effort. She knew, though, that ultimately she did not envy Purdue. There was never a doubt in anyone's mind about which of the two overachievers was the more likely to succeed in the real world beyond law school: Amy Powell Hill. For all Purdue's quick intellect, there was a fragile quality about her that suggested she was too easily bored, too distracted by life itself to endure the daily grind of the treadmill that put beginning lawyers on the road to success.

A. P. Hill sprinted off into the soft darkness of the suburban Danville street, savoring the quiet and the feel of cool night air in her nostrils. The trick was to push yourself so that you had to concentrate on taking one more breath, one more step. If you were lucky, the stitch in your side and the sharp twinge in your lungs would drown out whatever troubles you had taken with you when you set out to run.

Purdue was smarter, quicker, better. The old thoughts settled into a rhythm matching her heartbeat as she ran. Smarter. Quicker. Better. A. P. Hill told herself with more insistence that she did not envy the mental capacity of P. J. Purdue. There was more to success than mental agility. She knew that her own capacity for diligence, hard work, and an eye for painstaking detail would take her far. If Purdue had ended up making the most money, she could live with that. She just wished she could get over the feeling that whatever Purdue was doing would turn out to be more fun than A. P. Hill would ever have.

She tried to outrun this thought for a mile and a half, but when it showed no sign of leaving her consciousness, A. P. Hill gave up. She touched her toes a few times in the deserted street while she caught her breath, then she jogged back to her building at a slower pace. It was late, and she still had laundry and paperwork to do before she could call it a night. It would take half a pot of tea to keep her awake enough to finish her chores.

When A. P. Hill rounded the corner of her street, she saw Edith sitting on the front steps of the building, reading a supermarket tabloid in the glow of the streetlight. Catching sight of her, Edith grinned and waved the paper aloft. "Found your friend!"

A. P. Hill was curled up on her sofa with her legs tucked up under her. "I don't believe it!" she said again.

Edith shrugged. "Well, it is a supermarket tabloid. I don't believe some of it myself. Clintons Adopt Alien Baby . . . Elvis and Liberace Frozen in Michael Jackson's Wine Cellar . . . Sure. Okay. But some of the rest of it is just plain hard to swallow."

"It's incredible," Powell Hill said again. She did believe it, though. The news story had a cold ring of plausibility that fit the phone call she'd received earlier in the day. A. P. Hill found herself thinking, *So that's what she meant. But why had she called?*

The tea in A. P. Hill's William & Mary coffee mug had long since grown cold, but she sipped it anyhow, too preoccupied to notice the flat, bitter taste. She picked up the tabloid for the tenth time and peered at the grainy black-and-white picture of a young woman with short, light-colored hair. The headline read PMS OUTLAWS TERRORIZE SOUTHERN BARS. The PMS Outlaws. One of their early victims had given the pair this name, and it had stuck. According to the article, two young women, believed to be escaped convict Carla Larkin and her attorney, Patricia Jane Purdue, had eluded law enforcement personnel after Larkin's escape from a western North Carolina prison six weeks earlier. Since then they had been on the run, stealing money and cars from men they picked up in roadhouses.

"Are they sure it's her?" she murmured. "This picture could be anybody."

Edith nodded. "They're sure. She was Carla Larkin's lawyer. Did you finish the article? It says that Carla Larkin had left prison to go to a doctor's appointment—"

"Wait! Carla Larkin was a prisoner? What was she convicted of?"

"Armed robbery. Assault. Something unladylike. She wasn't a sophisticated embezzler or a country-club shoplifter, if that's what you're thinking. She was doing some hard time in a state prison."

"And Purdue was her attorney."

"Right. Larkin had to go to a clinic for a psychiatric evaluation—escorted by a guard, of course—and Purdue was accompanying her. When they reached the doctor's office, P. J. Purdue pulled a pistol and a roll of duct tape out of her briefcase and held the guard at gunpoint while Carla Larkin disarmed the guard, taped his mouth shut, and shackled him to the doorknob with his own handcuffs. Then they took off in Purdue's car, and the rest is tabloid history."

A. P. Hill shuddered. "Why would she do such a thing?"

Edith contrived to look vague. "Opinions vary," she said carefully. "But most of the stories refer to the two of them as a latter-day Bonnie and Clyde."

A. P. Hill wasn't interested in the salacious details. To her the career implications were horrifying enough. "Assisting a convict in an escape from prison," she murmured. "That's a felony! She'll lose her license to practice law. She's thrown away her career. Her whole life. She must be crazy!"

"I guess she has fouled things up pretty royally," said Edith. "But I don't see what you're so upset about. I thought you'd have a good laugh over this. I figured you'd say you were sorry, and put on your 'concern face,' but secretly you'd gloat a little that you turned out better than she did. Bill told me the two of you weren't exactly friends in law school."

"Well, no, we weren't. But this is a shock. I mean, her whole career. What a *waste*." A. P. Hill shuddered. Then another thought hit her. "Bill! Does he know about this yet?"

"Not from me," said Edith. "I didn't see him again after he went off house hunting. I didn't find out about this until after

47

work when I saw this paper in the check-out line at the super-market and recognized the name. Small world, isn't it?"

"She warned me," murmured A. P. Hill, scanning the article yet again as if she expected the words to rearrange them-selves into a more sensible story. "Purdue said to watch the me-dia for news of her. I wonder why she called me, though?"

"Well," said Edith. "Sooner or later, she's going to need a lawyer."

"Much madness is divinest sense."
—Emily Dickinson

Chapter 4

"Good morning," said Bill MacPherson to his law partner. "I've bought a house."

"Mmm," said A. P. Hill from the depths of the *Washington Post*. Her hand reached out from behind the wall of newsprint and groped for her coffee cup.

Bill obligingly shoved it into her grasp. He tried again: "You told me we needed a new place, so I got right on it. It's a very nice house, and I found that I could afford it. It has attractive tax benefits, too. Good price."

"Mmm."

According to the MacPherson & Hill office hours posted on the door, Bill had come in late; actually he had arrived a bit earlier than his usual time because he wanted to catch Powell before she went off to Richmond for the week. As always, A. P. Hill was there first, but today she seemed more preoccupied than ever. She barely stirred when the door opened, and she did not look up when he came in.

She was sitting at her desk, barricaded behind an open copy of the *Washington Post*, surrounded by other newspapers. In addition to her regular reading material, she had acquired a stack of other periodicals, including several supermarket tabloids and the current issues of *People* and *Newsweek*. She was so absorbed in her reading that she merely grunted when Bill wished her good morning, and her answers to his subsequent conversational gambits had been monosyllabic. For a morning person, Powell Hill was acting in a most peculiar way. Since Bill was definitely not a morning person, he fumbled with the canister of tea bags, and made only feeble efforts to communicate with her.

Bill microwaved himself a cup of tea while he considered the matter. According to a note on the reception desk, Edith had gone out to buy doughnuts, so he was left alone to cope with his partner's puzzling abstraction. When, in diffident tones, Bill made his announcement about the new house, he was anticipating an explosion. He had expected his news to be pounced upon with cries of alarm and demands for a cast-iron explanation of his fiscal impetuousness. ("You bought a house? In an hour?") But so far his efforts to apprise his partner of their new quarters had been met with a bewildering indifference. In the past A. P. Hill had displayed more interest in some of his necktie purchases than she was currently showing toward this monumental investment. Perhaps she thought he had simply made an offer to rent office space. He decided to feed her the details of the purchase in small increments, leaving the subject of price for last.

"It has eight thousand square feet," said Bill. "That's including the third floor, which has dormers and slanting walls. Servants rooms, the Realtor said. I thought we might use them for storing the files."

"S'nice." She turned another page.

"The house has seven fireplaces and oak paneling from a French chateau."

"Mmm."

"Cost close to half a million dollars. Of course it would cost twice that to build it from scratch. At least."

"Uh-huh." She reached for a supermarket tabloid.

"And it has an elevator run by a trained gorilla."

"Fine."

"The governor will be running a shoeshine stand in the marble foyer."

No reply.

Bill raised his voice by two notches: "Okay, Powell, I'm wasting my breath. You're not listening."

The silence that followed this remark finally caught A. P. Hill's attention. She lowered the paper and looked at him. "I'm sorry," she said. "I've got a lot on my mind. The trip to Richmond. Pretty high-powered case, you know. Cousin Stinky recommended me." She frowned at the thought of the attorney general of the Commonwealth of Virginia, known as "Stinky" only to his closest relatives.

For the first time that morning, Bill was able to see her face. She had rumpled hair, dark circles under her eyes, and no lipstick. He wondered if she had slept at all the night before. If so, it must have been in those clothes. The case she was working on must have been more difficult than she expected, he thought, although A. P. Hill did tend to take things too much to heart. She plowed into criminal cases as if losing one would mean that she would have to go to prison instead of her client. Obviously this was not a good time to add to her worries.

"Look," he said. "I don't mean to bother you. I can see you're busy. I just want to clarify something. You did say that I could handle the business of buying a house, right? On my own?"

He could see her attention drifting back to the newspaper. "Sure, Bill," she murmured. "I trust you. It's just a house, and it's your money. If we don't like it as an office, we call another Realtor."

"I may have some papers to sign this afternoon. Shall I go ahead and use my judgment? You haven't seen it yet, I realize, but I think it's important to close the deal as soon as possible."

"Whatever."

"The deal may go through rather quickly. The owner is a corporation and they're handling the financing themselves."

A. P. Hill turned another page. "Mmm."

Elizabeth MacPherson settled comfortably in the big leather chair in the office of the consulting psychiatrist, trying not to focus on her own troubles. Eventually, of course, she would have to talk about Cameron—that's what she was here for, after all. But not yet. The tissue box was within reach, she noted, but this was her first session with this doctor, and she felt reluctant to unburden herself without any preliminaries. She felt that to begin the counseling session with tears and a litany of sorrow might come perilously close to whining, a form of self-indulgence strictly forbidden by her Scots Calvinist forebears. To play for time, she cast about for a more neutral topic to discuss. "What is Asperger's syndrome?" she asked.

The doctor looked down at his notes and then back at her with a puzzled frown. "You don't have it."

Elizabeth smiled. Dr. Freya would have said, Why do you ask? Then she would have wanted to explore the implications of Elizabeth's curiosity, wringing out every nuance, like a terrier worrying a rag. But Dr. Freya wasn't due to visit today, so Elizabeth was having a settling-in session with one of the staff physicians, Dr. Thomas Dunkenburger, whom Elizabeth was already thinking of as "kindly old Dr. Dunkenburger." Through her haze of grief and self-absorption, Elizabeth perceived him as a soft-spoken, elderly man with mild blue eyes and a gentle smile. She found his presence comforting. He doesn't take up much psychic space, she thought. He leaves you enough room to air your thoughts.

"Asperger's? I just wondered about it," she told him, thinking of yesterday's visit from Emma O. "I have a doctorate in anthropology, you know." She blushed at her attempt to establish parity with her therapist. "Well, forensic anthropology, actually," she admitted.

Dr. Dunkenburger nodded. "It's on your record. I hope we won't be needing your services while you're here. You wanted to know about Asperger's?"

"Somebody here mentioned the term, and I'd never heard of it."

The psychiatrist permitted himself a tight smile. "I'll bet you've seen it, though. It's actually classified as high-functioning autism—that is, it's a mild form of the disorder. Asperger's people don't live entirely in their own little world, but they're not quite at ease in this one, either. They're people who don't quite fit into the mainstream, and don't see why they should try. Asperger's types have their own pet subjects, and they tend to lecture others about their obsessions without making eye contact or pausing for comments from the other person."

He paused, but Elizabeth did not reply, because she was busy making lists of people who fit the description. Cousin Charles . . .

Dr. Dunkenburger went on. "They say whatever they're thinking, with little regard for tact or courtesy. And they don't seem to be able to empathize with other people, or to gauge other people's reaction to themselves."

Elizabeth considered this. "Like the people at a science fiction convention?"

Dr. Dunkenburger nodded. "Well, if you needed to observe some people with Asperger's, that might be the quickest way to find some. I've often thought that the three Lone Gunmen characters on *The X-Files* were typical Asperger's cases."

Elizabeth raised her eyebrows. "Oh, you watch *The X-Files?*"

"For professional reasons, certainly. That and *Star Trek* and *Babylon 5*. Futuristic television programs are a useful common ground with certain patients. If paranoids love spy thrillers, then autistic types belong in the constituency of science fiction." He paused. "Of course, the programs can be pretty interesting in themselves."

Elizabeth just looked at him, eyebrows raised.

Dr. Dunkenburger laughed. "Okay! Not everybody who's interested in science fiction has Asperger's."

"How do you treat it?"

"Well, you don't, for the most part. Asperger's people function in society well enough. They might be research scientists, or engineers, or computer specialists, and they are often highly intelligent. They just do their thing. Perhaps they don't have many friends . . . they have a tendency to show off their knowledge. They are the sort of people who read novels in order to find mistakes, which they can point out to the author to show how clever they are."

"I'll bet that makes them popular."

He smiled again. "Granted, their people skills are minimal. You'll seldom find one in a college fraternity or in a people-oriented job like politics or car sales, but they contribute to society in many valuable ways. Inventors . . . research scientists . . . It would be a dull old world if everyone were baseline normal."

"Fat chance of that."

He sighed. "Well, I'd be unemployed then, wouldn't I? As I said, though, you don't happen to have the disorder, so let's talk about something that does pertain to you. Your chart says that you are here for depression, but there is a recommendation that you stay here for a month. Hmmm." He frowned at the folder. "Now, usually with depressed patients, we stabilize them, prescribe medication, and send them home. . . ."

"Well," said Elizabeth. "About the medication . . . I may have mentioned to Dr. Freya that if she gave me a prescription for tranquilizers, I'd take them home and eat them like popcorn. . . ."

"Ah," Dr. Dunkenburger nodded. "References to suicide. Then you will be with us for a while. Have you settled in to the routine around here?"

"I suppose so," said Elizabeth. "Except for the blood tests and the morning medication ritual, it's a little like being back in college. Interesting people who are not entirely sane." This remark suddenly reminded Elizabeth of her family. "May I have visitors?" she asked.

"If you like. You cannot leave the campus, as we like to call it, but there is a reception room where people may come and visit with you, if the idea appeals to you. You are here for situational depression. Would you like to talk about it?"

"Well . . ." Elizabeth kept her voice carefully neutral. She didn't want to dwell on Cameron—not yet. Best to keep to an impersonal recital of the facts. "My husband is . . ." She hesitated for an instant over the word. Verb tenses were no longer something that she took for granted. Is? Too naive? Was? Too pessimistic? ". . . a marine biologist. One day he went off into the North Sea in his boat to study seal migration, and he was never heard from again."

Dr. Dunkenburger nodded sympathetically. "Presumed dead."

Elizabeth winced. "Well, not by me," she said. "Not at first. When he first went missing, I presumed everything but. Engine trouble on the boat. Caught in the Gulf Stream and drifted to Iceland. Eloped with Norwegian sex goddess. Eloped with a seal. I had a million theories, not excluding amnesia and flying saucers. All these scenarios ended with Cameron coming home." She sighed. "But . . ."

"But he didn't."

"No."

"It has been more than a few weeks now, I take it?"

Elizabeth nodded miserably. "Nearly two months. The searches turned up nothing."

"And now you have to get on with your life."

"Or find a life to get on with." Elizabeth heard her voice quaver. She held her breath until the urge to cry went away.

Dr. Dunkenburger tapped his pencil on his notepad. "Under the circumstances, I think it would do you good to have visitors," he said. "You need to be taken out of yourself every now and then. Have you been assigned a roommate yet?"

Elizabeth shook her head.

"Well, you might do with some companionship there, too. I'll see what I can arrange."

"Too bad Pierce Brosnan isn't crazy," said Elizabeth.

Dr. Dunkenburger regarded her thoughtfully. "Don't feel that you have to be charming," he said. "Putting up a brave front for your therapist is a waste of money, surely. We're here to help you deal with the pain. Besides, the world won't throw you overboard if you feel sorry for yourself every now and again. You're here to get better, not to practice a stiff upper lip."

Elizabeth nodded tearfully. "Sorry," she said. "It's second nature."

"Of course it is. We were all taught that it is good manners to mask one's pain. But remember: You have to hurt to heal."

At an interstate exit somewhere near Memphis, P. J. Purdue was sprawled across one twin bed in the Star-Lite Motel, studying a grainy photo of herself in a supermarket tabloid. The headline read PMS OUTLAWS STRIKE AGAIN! Purdue scowled at the unflattering shot. "This picture makes my jaw look puffy," she announced. She struck a pose. "Carla, look! Don't you think I look puffy?"

Carla Larkin set down the bottle of silver nail polish and leaned over to examine the photo. "I think it's the angle," she said after a few moments' scrutiny. "You look fine."

Purdue shrugged. She had never been particularly interested in her looks because the emphasis in her family had been on brains, but somehow being with Carla had made her more aware of her appearance. Not that she could compete with Carla, who was beautiful; Purdue just wished that her own image in the mirror would stop looking so reproachful.

Carla had that fine-boned perfection that either you were born with or you did without. She ate all she wanted of whatever junk food was available and never gained an ounce, and she moved with a natural grace that suggested a privileged upbringing and years of training in ballet—neither of which she'd had. It was Purdue, the judge's granddaughter with the expensive private education, who looked like a peasant. Purdue sometimes marveled over the irony of it without any rancor whatsoever. How could you begrudge anything of Carla Larkin?

The day they had met—Purdue stepping in as her court-appointed lawyer—Carla's beauty had shone through even the drab prison uniform, the seldom-washed hair, and the scrubbed face of a woman no longer allowed to keep makeup. She looked like a captive princess. In similar circumstances Purdue would have looked like a potato with frizzy hair. No stranger on earth would have been moved to help her. But Carla was different. She touched the world but lightly, wherever she was.

Purdue sighed as she looked at the unflattering news photo.

Maybe if she let her hair grow longer her neck wouldn't look so short.

Carla was smiling. "It's just a bad picture, hon. Don't worry about it. Hey, you still look good enough to make the lounge lizards lust after you."

"Oh, them." P. J. Purdue scowled at the thought of their string of victims. "I don't take that personally. Anybody under forty and breathing is the girl of their dreams. After three drinks, they'd still be interested even if I did look like this." She tapped the offending photo.

"Well," said Carla. "Mug shots are like driver's license pictures. They don't care if you're ready or not. Just point and shoot." She giggled. "Sort of like my ex-husband."

P. J. nodded. "Anyway, we don't want the photos to look too much like us. That would make us too easy to spot."

"So would a T-shirt that says PMS OUTLAW, but I want one anyway."

"No, you don't. You've been in prison already, and drawing attention to ourselves would be a sure way to get you sent back there. Have you forgotten what it was like?"

"I'm trying to." Carla Larkin shrugged. "At first I thought you could survive it with a positive attitude," she said. "When I first went in, I pretended that I was in the air force. We had to wear uniforms, get up at a certain time, eat together in the mess hall, do our assigned jobs. I just made believe that I was Private Larkin, USAF, doing a hitch in the service. . . ."

"Yeah, twenty years' worth. You could have made general by then."

"Well," said Carla, "You could have made attorney general if you hadn't broken me out of there."

"Maybe, but I never was one for playing it safe," said Purdue. "And it seemed like such a waste to keep you cooped up in there until you got old."

"Old comes fast in prison." Carla shivered. "They get like sheep, the institutionalized ones. Like canaries who think the cage is their home."

Purdue nodded. "And unlike some of my old acquaintances, who are probably pillars of respectability by now, I thought that our present course of action might be more fun than what I was doing before. Lawyers get institutionalized, too, I think. Anyhow, I still think of myself as practicing law. Enforcing it, anyway."

"How do you figure that?"

Purdue grinned. "When we take those guys' wallets, we're just collecting the fines for adultery and fornication. Just collecting the fines."

Carla Larkin looked at her watch. "Happy hour," she announced. "Let's go and collect the wages of sin."

"Yes," said Purdue. Her eyes sparkled. "But this time let's try a change of venue."

"We've passed all the restaurants on this road," said Edith, looking through the rear window back at a hamburger joint receding into the distance. Then she looked meaningfully at her wristwatch. "And my lunch hour is over in fifty-one minutes."

"I thought we could pick up fast food on our way back," said Bill. "I want to show you something."

They were speeding along a two-lane blacktop road that had slowly changed from suburban-commercial to rural-agricultural.

It was the same route that Bill had traveled yesterday with Holly Milton, but this time Bill was the tour guide.

"Lawyers!" grumbled Edith. "With lawyers, you can never assume. At precisely eleven fifty-eight A.M. you said to me: 'It's lunchtime, Edith. Let's go out.' And I leapt to a foolish conclusion. Call me crazy, but I took that statement as an implied oral contract, offering me a moderately priced midday meal at your expense, but no-ooo."

Bill did not take his eyes off the road. "I'll feed you, I swear!" he said. "At least . . . I'm not sure how much cash I actually brought with me. I may have to borrow some. . . ."

Edith sighed. "Let's go to the Gingerbread House then. They'll take your check. They know you of old. Now what is so all-fired important that I have to postpone lunch to see it?"

Bill hesitated. "I think it's better if I show you rather than tell you. Besides, there's something else I wanted to ask you about—out of the office. What's wrong with Powell today. Do you know?"

Edith shrugged. She hadn't been told not to tell Bill anything about the PMS Outlaws, but A. P. Hill was a deep one. Any explanations had better come from her and not through an intermediary. Before Powell Hill left for Richmond, she had left instructions with Edith that if Purdue called again, she should be given the number of Powell's cell phone and the switchboard of her hotel. "A. P. Hill is always worried about something," Edith hedged. "She broods. Sometimes I think the calcium in Tums is all that's keeping her alive."

Bill nodded. Had he not been so concerned about his cavalier expenditure of his entire savings—some half a million

---

dollars—he might have pursued the matter further, but just now his own troubles were uppermost in his mind. "That's why I brought you out here really," he told Edith. "Sort of a second opinion. If you think she won't like it . . ."

He had timed this speech to coincide with pulling into the driveway of the Dolan Mansion, as he now thought of it. When he reached the exact spot in the curve of the driveway where the white-columned house sat framed in the windshield like a scenic postcard, he stepped on the brake, letting the car idle through an otherwise unbroken silence. He waited.

Finally Edith said, "This is it? This—? You don't mean that you bought the woodshed out behind it or anything?"

"Nope. Bought the house," said Bill with a touch of modest pride.

"Bought . . . the . . . house," murmured Edith, still staring.

Bill took his foot off the brake, allowing the car to inch forward toward the grand entrance, as Edith continued to stare, her lips moving soundlessly. "So—do you think she'll like it?"

Edith nodded slowly. "If she's human—which at times I do wonder about—she will."

"Good. I brought my camera along. I thought we'd take a few pictures of the place. Maybe we could get some new business cards with a picture of the house on it. No, I guess we'd need a sign out front first."

"I'll call around," murmured Edith, still staring at the white-columned mirage framed in the windshield.

"Well, maybe you could take my picture standing on the front steps. I could send one to Elizabeth. Cheer her up."

Edith shook herself out of an architectural reverie. "Bill, this place must have cost you a fortune."

"Well, we did the math with the mortgage people, and they seem to think we can manage. I'm selling some stock to make a pretty hefty down payment. Remember, we won't have separate rents to pay any more. We'll be living upstairs." He smirked. "And the corporation was eager to find a buyer for the place. Tax reasons, I suppose. It was priced to sell. Besides, I drove a pretty hard bargain. Made them knock fifty K right off the price of the place."

Edith's jaw dropped. "Are you telling me that you got this place with a discount of fifty thousand dollars?"

"That's right."

Edith was silent for a moment, thinking how best to word her next question with skill and tact. After all, Bill MacPherson was her employer. He had many good qualities, but driving a hard bargain was not among them. Edith had seen Bill's haggling skills in action when the firm hired her as its office manager and general dogsbody several years back. She had come in, fresh from the community college, asking for seven dollars an hour. After a few moments of salary negotiations with "hardhearted Bill," Edith had ended up with eight. Her employer's present claim to have saved fifty thousand dollars on the price of a mansion made her wonder if the place glowed in the dark from a radioactive waste site, or if it were being held together by teetering pyramids of termites. She could not even venture a guess. "Tell me," she said at last.

The Cherry Hill cafeteria was filled nearly to capacity. Elizabeth stood a few feet past the food line, holding her tray of meat, two veggies, and Jell-O, looking for a place to sit. She had been a little intimidated by the thought of her first meal in a mental institution. Did people howl and throw food? On the way to the cafeteria, she had been greeted in the hall by a tiny, wizened woman who waved at her and said: "Praise the Lord, child. It makes the devil crazy." Before Elizabeth could muster a response, the woman cackled happily to herself and wandered away. She wondered if this were a portent of encounters to come, and if so, did one ever learn to take such experiences in stride?

Elizabeth had considered eating alone in her room, but she thought that might be against the rules, and since she couldn't be bothered to argue with bureaucrats in her present state of apathy, she decided to venture into the dining room and hope for the best.

The cafeteria seemed perfectly ordinary. People sat quietly at tables for six, eating and chatting and taking no notice of her whatsoever. A few patients stared off into space or muttered to themselves, and others had a ravaged look that seemed more in keeping with street people than campus residents, but on the whole the diners appeared rather ordinary. Elizabeth's anxiety did not lessen with this observation; it merely changed focus. Now the place felt like junior high school, where everyone knew one another, and she was the new kid. Lunchtime as a ritual of the institutional caste system. Which crowd did you want to hang with? Who were the popular people and who would it be social death to sit beside? (I am not paranoid, she told herself. I am severely depressed. Pick a form of insanity and stick to it, girl.)

Elizabeth noticed that the groups tended to segregate themselves at tables of all males or all females. She sighed. Perhaps we are different beings, she thought. The sexes come together for a few years between puberty and menopause, and then we drift away again, with nothing left to say to each other. She wondered if her time of gender isolation had been prematurely advanced by widowhood, or if she would some day come out on the other side. Lots of topics are gender neutral, Elizabeth told herself. The weather. Movies. News of scientific discoveries. Sometime I will find a man and make small talk with him, she promised herself silently. But not today.

She wandered closer to the women's tables, searching for a familiar face. A moment later she spotted the pudding face of Emma O., the patient who had come to see her the day before. There were five people seated at the table, all laughing and talking and paying Elizabeth no mind, but opposite Emma O. was an empty chair. With a smile of recognition, Elizabeth approached the table, resolving to make an effort to be sociable.

"Excuse me," said Elizabeth, pointing to the empty chair. "Is this seat taken?"

Before her new acquaintance could answer, a plump woman with a pink scrubbed face and gooseberry eyes smirked up at her. "Yeah, that chair is taken," she said. "A middle-aged woman is sitting in it."

Elizabeth took a step backward in surprise. Delusional, she thought. Or else they don't like me. Rejected by mental patients—how outcast can you get? Feeling the familiar sting of tears in her eyes, her shoulders sagged, and she turned to go.

"Come back, Sunshine!" Emma O. called after her. "Rose here was making a joke."

Elizabeth approached the table again, and Emma O. explained: "From a man's point of view, all the seats at this table would be empty. All, that is, except . . . that one." She nodded toward a pale but lovely young woman at the other end of the table.

Elizabeth had never seen anyone so fragile-looking and yet so beautiful. An angel carved in ivory might look like that, she thought: hair too pale to be called blonde, and skin so translucent that you could see the blue tracery of veins at her hands and throat. She was in that ephemeral stage of modern perfection that came just before death from starvation. An angel carved in ivory also might eat more than she did. The young woman had a full plate, and she was using her fork to make little trails through her mashed potatoes, making it seem as if the food had been picked at. At no time, however, did the fork go near her mouth.

"You can sit down," said Emma O. to Elizabeth, indicating the empty chair.

While Elizabeth set down her tray and took the seat, Emma O. picked up her fork and went back to eating, as if she had forgotten Elizabeth's presence altogether.

"I'm Rose Hanelon," said the dumpy woman who had joked about the empty chair. "It's no use expecting Emma Kudan to make introductions. The social graces are Martian to her. It would never occur to Emma O. that you'd even care who anybody else was."

The object of the discussion shrugged and went on eating her Jell-O.

"Asperger's people have to concentrate very hard on being sociable to think of things like introducing people," Rose explained. "They can focus on one person at a time, but more people than that puts a strain on their ability to socialize. We wrote out all the instructions on a card for Emma once, but she used it as a bookmark and lost it."

"How do you do? I'm Elizabeth MacPherson," Elizabeth said meekly. She smiled and nodded to the other occupants of the table, careful to observe all the social niceties, lest she be mistaken for an Asperger's patient herself. She had already concluded that rudeness was a hallmark of the condition.

Rose nodded. "You're here for depression. Emma told us. It wouldn't occur to her that you might not want people to know. That's Lisa Lynn beside you. She's a little hyper today, so if you talk to her, don't expect to get a word in edgewise."

Lisa Lynn was a thin, mousy-looking young woman. "Hello," she said, accompanying her smile with a tentative wave. "Pardon my fidgets. We're adjusting my medication," she said. "Which is good because with the old one I was getting these side effects that—"

"Hold that thought," said Rose, drowning her out. "Beside her is old Mrs. Nicholson, who may or may not know we're here. Anyhow, she doesn't care. Just watch your dessert if you ever sit next to her. And last but far from least is Sarah Findlay, the shining light pretending to eat at the end of the table. Somebody in here nicknamed her Seraphin, and it stuck."

Emma O. looked up. "Seraphim is the plural form of the word, of course, but it's such an apt play on words that everybody uses it. I expect you can see why."

Elizabeth looked at the frail beauty and nodded. "Angelic. Yes. She looks like a movie star."

"Which is very unfortunate in terms of role models, don't you find?" said Rose softly. "Be beautiful if it kills you."

"It's crazy, isn't it?" Elizabeth agreed.

"Crazy?" Scenting a debate in the offing, Emma O. set down a fork full of mashed potatoes. "Seraphin is the sanest woman in here. The one most in sync with the world, anyhow, which is what reality is: consensus. If you want to see someone out of touch with reality, look at Warburton over there, carrying her tray to the drink table. It's a wonder she can lift it. Now there's crazy on the hoof."

Elizabeth saw a heavyset woman in a white uniform carrying a lunch tray laden with plates, little bowls of vegetables, and desserts. "Are you referring to that staff member?" she asked.

"Right. Warburton. Look at her. How old would you say she is, just offhand. Top of your head guess."

"Well, she's a bit far away," said Elizabeth. She studied the waddling woman. "I don't know. I'm too far away to see her hands. Hair color tells you nothing these days. Fifty?"

"My point exactly," said Emma O., grinning wickedly. "Warburton is thirty-seven. Just. Birthday last month. Looks sixty, poor beast. Never going to get promoted—it'd be too cruel to tell her why, though. And you know what else? She's only four years older than Seraphin."

Elizabeth turned to stare at the beautiful doll-like girl at the far end of the table. Apparently oblivious to the conversation of her table partners, she was breaking her bread into tiny pieces, and placing them carefully at intervals on the plate. Sarah Findlay looked like a delicate child. You had the urge to protect her, to fuss over her. Elizabeth was willing to believe that the girl was in her early twenties, but . . . thirty-three? She shook her head. Warburton and the anorectic girl could have passed for grandmother and granddaughter, so vast was the difference between them.

"That's right," said Emma O., who seemed to be particularly gifted at reading facial expressions. "Chronological age be

----

damned: Warburton is old and Seraphin is young—John Keats got it wrong, you see."

"Keats? The poet?"

"S'right. 'Ode to a Grecian Urn.' Ever read it? Well, in it, he said, 'Beauty is truth, truth beauty.' But beauty isn't truth. It's *youth*. Beauty is youth, youth beauty. And it's worth starving for if you want everybody to love you. Greatest power there is."

"But . . . if you starve yourself— . . . doesn't that mean that you don't love yourself?"

"Doesn't matter. You can never love yourself enough to make up for the indifference of others. Look at poor Warburton shoveling it in. She can never fill the void inside her with food. And the more she eats the more powerless she becomes."

Elizabeth looked down at her plate, at the congealing mashed potatoes and slabs of roast beef drenched in viscous brown gravy. She wasn't hungry any more. She wondered how Emma O. could manage to eat so heartily, given her obsession with beauty, but perhaps it would be rude to challenge her on that point.

After a moment's pause, Elizabeth said to Rose, "I'm new here, so I'm not sure if it's the done thing to ask people what they're in for."

Rose Hanelon gave her a pitying smile. "You're officially crazy, my dear. Now you can ask anybody anything you damn well please."

Before Elizabeth could put this new freedom to the test, however, Emma O. finished her gelatin, and asked, "You had a session with a shrink today, didn't you? Which one?"

"Kindly old Dr. Dunkenburger," said Elizabeth.

Emma looked as if she were about to say something, but

then she shrugged. As she got up to refill her water glass, she muttered, "I have Dr. Shokie. Fat lot of good he is."

"I hope you'll be in group with us," said Lisa Lynn. "You really get to know people in group."

"I don't think I'll be doing group therapy," said Elizabeth carefully. "You see, I'm not really—"

"Crazy." Rose beamed at her. "Isn't that what you were going to say?"

"Not at all," said Elizabeth, thinking fast. She didn't want to offend these people, who would be her friends, even if it was for only a month. A month could be a long time. "I was going to say that I'm not able to be helped. My husband is dead, and talking about it is not going to bring him back."

"Yes," said Lisa Lynn. "But the therapy is for you. Not for him."

"They'll insist on assigning you to group," Rose told her. "It's a standard part of the treatment here, so you might as well come to ours. We have a session after lunch. Warburton is our group leader."

"Well . . ." said Elizabeth, "I'm not sure. . . ."

Rose Hanelon gave her a wolfish grin. "You'd better come to our group. We're the cool people."

The PMS Outlaw gig had a lot in common with the cocktail party circuit in her old life, thought P. J. Purdue. A lot of lies were told over many little drinks, phony compliments passed, and one way or another somebody was going to get screwed. And then as now it was all strictly business.

She sipped her drink, watching Carla bat her eyes at an owlish young man with a stained tie and a briefcase in his lap.

Carla was a natural at the pickup con. She acted as if she had been doing it all her life, which perhaps she had. Growing up poor with a succession of unofficial stepfathers, Carla had learned early on that love was not something you ever got for free.

One way or another you pay your way in life, Carla often said. Being pretty is the cheapest way to go. Purdue wouldn't know about that. Early on she had opted for smart, which wasn't as cushy a ride as pretty, but it sure beat the hell out of "desperately nice and sincere," always a popular choice among women. The meek shall inherit the earth, all right, thought P. J. Purdue. One heaping spoonful at a time.

Carla was indeed a beauty, but she'd needed some guidance from Purdue to dress the part for the caper of the day. Teased hair and raccoon eye shadow were all right for roadhouses, but razzle-dazzle wouldn't do the job in a rock-bed Republican country club.

They had found the place by reading the local newspaper, which had given up carrying world news altogether, so hopeless was the prospect of competing against the big-city dailies that everyone subscribed to for "real news." The purpose of the small-town publication was to keep track of the community's weddings, births, and funerals (not necessarily in that order); to chart the activities of local government; and to chronicle the social scene for the area elite. All pretense of national coverage had vanished from the pages of the local twice-weekly: it had given pride of place on page one to the country club golf tournament, as if wars, tornados, and presidential elections were things that happened to other people.

Carla was working alone at first. Two women on the prowl would raise too many eyebrows in a staid private dining room.

No one had questioned their entrance, though. They walked in, well dressed and confident, as if they had arranged to meet some- one. "Don't trouble yourself about us," Purdue told the waiter as she commandeered a table. "He's late. We'll keep an eye out for him." Purdue could manage more well-bred hauteur than the av- erage duchess. It had served her well in courts of law, but it was an even more useful talent when possessed by a fugitive.

Carla was wearing the little black dress they had bought at a department store sale in a mall two states back. Her only jew- elry was a single strand of pearls, which happened to be real be- cause Purdue, who had inherited them from her grandmother, had been wearing them on the day of their original getaway. Well-cut black dress. Blonde hair. Pearls. Now if only she could get the patter right.

Carla had moved away from the nervous-looking young man. Bad prospect. Conveying this message to Purdue with the briefest of glances, she sauntered with deliberate casualness toward an older man in golfing clothes, who was sitting alone at a table. His face was not visible, but he kept spearing forkfuls of chicken salad from behind an open *Wall Street Journal,* and from the look of his blue-veined hands he was well past sixty. Still young enough to dream, Purdue thought approvingly.

She held her breath as she watched her partner's initial ap- proach. Sloe-gin smile, soft voice, one well-manicured hand ges- turing toward the newspaper. Good . . . good . . . After a few more moments of smiling conversation, Carla slipped into the chair beside the golfer. Now she assumed a pose of rapt enchant- ment, saying very little, but looking as if the old duffer's remarks were pearls of wisdom. Things should go off without a hitch now. Carla had been accepted in her role, and the old fellow would remember her as a sparkling conversationalist, as people usually do when you allow them to do all the talking.

Purdue turned her attention back to her drink. She didn't want the mark to catch her staring at him. She wondered how long it would take Carla to get down to business. Purdue sipped her vodka martini, wondering idly why she derived such pleasure from the fleecing of their victims. There were other ways the pair could have supported themselves, even illegally. They could have sold phony gold-mine stock to greedy investors, or wheedled lonely senior citizens out of their life savings with bogus investment scams by telephone. Purdue had not even considered such ventures. There was no satisfaction for her in bilking gullible fools whose only crime was ignorance. She wanted the shallow men, the self-styled Romeos, the ones who thought they were the predators. Purdue recognized her own satisfaction in the humiliation of these men as a species of rage. Where had it come from, though? Was this for Daddy, who thought that the honor roll was nice but not good enough to compensate for the fact that the teenage Purdue was not a pretty, giggly blonde? Was it for every boy who made fun of her in high school, and for every loathsome blind date she had endured in college? Well, no matter. She would show them all.

She looked up in time to see Carla smiling and nodding in her direction. She leaned over and whispered something in the businessman's ear, and he grinned and reddened slightly. Then the two of them got up, and, hand in hand, they approached Purdue.

"I'd like to introduce you to someone very special," said

Carla. "This is Sam Jenkins. Mr. Jenkins is a banker." She giggled as she added, "I don't know when I've met anybody more
captivating!"

Carla gave a little smirk when she said the last word, and
Purdue looked startled, thinking of the handcuffs stashed in her
evening bag, but a glance at their prospective victim reassured
her. Mr. Jenkins suspected nothing but a unique and delightful
evening of fun. Well, it would be memorable, they'd guarantee
him that.

"It is indeed a pleasure to meet you," said Purdue, extend-
ing her hand. "My name is Hill. A. P. Hill. I'm an attorney from
Virginia."

"She's a criminal lawyer," said Carla Larkin, and they
laughed merrily at the wordplay that Mr. Jenkins would come to
appreciate only later.

"Elves are one of the things they
give you
When you go mad.
They come on the Welcome
Wagon,
Sit in your mind,
And tell you what sane people
are up to."
—Sign on Emma O.'s door

Chapter 5

Group therapy at Cherry Hill was held in a sunny first-floor room whose curtainless windows overlooked an expanse of green lawn. Metal folding chairs stood in a semicircle, facing a chalkboard mounted on one cinder-block wall, while above it a plate-size Seth Thomas clock measured the minutes of the session.

Following her new friends into the room, Elizabeth chose a seat near the window with a good view of the flower beds, in case listening to other people's troubles became tedious or threatened to distract her from her own sorrow. Elizabeth did not plan to contribute anything to the afternoon's discussion herself. She felt that since bereavement was an indisputable, incurable fact, it did not qualify as a mental imbalance. Besides, her grief was too private to be shared, but she congratulated herself on being a good

----

sport by coming along to group therapy to provide an audience for the others.

She counted the chairs. Judging by the number provided, twelve people would be participating in the session, which would practically guarantee an argument. Even among sane people, in a group of that size at least one person always takes the outrageous position just to antagonize the rest. Elizabeth already knew four of the other six women present: Rose, Emma, the beautiful Seraphin, and the fidgeting, still hyper, Lisa Lynn. One by one, four men straggled in and took their seats, leaving one empty chair.

One trim, dark-haired young man in jeans who appeared to be in his mid-twenties sat down next to Elizabeth. "Hello!" he said with a shy smile. "I don't believe we've met."

"No. I'm new here." Elizabeth smiled back at him before she remembered that this was not the place to cultivate new male acquaintances. For all she knew this personable young man could be a recovering ax murderer, or a raving psychotic. Still, she thought, looking at the other three patients, he seemed the most agreeable one of the bunch. Besides him, the other men in the discussion group were: an elderly fellow in a bathrobe who stared at the floor; a portly, red-faced man who kept beaming at everyone; and a scowling young man who kept tapping the floor with his foot. Given the choices, Elizabeth decided that on first glance she could consider herself lucky to be sitting where she was—later on, she thought, as details of the men's individual disorders were disclosed, she might revise both her opinion and the seating chart.

"Name's Matt Pennington," the young man was saying. "First time in group?"

Elizabeth nodded, wondering what sort of small talk one made when all you had in common was insanity. "First time. Yep. It's a little unnerving, the thought of opening up to strangers."

Matt smiled. "Who else can you open up to?"

"I don't know," murmured Elizabeth. "I'm of Scottish heritage. With us it isn't encouraged at all. Ever."

"I'm having electric shock treatment."

Elizabeth gasped, picturing lurid Hollywood scenes of snake-pit asylums. "Is it voluntary?" she asked. Because if electric shocks were a standard, compulsory part of treatment at Cherry Hill, she would go to her room right now and start packing.

"Did you come here voluntarily? I mean, the cops didn't drag you in here for assaulting somebody, or anything?"

She shook her head. "I checked myself in for depression. Situational depression, that is. I mean, things are really as bad as I think they are. It's not all in my head."

"Oh, well, ECT—that's what we call shock therapy these days—is certainly used to treat depression, but it wouldn't be done without your permission. Might help you, though. You should consider it."

Elizabeth shuddered. "I did," she said. "For a tenth of a second. No way."

"It isn't too bad," Matt insisted. "You're not awake for it. You've probably seen the old snake-pit movies about mental hospitals, but ECT is certainly not torture. The way my doctor explained it to me is: your brain gives off electrical waves, and shock treatment is one way of trying to stabilize those waves. The funny thing about it, though, is that it plays tricks on your memory. Short-term memory, I mean. Like—I cannot for the life of me remember what I had for breakfast."

"Oatmeal, I expect," murmured Elizabeth, turning away. All but one of the patients' chairs were now occupied, and the clock said 1:29. Class would begin at any moment.

As promised by Emma O. and Rose, Nurse Warburton appeared presently, clipboard in hand, and took her place as the mediator of the discussion group. She began by introducing Elizabeth and prompting the group members to call out a greeting to her in discordant unison. That alone would prompt one to feign a recovery, Elizabeth thought. She managed a feeble smile and a stifled wave in response to the halfhearted chorus of hellos.

"Tell us about yourself, Elizabeth," Warburton prompted. She didn't sound very interested, but apparently a novice speech was expected of newcomers to the group.

Elizabeth wondered whether she ought to stand. No, she decided. If you can't dispense with formality even when you're crazy, what's the point of it all? Still sitting in the metal folding chair, she said, "I'm Elizabeth MacPherson. I'm a forensic anthropologist, and I'm here for depression."

"No wonder," said the old man in the bathrobe. "A forensic anthropologist—ycch! You work with human remains, don't you? That would send anybody up the wall."

Elizabeth stared at him openmouthed. She hadn't expected such rudeness, even if the man was crazy. He looked seventy, and there was an unnatural smoothness to the skin of his face which suggested that at some time in the past he had undergone skin grafting operations, probably as a treatment for burns. He was not badly disfigured, but he did look unusual enough to warrant curious stares from strangers.

"Have you ever thought about teaching kindergarten instead?" the old man was saying.

Elizabeth narrowed her eyes. "I like my work," she said. "I'm only here because my husband died."

The man in the bathrobe shrugged. "I hope you buried him."

Warburton felt the discussion slipping from her grasp. Before Elizabeth could frame a blistering reply, she said, "I'm sure we'll learn more about Elizabeth in the days to come. Now before we get down to business, why don't the rest of you make her feel part of the group by telling her who you are."

With varying degrees of reluctance, the adults-turned-kindergartners mumbled their set pieces.

One of Elizabeth's lunch table partners went first. "Rose Hanelon, journalist and alcoholic." The middle-aged woman smiled. "The two are not always synonymous. In my case they are."

Seraphin, the waiflike beauty, gave Elizabeth a tentative wave. "Sarah Findlay. Depression, I guess."

"And liar," put in one of the men. "She doesn't eat enough to choke a cat." A warning look from Warburton silenced him.

Emma O. held up her white-scarred wrists. "E. O. Kudan. Technogeek. Escape artist."

"Matt Pennington. Architect—um . . . currently unemployed. I suffer from depression."

"Or, an acute perception of reality," said the scarred man in the bathrobe.

"Wait your turn, Mr. Randolph," said Warburton, putting an edge in her voice.

"It is my turn, O Elephant Bride. Hillman Randolph. What am I here for? Perhaps because I annoy the oafs in the outside world. Or because my countenance mars their pretty little world."

Deciding to let that one pass, the discussion leader turned to a faded older woman who had been staring at the floor. "Mrs. McNeil?" she said. At once she corrected herself: first names only in group. "Beulah?"

A colorless woman in a worn sack of a dress looked up shyly as she spoke. "I'm Beulah. My son and daughter-in-law insisted I come here for a while. I've been active in church all my life, you see, but just lately I've been called to go and preach the word of God to strangers. . . ."

"At the top of her lungs. On street corners," Matt whispered to Elizabeth, who nodded in sudden comprehension.

"It just embarrasses me so much to make a spectacle of myself like that, but they tell me I must. They keep at me until I do it. The voices, I mean." Her own voice trailed off into an anguished whisper. "The voices."

"We'll get back to the voices later, Beulah," said Warburton. "Clifford, you're next, please."

The scowling young man rubbed his stubble of beard and flashed an unpleasant smile. "Cops put me here," he said. "Evaluation-before-trial kind of crap. Street cops risk getting their heads shot off for twenty grand a year, and they're trying to tell me that I'm crazy." He leaned back in his chair and shot a triumphant glance at Hillman Randolph, who pointedly ignored him. " 'Course if it keeps me out of prison, I'll give 'em all the crazy they want."

Warburton simply stared at him and waited. Finally the young man mumbled, "Clifford Allen. Alleged burglar. That's all I'm going to say."

"All right." Warburton nodded to the portly man with the beaming smile on his round face. "Steve?"

The portly man upped the wattage of his grin, and said, "Steve Monroe. Attorney at law."

"I'm pretty sure that's curable," said Emma O.

Warburton glowered, as only a plain fat woman can. The badinage stopped.

Elizabeth felt an odd sense of detachment from this assembly of strangers, as if she had wandered into an audience participation play whose plot she could not fathom, but she was prepared to be entertained. She drifted away into contemplation of her own situation and missed the rest of the introductions. Perhaps the medication was working. She was still aware of her grief, and the fact that it ought to cause her pain, but there, too, the detachment made her feel as if she were observing someone else's troubles or remembering the emotions generated by a favorite book or film. Her bereavement was still there in the forefront of her mind, but it wasn't personal just now. She knew it, rather than felt it.

Elizabeth wondered if a dulling of the emotions helped one to get over a death or merely postponed the grieving. Sooner or later she would have to stop taking sedatives . . . wouldn't she? And when she did, would the sorrow flow back undiminished from the first pang of loss, or would the passage of time have distanced her beyond its reach? She decided that worrying about future emotions was borrowing trouble. Just get through today, she told herself. Eat, and sleep, and take your pills.

In the kitchen of the newly purchased mansion/office of MacPherson & Hill, the previous owner, the notorious Jack Dolan, was nodding happily over a cellophane-wrapped chocolate brownie. A steaming mug of sugared tea sat on the table within arm's reach. Edith had made it for him, when on thirty seconds' acquaintance he told her plaintively that he hadn't had any breakfast. He was counting on her not noticing the paper wrappings from his fast-food breakfast biscuit in the trash can. He liked this new visitor. When he said he was hungry, he thought he saw tears in her eyes. With a horrified squawk and a reproachful look at poor old Bill, the lady had searched the refrigerator, and, while the selection was meager, she'd managed to rustle him up a snack, promising to bring proper groceries the next time she came. Yep, she was a keeper all right. He hoped she could cook.

Now fortified with his makeshift meal, Mr. Jack had returned to his nap. He hoped these people would be gone by four, when the pizza delivery boy was due to arrive with his dinner. While he dozed, his visitors discussed him in anxious whispers.

Edith hissed, "What do you mean, the old man came with the place?"

Bill motioned her into the dining room, letting the swinging door to the kitchen close silently behind them. "Keep your voice down!" he said. "I don't want to upset him."

"You're upsetting me," said Edith. "Is he starving?"

"No. I am. I notice you didn't offer me any tea."

"It's not in my job description," said Edith, waving aside

his hunger as a minor point. "You bought a house with an old man in it . . . like a . . . like a garden gnome?"

"All right, I admit that it's a bit unusual as real estate transactions go, but I did save us a lot of money. And I thought it might be the best thing for him, really." He explained about Mr. Dolan's children who lost the house in a land deal, and how the old man had refused to be moved from his home. "He has no place to go," said Bill. "And I felt so sorry for him. Poor, helpless old man, well past ninety. He doesn't want to go into a nursing home, and who can blame him? How could I turn him out of the house he built?"

Edith sighed. He couldn't. Of course, he couldn't. He was Bill, the ultimate soft touch. She and Powell Hill would probably have to send him to the beach before they called in the termite exterminators. "So instead of a guard dog, you have an elderly tenant in your Tarafied law office. How do you see this working?" she asked.

"Well, I don't know. Mr. Jack seems pretty happy on the sunporch, and the offices will be in the front parlor, so he won't be in the way." Bill was giving her that he-followed-me-home-can-I-keep-him look. "There are extra rooms upstairs, and I wouldn't mind giving him one of those, but I don't want to take a chance on his falling down the stairs and getting hurt. He's pretty feeble. I don't think he can handle stairs anymore."

"I just hope he's housebroken." Edith sighed again. She supposed that her law-firm duties had just been enlarged to include nurse/caretaker for an elderly man. Still, the place was magnificent, she thought, looking around at the golden oak paneling and the high ceilings of the elegant dining room. It would cost millions to build such a house from scratch today.

Another thought occurred to her. "You've checked this out, haven't you? Structurally, I mean. Somebody has made sure this house isn't built on a landfill or an earthquake fault? Quicksand? Anything like that?"

"All clear," said Bill. "Outside inspector. Seller's guarantee."

Edith shrugged. Miracles do happen, she thought. Perhaps Bill had made a sensible buy, after all. She hoped that A. P. Hill would see it that way.

"Mr. Jack has had a really interesting life," Bill was saying. "The Realtor told me that back in the forties he got into trouble with the law. He may even have been in prison."

"Oh, fine," said Edith. "Dream houses always have some kind of a catch to them. The problem with this one is it comes with a little old convict. We'll all be murdered in our beds."

"No," said Bill. "I got the impression that Mr. Dolan was a white-collar criminal. Not violent. Anyhow, I doubt if he could even lift an ax any more. . . ."

Edith was unimpressed. "Let's hope you don't have to be his lawyer as well as his landlord." She sniffed.

A. P. Hill sat at the desk in her hotel room, going over the papers for the case that had brought her to Richmond, but she was unable to concentrate on the details because her thoughts kept straying to memories of her conversation with P. J. Purdue. Should she report the call to the police? She sighed. Why bother? Purdue had given her no idea of her whereabouts, and the call would not be traceable. Was there anything she could have said that would have convinced Purdue to give herself up? Again, no. At the time of the call, Powell had not even known that her old classmate was a fugitive from justice. There isn't much you can do when you don't know what's going on.

She tried pacing up and down in the hotel room to clear her head. Then she began her exercises. Twenty sit-ups later, she turned the television on for noise. The problem with exercising alone is that there's nothing to do with your brain, and it goes on in third gear while the rest of your body struggles along in first. Purdue and Larkin would not be evicted from her brain.

She sighed and pulled out the case folder she had started on the PMS Outlaws. Might as well consider the case. She wasn't going to get anything done otherwise. She read a summary of the escape and an account of the first robbery. The state had plenty of witnesses, that was certain. The guard who had been disarmed at the doctor's office had been frightened and humiliated when two women handcuffed him to a doorknob and made their escape. No doubt he had endured a considerable amount of ridicule back at the department for letting a couple of "ladies" get the best of him. He would be only too eager to testify for the prosecution, and there could be no question of mistaken identity with that particular witness.

The second victim of Purdue and Larkin was one Randy Templeton, a factory worker. The pair had picked him up in a roadhouse with promises of kinky sex, and then they'd left him handcuffed to a pipe in the basement of the bar. He had been rescued around three A.M. when the cleaning crew shut off the jukebox and heard cries for help from beneath the floor. The police had to send for a plumber to cut the pipe in order to free the nude and shivering Randy Templeton from his awkward position. Aside from bruises on his wrists from the handcuffs, Mr. Templeton was not injured, but his humiliation was painful indeed. A weapon had not been used in his abduction, but still he had been robbed of more than three hundred dollars. Or so he claimed. A. P. Hill doubted that Randy Templeton saw that much cash in a month, let alone one evening, but even if the charge were reduced from grand larceny to petty theft, it still meant serious trouble for the assailants.

Three days later, just over the Georgia line, the pair had struck again, this time luring a newly divorced car salesman out of a Laundromat. The owner of a local pig farm had found the salesman handcuffed to the steering wheel of a junked car body in the weeds just off a dirt road. The victim's car and wallet had left with the two pretty women whose descriptions matched those of the suspects in the roadhouse robbery.

Where were they getting all the handcuffs, A. P. Hill thought to herself. Would it be possible to trace them through the purchase of new ones?

Next she considered the matter of jurisdiction. The first crime had been committed in Alabama, when P. J. Purdue had assisted in the escape of a convicted felon. Was that a state or federal offense? Now they were robbing people and crossing state lines. What about extradition between states? No one had been killed or held for ransom, though. State or federal? And if . . . when . . . the pair were caught, what kind of prison time would they be facing? She hoped the pair would be tried in a state court and sentenced to a state penitentiary, because federal sentences do not allow for parole. Twenty years is a long time to sit while the world goes on without you.

A. P. Hill had met scores of criminals. She had defended

---

murderers without a moment's qualm, but this case was different. In her law practice, she met her clients only after they were
already accused of crimes, but P. J. Purdue was someone from
her student days. Not a case. A person. A. P. Hill could handle
weird cases or personal cases, but not both. And who appointed
you P. J. Purdue's lawyer? she asked herself sardonically. In order to represent her, first she would have to find her.

Elizabeth was watching the clock on the wall of the group
therapy room. Forty-five minutes to go. She hadn't felt this anxious to leave a room since high school algebra. The introductions were over now, and presumably a real discussion of
problems would begin. Were any of these people ax murderers,
and if so, would she feel any better for knowing who they were?

Nurse Warburton gave the group a grudging smile. "Now
who would like to go first?" she said. She looked expectantly at
Elizabeth, who shook her head and looked away. "Anyone?"

Seraphin's hand wavered tentatively, as if she lacked the
strength to fully extend her arm. "I ate some lunch today," she
said softly.

"And how did that make you feel?"

The girl closed her eyes. "I try not to think about it,"
she murmured. "Food is so heavy. I'm afraid it will close up my
throat and never go down."

This statement was followed by a few moments of silence,
as everyone except Seraphin considered the consequences of
not swallowing food. Finally the elderly woman in a faded sack
dress raised her hand. "I've been thinking about God," she said
with a tremulous smile.

"What about God, Beulah?" asked Warburton, almost

quickly enough to drown out a groan from the men in the group.

She twisted her hands in her lap. "Well, what if God's values are really different from ours? I mean, I've tried to live a good life, and do my duty and not hurt anybody, but how do I know if that's what God really wanted? What if He wanted something else altogether?"

"Yes!" said Emma O. "Good point! What if God only cares about . . . say . . . fashion? What if He spends His time obsessing about how we look? After all, He supposedly created us in His image . . . B.C. . . . . Before Chocolate. So what if you turn up in heaven on Judgment Day, and God says, 'About that time on August fourteenth of last year when you took My name in vain . . . on that occasion you were wearing a lime-green polyester skirt with a fuchsia blouse and a brown plastic belt. What were you thinking?' "

Beulah McNeil blinked furiously. Her spiritual train of thought had been derailed, and she was bewildered by the turn it had taken.

"Surely in the ten commandments He specified His priorities," said Steve, the lawyer. He seemed poised to lecture the group on the contractual obligations of the deity regarding the specifics of sin, but before any celestial preferences could be discussed further, the door opened and a slender young man wafted in. "I'm sorry I'm late," he said. "Of course, it's no use expecting me to be on time. I simply cannot force my body to bow to the beat of artificial timekeepers. I know that it's madly selfish of me to miss everyone's discussion at the beginning, but there it is. I am inconsiderate. It's the way I'm made."

Everyone else in the group nodded and went back to a listening posture, but Elizabeth continued to stare at the newcomer.

Warburton looked stern. "Richard, what have we said about punctuality?"

Richard sighed theatrically. "It is a sign of maturity and a mark of respect for your fellow patients. I know. But it's no use expecting me to obsess about a few paltry minutes. I was deep in contemplation of Beauty."

"Oh, is the Disney channel on?" asked Emma with a straight face.

Richard's stare in her direction was forbidding. "I was referring to the garden. I will sit down now and not continue to monopolize the session, although I'll probably talk too much anyway, even if I promise not to. My brain is a wellspring of thoughts and ideas, and I feel I simply must share them." He stopped abruptly as he noticed Elizabeth. "Hello, you're new here," he informed her. "My name is Richard Petress, and I expect you think I'm a therapist or something, but actually, I am a fellow patient, not unlike yourself."

"Richard Petress, M.D.," said Emma O. "But in his case it stands for manic depressive."

Richard nodded, as if a compliment had been conferred. "I live in a wider spectrum than most people have in their humdrum lives. Like the butterfly, I dance with the rainbow and then the flame. Society seems to wish to cure me of this heightened perception—"

"Oh, can it, Petress!" said Clifford Allen. "We were discussing something." He turned to the nurse. "Warburton, I have a question for you. Do patients have any say in the menu planning here? There was a puddle of butter on my broiled fish at lunch. Butter! I specifically asked for my meat to be cooked without oils of any kind. And I would prefer a salad without dressing instead of cooked vegetables . . ."

The harangue went on. Elizabeth whispered to Matt Pennington, "Is he phobic about food?"

"Who, Clifford?" Matt shook his head. "You know how some men love to tinker with sports cars? Soup up the engine and so on?"

"Yes."

"Well, Clifford is his own sports car. His body, I mean. He's always fussing over it as if it were a brand-new Jaguar. He scrutinizes every forkful of food, and he exercises for hours at a time."

Elizabeth studied Clifford Allen with interest. He was well muscled, younger than thirty, and sleekly fit without an ounce of fat. He looked in perfect health. Of course, it's sometimes difficult to judge people's medical conditions by appearances. He might have a heart condition, she thought. "Is he ill?" she asked Matt.

"No. Well, not physically. In fact, I'd say his body is as good as it's going to get, but that doesn't stop him from taking four showers a day, and obsessing about every item on his meal tray."

"But I thought he was here because he's a suspected thief."

"Well, he is. His obsession with his body is his personality, not his problem." Matt smiled. "In California it's people who aren't like that who are considered crazy. So maybe Clifford is just geographically challenged. He's in the wrong state. But, anyhow, that isn't his problem."

A sharp voice ended their private discussion. "Elizabeth, you haven't said anything to the group yet. Is there anything you'd like to talk about?" Warburton's expression was a careful neutral, but Elizabeth felt that she had just been punished for whispering in class.

Elizabeth sighed. "I'm sad," she said. "I was so happy. I guess I expected life to be like a fairy tale. You know: 'And they lived happily ever after.' "

"Life is like a fairy tale," said Emma O. "Fairy tales are very realistic. They all begin with, 'Once upon a time there was a beautiful . . .' whatever. Princess. Miller's daughter. Robber girl. Doesn't matter. The operative word here is *beautiful*. If you're pretty enough, the prince comes, the frog takes pity on you, and the fairy godmother does a few magic tricks for your convenience. That's what makes for the happy ending. Ugly people need not apply."

"Pretty people aren't guaranteed happiness," snapped Elizabeth. "Some of them die young."

"And then they make the cover of *People* magazine, and total strangers weep for them. If that's not a fairy-tale existence, I don't know what is."

"Can any of the staff doctors here check my cholesterol?" asked Clifford Allen.

Jack Dolan nodded happily on his sunporch. He liked to feel the warmth of the westering light on his face, and as he leaned back against the soft-cushioned back of his wicker arm-chair, he slipped in and out of awareness, more at peace than he had been in many months.

He wasn't as young as he used to be. Hell, he'd been old

four presidents ago. It had been a long, eventful life. He'd been
born in 1908 on a farm in southside Virginia, which is what they
call that part of the state bordering North Carolina. Times were
tough in his youth, and making illegal whiskey during the Pro-
hibition years was one good way for a farm family to get a little
extra cash. The Treasury cops seemed to think moonshining
was some high and terrible crime, damn near treason the way
they carried on about it, but as far as Jack Dolan could see,
moonshining was just an agrarian form of tax evasion, and he'd
never met anybody yet who didn't do a little of that when times
got tough. The really expert bootleggers were the ones up north
who dodged the tax man by importing the forbidden whiskey
from Canada. Those fellows ended up with fortunes, and fine
houses, and sons in the U.S. Senate. Jack had never attained
that exalted degree of success, but he had done well for a farm
boy who never got past sixth grade.

The children were less of a success, though; he had to admit that. Maybe he'd given them too much money, or maybe
they'd got above their raising, with their private schools and
flashy cars as soon as they were old enough to drive. Well, things
might have been different if John hadn't been killed in Vietnam.
He always was the best one of the bunch, and maybe Jack had
doted too much on the oldest boy and the others resented it. Or
maybe the time he'd spent in prison when the feds finally caught
up with him had soured his children and cost him their respect.
Too late to worry about that now, though. He hadn't seen the
young'uns in ... must be seven years, he thought. Not since
Alice died and they came to pick over the furniture before he
sold it all in a tag sale.

Although he still retained his habit of hiding any real emotions, Jack had been worried lately. He was past ninety, and although he had boasted the constitution of an ox for nine decades now, he knew that health was no longer a thing he could take for granted. Living alone was dangerous at his age. One fall could leave him helpless on the floor, dying by inches out of reach of the telephone. Of even greater concern, though, was the possibility that he would be taken ill and hospitalized. He didn't like the idea of being given anesthetic. He'd heard that people said things under anesthetic—things that they didn't want other people to know about. That thought made him uneasy. He hoped he'd never be sick enough to risk it. Another danger of hospitals was the fact that they were full of social-working busybodies who might decide that when he recovered he would not be allowed to return to the mansion.

The young man who had bought the place seemed like a nice fellow, though. He didn't ask too many personal questions, which was good. He might be useful to have around. At least he wasn't stingy with the groceries. Maybe the young man or his lady friend would turn out to be decent cooks. Mr. Jack was getting tired of living on fast food. Besides, when he walked to the grocery store he couldn't carry very much back with him. Five pounds of sugar at a time was about all he could manage these days. He was going to need a lot more than that.

*"Show me a sane man and
I will cure him for you."*
—Carl Jung

Chapter 6

Elizabeth MacPherson wondered what day it was. Not that it mattered, really. Eat, sleep, and take your pills. The days at Cherry Hill had begun to slip by in an amiable haze, and somewhere in the drift of days she had stopped marking the time until her month was up. She had settled into a routine now—rest, meals, therapy, and group sessions, all punctuated by sedatives designed to take the edge off reality. Elizabeth could see how people could come to prefer this soothing cocoon of a life to the endless struggle of the sane world.

As the days slid past, she found herself getting to know the members of her group, as little by little they disclosed bits of information about their problems. They no longer seemed exotic creatures to her; now they were her comrades, no stranger than anybody else's friends. She had pegged Richard Petress for problems relating to gender confusion; the vain and caustic Clifford

----

Allen was probably a sociopath; the waiflike Seraphin wouldn't eat, and wouldn't say why. Rose, the newspaper woman, was an alcoholic, Emma O. wanted to die, and old Mrs. Nicholson had left reality through a door marked ALZHEIMER'S. Not exactly the social set Elizabeth would normally have chosen to spend her days with—ah, but normal had nothing to do with it. As it was, there seemed to be a certain satisfaction in joining a group in which you were the least disabled. Elizabeth knew that among her friends and family outside Cherry Hill, she was the afflicted one, while their lives seemed to be progressing smoothly. She'd felt everyone mentally tiptoeing around the minefield of her grief, which had only heightened her sense of loss and isolation. Here, though, everyone had problems to overcome, and she was accorded no special treatment. Others were worse off than she. As a triumph, such a distinction was minuscule, but it offered a flicker of hope for a future recovery. She was not pushing herself to rejoin the world yet, though. Easy enough to suck in one's sorrow, grasp a prescription for pills, and go back to life as one of the walking wounded, but that would serve no purpose. Go back to what?

As kindly old Dr. Dunkenburger kept reminding her, the important thing was to feel better, not to rush back to the rat race just for the sake of pronouncing oneself cured. Not that she was anywhere near cured. In fact, the members of her group accused her of having a tendency to wallow in her grief, resisting any efforts to bring her out of her depression. In art therapy she drew nothing but charcoal seascapes of a small boat tossed by towering waves.

After studying the tenth rendering of the stormy boat scene, Emma O. had announced, "This is not therapy. This is an

---

exercise in masochism. Why do you dwell on this scene of your husband's disappearance? It's almost as if you had to remind yourself that you're supposed to be sad."

Elizabeth made no reply, but for the rest of that class period she painted stick-figure deer at rest under sprawling oak trees. Nobody could find anything objectionable about that. Today, though, she was going to try a more ambitious project.

Art therapy class was apparently designed in the hopes that the patient would draw road maps to his subconscious, thus shedding further light upon his own particular disorder. Rolls of paper and several kinds of drawing materials were made available to small groups of patients in a sunny room with cinder-block walls, a tile floor, and large rectangular windows overlooking the back lawn and the woods beyond. Hardly anyone ever drew the view, though. Apparently their inner vistas were more compelling than the well-tended institutional landscape beyond the glass.

Seraphin did not even face the window as she worked. She stood with her back to the daylight, frowning in concentration at the penciled outline of a portrait on her easel. She always drew the same face: a young woman with short, light-colored hair, and fine-chiseled classic features. Sometimes the woman was a figure in a larger scene; sometimes her face alone looked out from Seraphin's drawing paper, but the features never altered, except to be rendered more skillfully by the artist, as practice sharpened her proficiency. Except for her slender figure, the woman in the pictures did not resemble Seraphin herself. Elizabeth wondered who the subject was. In today's drawing the fair-haired woman was kneeling before an altar. In the background of the sketch a lightly penciled suggestion of

----

Gothic arches and a stained-glass window of a sword-bearing angel implied that the setting was a cathedral somewhere.

Elizabeth could not resist a guess. "It's a lovely drawing. Is it Joan of Arc?"

Seraphin shook her head and went on sketching without bothering to reply.

The other group members had begun to work on their own projects. Rose Hanelon specialized in caricatures of political figures done with bold strokes of a felt-tip pen. She had the cartoonist's knack for making her subjects recognizable in a few deft pen strokes. In the last class she had drawn Al Gore as the Tin Man in *The Wizard of Oz*. Now she seemed to be working on a religious painting. The rough outlines of a crucifixion scene had begun to take shape on the white poster board. This seemed most unlike Rose's usual sardonic sketches. Elizabeth wondered if this signaled a breakthrough in therapy.

Beside her Emma O. was putting the finishing touches on a fantasy watercolor depicting a dark-haired man with pointed ears gazing out a porthole at the rings of Saturn. Elizabeth was careful not to show any interest in this particular work, because Emma O. met any display of curiosity with an earnest and complete synopsis of whatever *Star Trek* episode had inspired her current drawing.

The other members of the art therapy class drew abstract patterns or stick figures with varying degrees of skill and perseverance. Beulah McNeil made clumsy renderings of crosses entwined with flowers, often adorned with a carefully lettered Bible verse. Clifford Allen drew detailed maps and house plans in a tiny, secretive scrawl. Nobody bothered to ask him why.

Elizabeth was pleased with herself for deciding to change

her drawing habit. Perhaps, if art therapy meant anything at all, this departure was a step toward wellness. She pulled an envelope out of her pocket. "I got a letter from my brother, Bill, this morning," she announced. "And I've decided to paint something different today."

The other members of the class gathered around her easel, their green artist smocks reflecting a rainbow of smeared paint. Elizabeth opened the envelope and handed a photograph around to her fellow artists, who made noises of polite interest as the photo passed from hand to hand.

Clifford Allen was the first to comment on the snapshot. "Mount Vernon," he said with that little sneer that never quite left his voice.

"Mount Vernon is not made of brick!" said Elizabeth. "But you did get the state right. This house is also in Virginia. It was just purchased by my brother, Bill, who's an attorney."

Clifford looked at the photo with more interest this time. "Some house! Looks like it would have a lot of valuable stuff in it."

Elizabeth hesitated between family pride and caution at arousing too much interest in her brother's property. In group therapy sessions Clifford had disclosed the fact that he was a burglar. His outlaw trademark had been to defecate on the floor of each place he burgled, as a hostile memento for his victims. ("A housebreaker who isn't housebroken!" Rose Hanelon had quipped. "I wish I could have written the headline for that story!") Opinion among his fellow patients was divided over whether Clifford was really mentally disturbed, or whether he had got himself committed in an effort to avoid a lengthy jail term, but Lisa Lynn seemed to speak for the majority when she announced that anyone who relieved themselves on strangers' living room rugs was not what she would call sane.

"It is a lovely house, isn't it?" Elizabeth smiled politely as she took the photograph back from Clifford. "But I'm afraid that the house cost so much that they probably can't afford anything worth stealing," she told Clifford. "My brother lives here, but it's also his law office. I thought I'd do a painting of it and give it to him for a present."

Rose Hanelon looked at the photograph. "Impressive," she grunted. "Looks like quite a find. You don't want to show that photo to old Mrs. Nicholson, though."

"Why not?"

Rose shrugged. "She cries when she sees large, expensive houses. You know the magazines that have decorating articles or photo spreads on gardens? We have to hide them from her. *Architectural Digest* makes her sob."

"Oh, me, too!" said Elizabeth. "Some of the contemporary designs in there are simply dreadful. Especially the ones in the Southwestern style, where they have huge stucco buildings with pastel trim, set in landscapes of rock gardens and cacti. To me they look like Ramada Inns set down in boxes of cat litter."

"Southern woman," said Rose. "You think anything that doesn't have Corinthian columns is a waste of money. But I think that Mrs. Nicholson cries over the houses she likes. Beats me why, though."

"Well," said Elizabeth, "she seems to be in her own world. At breakfast this morning she was reading the hallmarks on her fork. When I asked what she was doing, she explained them to me in a very pleasant, lucid tone: Lion passant for sterling, capital letter signifying the year, thistle for Scotland. . . ."

Rose Hanelon frowned. "The flatware here is institutional stainless steel."

"I know."

They sighed, wondering what the rest of Cherry Hill looked like in Mrs. Nicholson's version of reality.

Matt Pennington was the last to arrive for class. He wandered in, looking a little dazed, as he always did on the days when he had electro-convulsive therapy. He took out his pens and drawing pad, staring at it thoughtfully. Then he looked up and saw Elizabeth watching him. "Hello!" he said. "You must be new here! My name is Matt Pennington."

"Yes, Matt, I know," said Elizabeth. "We've met." In point of fact they had been sitting next to each other in group for more than a week. By now she knew a good deal about Matt's childhood, his education, his career goals, and his inner fantasy life. She knew that in art class he drew designs for ships and skyscrapers with the practiced skill of a trained architect. What she did not know was why he did not seem to recognize her now.

"We've met?" Matt smiled in polite disbelief. "I think I'd remember if we had. Attractive young lady like you. What did you say your name was?"

"Elizabeth . . ." she said on a rising inflection, expecting him to supply the rest, but he simply smiled at her and nodded.

"Pleased to meet you, Elizabeth," he said. "I guess I'll see you around."

Elizabeth turned to Clifford Allen who was watching her with his usual sneer. "What was that all about?" she said softly. "He's been sitting next to me in group for days now!"

Clifford gave her a cold smile. "Guess you're not memorable."

Between her family connections and her own career, A. P. Hill thought she must know every attorney in Richmond. That was impossible, of course. When the state legislature was in session, the lawyers in Richmond must outnumber the pigeons, but it still seemed that she was acquainted with a great many of their number. Occasionally, this was a pleasant circumstance. After a long, tedious day in court, she had a fair chance of finding someone to have dinner with, and if her companions ended up talking shop, that was all right, too. Powell Hill's stock of nonlegal small talk was generally exhausted after three remarks about the weather.

She had just finished an excellent dinner in fashionable Shockoe Slip, in a restaurant called The Frog and the Redneck, a trendy establishment whose cuisine was more politically correct than its name. Her dinner companions had explained that they loved to entertain guests there, because the name of the restaurant fit them so well. The "frog" was Katy DeBruhl, who as an undergraduate had been a French major. After law school, Katy had worked as a staff member for A. P. Hill's Cousin Stinky, as the family privately called Virginia's attorney general. Now she worked as a prosecutor for the Commonwealth Attorney's office in Richmond. Her "redneck" companion was Lewis Paine, a tall, sandy-haired police lieutenant from Martinsville, who preferred stock-car racing to opera.

"You seem awfully far away tonight, Powell," said Katy DeBruhl. "Are you worried about your case?"

"No." A. P. Hill took a sip of her wine. The case had been straightforward enough. She worked Microsoft hours to prepare for every contingency, and then she went into court with the attitude of a pit bull, and everything worked out to the client's satisfaction. Her legal business in Richmond did not trouble her. The news did.

"I was thinking about a story I heard on the radio," she told her dinner companions, trying to sound casual. "A woman lawyer somewhere down south broke her client out of prison, and apparently the two fugitives have committed some robberies along the way. The suspects are still at large. Two women our age. One of them's a lawyer." She told DeBruhl and Paine about the PMS Outlaws, carefully omitting the fact that she was personally acquainted with one of them. "I suppose it fascinates me because I have never heard of anybody so completely trashing a charmed life. I'm referring to Patricia Purdue. The lawyer. She's our age, Katy. She had a promising legal career, a bright future. She was attractive and smart. And now she's thrown it all away forever."

Katy DeBruhl nodded. "Forever is right. Aiding in the escape of a prisoner is a felony. If she is convicted, she'll never practice law again. That is a waste. Does it make any sense to you, Lewis?"

Police Lieutenant Paine shrugged. "I don't find it rational, if that's what you mean, but in my job, I see so much stupidity that nothing surprises me any more. Except for one thing, this fugitive story isn't particularly unusual."

"What, lawyers breaking clients out of jail?" Powell Hill's expression suggested that he had uttered blasphemy. "Not unusual?"

"Not specifically that," said Paine. "I meant women becoming emotionally involved with prisoners. Female guards will get crushes on the prisoners. They become pen pals with them, slip the guys nude photos of themselves. The jailers find them all the time when they do shakedowns of the cells. A jailer once told me that it isn't unusual for women to drive into the parking lot of the jail and . . . um . . ." Remembering that his dinner companions were female, Paine edited his remarks. ". . . they expose themselves to the prisoners looking out through their barred windows. I don't mean wives and girlfriends of the prisoners. I mean college girls and suburban matrons in expensive cars. I guess it's a dangerous thrill: taunting the human animals in the zoo."

Powell shuddered. "Is that true?"

"Happens all the time."

"Well, it's insane," she said. "Killers. Sociopaths. Aside from the degrading aspect of it, which goes without saying, I cannot think of any stupider way to ask for trouble."

"It's the Little Red Riding Hood syndrome," said Katy DeBruhl. "Some women like to walk with wolves for the emotional high you get from the danger. I'm not saying I approve of it, but I can see how it might happen. Some women like to live close to the edge. The tiger is behind bars so it's safe to flaunt yourself at him."

A. P. Hill nodded. "You have a point, Paine, about the emotional attraction of prisoners. I remember reading about a woman in Florida who married Ted Bundy while he was on trial for murdering more than two dozen women. Go figure."

Lewis Paine was staring at the flickering light in the glass candleholder in the center of the table. "Little Red Riding Hood," he mused. "I knew a nun once who belonged to an order that visits prisoners as part of their charity work. This was years ago—I forget the name of the order. They wore those hats like the Flying Nun, though. Anyhow, Sister What's-Her-Name fell in love with one of the prisoners. An armed robber. He swore he was innocent, of course, and she believed him. I mean, who'd lie to a nun?"

"Every man in that prison," muttered A. P. Hill.

"Right. Of course. She didn't know that, though. She was a sweet, trusting woman. She thought the guy had been framed. Anyhow, she wrote to the governor, held press conferences on the robber's behalf, swore he was innocent, and said that she would personally shepherd him back into society."

"What did the Church think of that?"

"I imagine that someone tried to talk her out of it, but they didn't get very far. She resigned from the order, or whatever it is they do to get out of being a nun. She was plain, plump, and forty-something, and she'd been in the convent since she was eighteen. She knew nothing about living in the present decade. Chronologically she was forty, but really, she'd turned eighteen about twenty-two times. Still a naive kid at heart. So she left the only home she'd known for twenty-some years to stand by her man." He sighed. "We joked about it at the time. Said that both of them got paroled the same week."

A. P. Hill looked up. "The nun got the prisoner released? She actually got him out?"

"Oh, yeah," said Paine. "He was only a robber. Hadn't killed anybody. No big deal. Prisons are overcrowded anyhow. They were probably glad for an excuse to turn him loose."

"Heaven help her," muttered Katy.

"One look into those dead shark eyes of his should have

told her that he was past praying for," Paine went on. "Classic sociopath. Knows what you want to hear, and gives it to you, pitch-perfect. You must have defended guys like that."

They nodded.

"But, yes, she got him out. He'd told her they were going to get married as soon as he was released. She picked him up at the prison on Friday. They had a weekend honeymoon without benefit of clergy—and Monday morning she woke up in the motel to find that the Robber Bridegroom was gone, taking every cent she had along with him."

The two lawyers looked at each other. Their reactions were a study in contrasts. A. P. Hill narrowed her eyes and set her jaw, as if she were imagining herself in that situation, and picturing in Technicolor the retribution that would follow. Katy DeBruhl brushed away a tear with the back of her hand, and said, "The poor Sister! Did she return to the convent?"

"No. I don't know whether she tried to or not. She certainly wasn't equipped to manage on her own, though. I guess she knew that. We found her in the motel room with an empty bottle of pills on the nightstand. No note. I mean, what was there to say? The robber's still out there somewhere. Technically, of course, it wasn't murder, so we couldn't take him back into custody. I'm sure he returned to business as usual."

Katy's eyes flashed. "I'd have been tempted to stash a bag of heroin in his hip pocket and bust him for drugs just to get him off the street."

"Nah," said Paine. "He'd already ruined one life. Why make it two?"

A. P. Hill was still thinking about the PMS Outlaws. "So

you think Purdue, the lawyer in the news, became emotionally involved with the woman prisoner, and that's why she helped her escape?"

"All I know about the story is what you've told me," Paine reminded her. "That doesn't qualify me to make a judgment, but if I had to make a guess based on those facts, I'd say it was an elopement."

"But they're picking up guys!"

The lieutenant shrugged. "That's just business. Just a way to make a fast buck. Nothing personal about it."

A. P. Hill digested this information. After a few moments' thought she said, "How would you go about catching them?"

"Are they headed this way?"

"Not that I know of. It's a theoretical question. I know how to defend suspects. I don't know much about the process of capturing them. Say you're FBI, Lewis. What do you do to apprehend the suspects?"

Paine laughed. "It would give me a good excuse to hang out in bars, wouldn't it? I could sit around hoping to get picked up by two women." He looked hopefully at his dinner companions.

"Don't even think about it," said Katy DeBruhl.

"Seriously," said A. P. Hill.

"Okay." Paine's smile vanished, as he shifted into the thought patterns of pursuit. "What would I do? I'd get a list of all the close friends and relatives of both women, and I'd ask local law enforcement people to keep an eye on their houses, just in case the two ladies stop by for an unannounced visit, and I might tap their phone lines, too. If the renegade lawyer has a telephone calling card, I'd get the phone company to give me a list of the numbers she's calling. I'd check the purchase on her credit cards, if she's dumb enough to keep using them."

"I think she's using other people's credit cards," said Katy.

"That works, too, as long as we know their names, and I presume we do, if the victims reported the robberies to the police. Every time one of the women uses a stolen credit card, you can put a pin in the map, and after a while you ought to be able to tell where they're headed."

"And what happens when you find them?"

Lewis Paine was silent for a moment. Then he said, "Well, you hope they are unarmed and that they're willing to listen to reason."

"And if not?"

He shrugged. "If not . . . Well, there was a poem written in the Thirties by another lady outlaw. . . .

> *"Someday they'll go down together.*
> *They'll bury them side by side;*
> *To some it will be grief; to the law a relief,*
> *But it's Death for Bonnie and Clyde."*

"Is this your photograph, young lady?"

Elizabeth looked up from her sketch to see the stern leathery face of Hillman Randolph looming over her. The old man was brandishing the snapshot of Bill's new house, which had been making the rounds of the art therapy class. "Yes," said Elizabeth with careful politeness. Hillman Randolph's expression was always one of unremitting severity, and his scarred face did not help matters. It was impossible to tell if he was angry by looking at him. Elizabeth decided to risk no further comment until she could gauge his mood.

"I know this house," Mr. Randolph said, tapping the photo. "It's in Virginia."

Elizabeth sighed. "It is not Mount Vernon."

He scowled. "Any fool can see that! Never said it was. This house is in Danville, Virginia, or near it, anyhow."

She stared up at the old man in astonishment. "Yes, it is, but how did you know that?"

The old man beamed triumphantly. "I knew it! My job used to take me all over the Southeast. Never will forget that house!"

Elizabeth tried to picture Mr. Randolph as a young traveling salesman, but unless the old curmudgeon had been more genial in his youth, she didn't think he could have been much good at it. "What did you do for a living?" she asked.

"Well, I guess it's all right to tell you now. After all, it was a long time ago, and I'm retired," he drawled. "I was one of the government men. Federal law enforcement."

Elizabeth nodded. She could indeed picture Hillman Randolph as a federal agent: no people skills required. The customer is always wrong.

"Yeah, I knew that place well," the old man was saying. "Belonged to a fellow named Dolan."

Elizabeth smiled. "Yes, I've heard about him. He's quite a character. I haven't met him yet."

"Well, he always was a twisty son of a gun, but unless he figured out a way to outwit the Grim Reaper, I don't think you're going to get a chance to meet old Jack Dolan. He was a personal crusade of mine. I wanted to nail him so bad I could taste it. We put him away for a couple of months once on a tax charge, but that was nothing. Never had the chance to do any better than that. Jack Dolan went up in flames in a car wreck in . . . oh . . . 1953, I think it was."

Elizabeth stared. "But that's impossible. He's still living in that house. My brother said so!"

"Your brother says he lives with the late Jack Dolan." Mr. Randolph gave her a pitying smile. "And you're the family member they locked up for being crazy?"

The real estate transaction moved swiftly, thanks to the large down payment made possible by liquidating a portion of Bill's stock portfolio, and even more to Sunshine Properties' pressing desire to be rid of their white elephant of a mansion. The bank president, who knew Bill socially, expedited the paperwork for the mortgage, and permission was given for the purchasers to begin to clean the house and move in their possessions.

A. P. Hill was still out of town. She phoned in once a day for messages, and Bill gave her progress reports about the house, but she wasn't very forthcoming about the case she was working on. "It's going to take longer than I expected," she told Bill. "Can you manage without me?"

Since A. P. Hill routinely worked six-day weeks and twelve-hour days, and since she had not taken a vacation since the firm opened for business, Bill assured her that he could manage without her. It was a nuisance for her to be gone when there was so much work to do on the house, but he would have to make the best of it. Besides, if Powell Hill had a fault, it was a tendency to be opinionated and dictatorial. This way after Bill made all the decisions, he could argue with perfect truth that he would have consulted her about, say, the dining room wallpaper, but she hadn't been around to give him the benefit of her wisdom.

Bill and Edith had taken to spending evenings and weekends getting the place ready to become their new office complex. They gave the downstairs walls a fresh coat of paint, scrubbed down the floors and the woodwork, and began moving files and bits of office furniture into the cavernous old parlor, which swallowed up their meager possessions and still looked empty.

"It's like putting peas in a pumpkin," Edith remarked. She leaned on the mop, and surveyed the room with a critical eye. "Not only do we need more furniture, we need better furniture. These beat-up metal desks just ruin the ambiance."

"It was all we could afford," Bill reminded her. He was perched atop a stepladder, putting new lightbulbs in the brass chandelier. "And now that we've bought this place, it's still all we can afford. Just be glad they're paid for."

Edith frowned. "Maybe we could put them close to the walls, and arrange plants in front of them to hide the dents."

"Can we afford plants?"

"I have a shovel. What time does the park close?"

Bill frowned. "I don't have time to take on any new larceny cases just now, thank you. Maybe I'll hint to Mother for a housewarming gift of greenery."

Bill was screwing in another lightbulb when Mr. Jack wandered in, nibbling on a Popsicle he'd liberated from Edith's refreshment stash in the freezer. "How's it going, boys?" he asked genially, peering up at Bill.

The lightbulb did not work. "It's not the bulbs," muttered Bill, indicating the still unlit light fixture. "I think the wiring is bad on this thing."

Mr. Jack put his hand to his ear and called out, "Say what?"

"I said: *We need a new chandelier!*" Bill yelled back.

"Oh," said Mr. Jack, digesting this information. He shook his head. "Nope. Nope. I don't agree with you there."

"You don't?"

"Nope. Give you three reasons. Number one: You can't afford one. Number two: None of us knows how to play one. And number three: What you really need in this room is a new light fixture!"

Before Bill could find out if Mr. Jack was putting him on, the old man ambled out again, humming to himself.

"I hope he doesn't start answering the phone," said Edith.

As if in answer to her remark, Bill's cell phone, propped up on the mantelpiece, began to ring.

"Can you get that?" he asked from the top of the ladder.

Edith set down the mop and lunged for the phone. "Bill MacPherson's cell phone," she said into the receiver. "I'm not an answering machine. If you want him, say so." She listened intently for a few moments, and then said, "We're fine. Well, we're getting enough exercise anyhow. How about yourself?"

"Who is it?" asked Bill, easing down the ladder.

"It's your sister." Edith cupped her hand over the mouthpiece. "I didn't think people in asylums were allowed to use the telephone."

"She's a voluntary patient," Bill reminded her. "She isn't dangerous. Hello?"

"Hi, Bill." Elizabeth sounded tired. "I got your letter. Thanks for the picture of the house. I can't wait to see it in person."

"It is pretty amazing, isn't it?" said Bill. In his voice pride of ownership struggled with modesty. "We just happened to be in the right place at the right time."

It occurred to him that burbling about one's own good fortune is extremely bad form when speaking to someone newly bereaved. "Well, never mind that," he said. "The house needs repairs, and we have a lot of work ahead of us. We're scrubbing a few square miles of floors. I have aches in muscles I didn't know I had. But how are you?"

"Oh, you know . . . one day at a time. Don't let's talk about that."

"Is the therapy helping?"

"It's hard to tell, Bill. I take the pills, and I still feel like screaming, but who knows how bad I'd feel if I weren't taking them? . . . Anyhow, that is not what I called about."

"I'm sorry I haven't been able to visit you, but—"

"Bill. Shut up." There was a gratifying silence at the other end of the phone. Elizabeth took a deep breath and plunged on. "I wanted to talk to you about the old man who lives in your house. Have you asked to see any identification?"

"Umm . . . no." She could hear the bewilderment in Bill's voice.

"Well, could you?"

After a long pause, Bill said, "I don't think he has a driver's license. The Department of Motor Vehicles gets very nervous when people over ninety take to the highway."

Elizabeth sighed. She was going to have to explain. "Look,

Bill, ask Mr. Dolan if he remembers a man named Hillman Randolph. You'd better write it down. Mr. Randolph isn't ninety, but he's pretty old, and he says that he knew the fellow who built your house back in the nineteen forties."

"Really? Where did you meet him?"

"In here. That's not important. Never mind about that." Elizabeth thought the time had come to talk very fast to forestall the inevitable and uncomfortable questions that were about to arise. "According to Hillman Randolph, Jack Dolan died in a wreck in the Fifties."

Another long pause. "I don't think he's a ghost," said Bill mildly. "He eats Popsicles."

"Of course he's not a ghost, Bill! But he may be an imposter."

"With rubber makeup, you mean? Like Dustin Hoffman in *Little Big Man*? This guy deserves an Academy Award, then, because he looks every single minute of ninety-two, and I've seen him up close, and I'd swear it's really skin."

Elizabeth sighed. Trying to explain things to Bill could drive you crazy even if you weren't already in a mental institution. Stay calm, she told herself. Hysteria negates your argument. "The substitution may have happened a long time ago," she said quietly. "At the time of the car wreck Mr. Randolph mentioned."

Something suddenly occurred to Bill. "Mr. Randolph? Isn't your friend there Dr. Randolph?"

"No. He's not on staff here. He's a patient."

"I see." Bill's voice took on the warm, comforting tones of one who has just realized what is going on, and who will now agree with anything and everything you say.

Elizabeth winced. "I am not hallucinating, Bill."

"No. Of course not. You sound great. Just like your old self! And, hey, thanks for this hot tip. I'm going to look into it first chance I get. Of course, Edith and I have a lot of painting and furniture moving to do just now, and Powell is in Richmond taking her sweet time over that corporate case of hers, but just as soon as things settle down here, I'll get right on it." Elizabeth recognized his tone of voice. It was the one he had used to discuss the Easter Bunny with her when she was four. There was no reasoning with him now. His mind had slammed shut.

"You are taking your medicine on schedule, aren't you?"

"Yes, Bill. In fact, I think it's time for a pill right now. Goodbye."

Bill switched off the phone and leaned wearily against the mantelpiece. "Poor kid," he said to Edith. "She's lost touch with reality."

*"A paranoid-schizophrenic is
a guy who has just found
out what's going on."*
—William Burroughs

Chapter 7

Elizabeth was in art therapy again. She stood before the easel in a few moments of silent contemplation before she set to work. As usual she began her charcoal drawing of a storm-tossed boat, but this time among the foam-capped breakers, she sketched in the head of a seal. In this view of the shipwreck, pictured a thousand times in her imaginings waking and sleeping, the boat was far in the distance, under dark clouds, like fists in the sky above it. Now the face of the seal loomed large in the foreground of the sketch, peering out at the viewer with sad, knowing, human eyes.

Long ago the Scots and the Norsemen believed that seals were drowned sailors held forever in the ocean that was life—and death—for them. For this reason, they considered it unlucky for anyone to kill a seal. Her late husband, Cameron, who was a marine biologist, had also hated those who killed seals, but he called his beliefs "ecology," and his opinions on seals had nothing to do with mysticism. Still, he had told her the old Scots stories of the drowned souls who came back as seals, and of the other seal creatures, the Selkies, who took the form of seals while they were in the ocean, but who transformed themselves into men when they came on dry land to marry a human maiden. After a few years together, the Selkie lover would leave his human bride and return to the sea, to his other form and his other life in the depths.

"Interesting that people once believed seals were human," Cameron had told her once. "I suppose it's the eyes that made them think of it. They do seem quite sentient when they look at you with that long-lashed stare. The odd bit is that seals were once land creatures—a long time ago, of course. Much too far back for our ancestors to have seen it, of course, but once upon a time the pinnipeds lived on dry land. If you dissect a seal, you'll find that attached to the skeleton it has tiny, atrophied leg bones under the flesh near the tail."

"So they are slowly emerging from the sea and turning into land animals?" Elizabeth had asked.

"No," said Cameron. "They've thought better of it. Seals seem to be at midpoint now between sea creature and land animal, but at some point they changed their minds about making the transition, I suppose. Each generation of seal spends more time in the water than the one before it, and some day—past the era of man, I suppose—they will complete the transformation and go back to the sea for good. Isn't it funny that people sensed the transformation? They got the details wrong, that's all."

Elizabeth could imagine an abandoned wife or the widow of a drowned sailor standing on the beach, staring into the eyes of

----

a seal, searching for a spark of recognition, wanting to believe that some part of her loved one remained. She wondered if such a belief would bring more consolation than the knowledge that one's man was forever lost. If you believed such a thing in these enlightened times, you would be thought mad. Well, here she was in a madhouse: surely she was entitled to the consolation of mysticism, and yet, for all the comfort it would have given her, she could not believe in any thing so gentle, so comforting as a transmigration from man to seal. Cameron was gone. Apparently her problem was that she was unable to be crazy enough. Still she dreamed of seals, and their sad eyes stared at her, as if at any moment they would speak and put an end to her pain of not knowing.

She was staring into the sad eyes of the seal when Rose appeared behind her. "Back to boating accidents, huh?" she said. "Well I have some news that might take your mind off your troubles. They sent me in to tell you that you have a visitor."

A. P. Hill seldom returned to her alma mater: all her friends had left when she did. Team sports did not interest her, and she had graduated too recently to be troubled by invitations for class reunions. She remembered her years in Williamsburg as neither happy nor unhappy. She had existed in a haze of hard work, punctuated by punishing physical workouts to keep her senses sharp. Now her memories of the city fit into an impressionistic collage of library stacks, bike paths, and autumn scenes. The old colonial capital held its elegance and charm in the suspended animation of life support, thanks to the efforts of a well-endowed charitable foundation that ensured that the buildings of Old Williamsburg were preserved with no taint

----

from the present century to sully the dream of the past. Memories of college were much the same. You expected your classmates to stay frozen in time, in the image you had of them during your student days. When one of them achieves tabloid notoriety, it disturbs not only the present, but also the past, challenging your memories of how things were and making you wonder what else you missed.

The drive from Richmond to Williamsburg takes less than an hour on I-64 east, traffic permitting. A. P. Hill traveled the distance without noticing her surroundings, so intent was she upon dredging up memories of Purdue from undergraduate days.

What could she remember about Purdue? She pictured the sharp little face under a strawlike thatch of blonde hair, and the black outfits that Purdue had invariably worn. Had she dated anybody back then? A. P. Hill could not remember Purdue ever going out with anyone, but she had taken an interest in the young men who used to call the pay phones on the halls in the dorm in search of a blind date. After several of their hallmates encountered lechers or losers in the blind-date lottery, P. J. Purdue had posted a list by the phone, describing the usual callers by name and detailing their objectionable qualities ("Breath smells like Lysol.") When some of the callers got wise to the loser list and began using aliases, Purdue calmly inserted the callers' current aliases beside the original names.

So the anger was there, even in her undergraduate days. But why? Where had it come from? Did it matter? In the back of her mind the seedlings of a plea of mitigating circumstances began to take shape.

A. P. Hill parked the car and began walking the familiar

paths of campus, heading more or less for the library because
she instinctively searched for the answers to things in the nearest library, but before she could reach it, her cell phone rang.

"A. P. Hill," said Powell, feeling the spell of the past evapo-
rate as she spoke.

After a short pause a familiar voice said, "This is Katy
DeBruhl. Where are you, Powell?"

"Williamsburg. Why?" Something in Katy's voice told her
that this was not a social call.

"Are you coming back to Richmond this evening, or are
you on your way back to Danville?"

"I'm not sure, Katy. Why?"

Another pause. "Lewis Paine asked me to call you," Katy
said at last. "Do you remember that case we were talking about
at dinner the other night? The one where the woman lawyer ran
away with a client?"

"What about it?"

"Well, it seems the pair has struck again. This time their
victim was a well-to-do banker somewhere west of Memphis.
Anyhow, after that police department took his statement, they
contacted Richmond."

A. P. Hill felt a prickling on the back of her neck. Here
it comes, she thought, although she had no idea what was coming. Just that it wasn't good. "Why did they contact Richmond,
Katy?"

"Well, it seems that one of the pair told the banker that she
was a Virginia lawyer. He was quite clear about it. She said that
her name was A. P. Hill."

Powell clenched her teeth.

"We thought it seemed rather a strange coincidence, your name turning up like that after we'd discussed the case. You didn't mention that you knew them."

"Acquaintances. I haven't seen Purdue in years. Not since law school."

"Well, of course, we know it wasn't you in that robbery, Powell. You've been in court here in Richmond every day this week, but Lewis did think it was interesting that you should be talking about the case, and then one of the fugitives uses your name for an alias. He'd like you to come in and talk to him about it—at your earliest convenience. And you know what that means."

"I know." Powell figured she had about twelve hours to turn up in Lewis Paine's office before he sent someone after her—politely, of course, but she would not be given the option of declining the invitation.

"I have some business to finish here in Williamsburg, Katy. Tell Paine I'll be back at my hotel at nine o'clock tonight. He's welcome to come and see me there, but I warn you that I won't be any help."

"I'll let him know," said Katy. "Oh, and Powell, I'd be glad to come along, if you think you need to be represented by counsel."

"Thanks, Katy, but I think I can handle this on my own. It's not a crime to be impersonated. And it isn't Paine's jurisdiction anyhow. He's just being nosy."

"I hope you're not planning to share that thought with him."

"No, Katy. I'll be as civil as I can. Thanks." A. P. Hill switched off the phone and shoved it back into the pocket of

----

her jacket. It had happened, just as she had feared all along. That one particular memory that A. P. Hill had been avoiding, even in her reminiscences, was now going to haunt her.

With narrowed eyes and an unbecoming scowl, she turned her back on the library and stalked off in search of the university alumni office. Now it was personal.

"Oh," said Elizabeth in a voice made leaden by disappointment. "It's you." She knew how dreadful she must sound before she had even finished speaking, but the disappointment made her cruel. A visitor, Rose had said, and Elizabeth had hurried from the art room, patting her hair down, and rehearsing words of welcome as she ran. Had it been insane of her to hope that it might be Cameron, to assume that he would suddenly materialize without warning on this side of the Atlantic like a migrating seal? At what point does the virtue of hope become the sin of obstinance?

The young man, who was just a shade too well dressed, met her scowl with raised eyebrows and a sardonic smile. "Yes, it is I," said Geoffrey Chandler briskly. "Don't apologize for that note of disappointment in your voice. People usually say 'It's you' in mixed tones of fear and dread, emotions that I endeavor to earn. It would be quite unsettling if anyone ever actually smiled upon encountering me unexpectedly. I'd wonder what unpleasant things they were getting away with that I ought to know about. And how is my little cousin the shut-in?" Geoffrey Chandler, a mainstay of his local community theatre, was often thought to be quoting Noel Coward even when he wasn't. It was an effect into which he put considerable effort.

Elizabeth took several short, deep breaths and tried to smile.

121

"Well, Geoffrey . . . I'm sorry if I was rude. I know that you drove a long way to see me. It's just that I . . . They told me that a young man was here to see me . . . and so I thought . . ." Her voice quavered.

"I had not expected to find you as bad as this," said Geoffrey quietly.

"It was a shock," said Elizabeth. "Except in time of war, we don't expect young men to die. I went numb for a while, I suppose. And the word widow . . . somehow I simply cannot . . ."

Geoffrey Chandler, who loathed tears as much as the next man, hoped to forestall the impending storm with a change of subject. He looked around at the primrose walls and chintz-covered sofas that graced the waiting room. "I have been here quite often, what with one thing and another," he remarked. "Visiting various people of my acquaintance. Really creative souls of a certain temperament generally matriculate through here sooner or later. Not that I counted you among their number, dear."

Geoffrey saw Elizabeth's eyes flash between tears, and he knew that the danger of hysterics had abated. "I believe they have redecorated since my last visit," he remarked. "That hideously flowered sofa appears to be comfortable. Shall we try it out?"

Elizabeth sat down, dabbing at her eyes with a tissue from a box on the end table. "You are odious, Geoffrey," she said, "but at least you came to see me, and I am sorry that I was beastly to you. Grief makes people selfish, don't you find? Actually, though, I did want to talk to you."

Geoffrey shuddered. "That remark, coming on the heels of

an observation about selfishness, frightens me more than you can possibly imagine. Obviously you have thought up some way for me to be useful to you. I tremble at the possibilities. I trust it goes without saying that blind dates are out of the question?"

Elizabeth gave him a tremulous smile. "Don't worry," she said. "I don't hate anyone here that much." For a moment she pictured Geoffrey and Emma O. forced to spend an evening together, and her smile became even broader. "It is good to see you, though," she said, laying her hand on his arm. "For the past few weeks I have been packed in the cotton wool of kindness until I can't feel anything any more. If you weren't your usual cobra-fanged self, I'd begin to cry again, and you would flee—in the politest possible way, of course, pleading another appointment, and I'd never get to ask you for the favor that I need."

"I need both my kidneys," Geoffrey put in. "Besides, the thought of organ transplants makes me queasy."

"You may keep all of your body parts, Geoffrey. I'm sure I speak for the world when I say that. I want you to investigate a disappearance." She saw his raised eyebrows and knew at once that the words "North Atlantic" were hovering on his lips. "Not that disappearance," she added hastily. "We've changed the subject, remember? This disappearance concerns an old man in Virginia. In fact, he's the man who built the house that Bill just bought."

"Has he disappeared?" said Geoffrey. "I just spoke to your brother the other day—to ask about you as a matter of fact— and I understood that when Bill purchased the house the old gentleman was included as an accessory. If he has subsequently

----

vanished, perhaps you ought not to call too much attention to it until you have inquired into your brother's alibi. Perhaps Bill is hoping no one will notice."

"No, Geoffrey. I don't mean that the old man has disappeared. He's still there all right. I'm just wondering exactly who he is."

"He's ninety, and you've forgotten who he is? Surely that is his prerogative."

"He says he's Jack Dolan, but I wonder about that. You see, something very odd happened today. Bill sent me a photograph of the new house, and as I was passing it around in art therapy class, someone recognized it. An old gentleman named Hillman Randolph claims that he once knew Jack Dolan in Virginia. He claims the man was a criminal. Anyhow, according to him, Jack Dolan died in the early Fifties."

Geoffrey's silence became an ice age. "Someone here said that?" he said at last. "Someone . . . here?"

"That's right."

"Someone here. A member of the staff, perhaps? Your physician?"

"Umm . . . no. Mr. Randolph is a fellow patient." Elizabeth added quickly, "But he used to be in law enforcement."

"Law enforcement. I see. Was he Wyatt Earp? Eliot Ness? The entire cast of *Gunsmoke*?"

Elizabeth sighed. It would be useless to tell Geoffrey that his remarks about the mentally ill were politically incorrect. Geoffrey always replied that political correctness was all very well, but he preferred other forms of hypocrisy. She decided to reason with him. "No, Geoffrey, Mr. Randolph doesn't think he was Wyatt Earp. He's old, and he has some sort of problem relating to his being disfigured, but he's not delusional. He doesn't seem given to telling tall tales. People with mental problems are not totally unreliable, you know. Aside from their one particular problem, they can be as sharp as anybody else."

" 'I am but mad north-northwest.' " Geoffrey nodded, cheered immensely by the opportunity to quote from *Hamlet*. "Yes, I take your point about that. Still, this story seems fairly improbable, don't you think? I mean, your man claims that Jack . . . what's his name?"

"Dolan."

"Right. The old fellow here claims that Jack Dolan is dead, but trustworthy people in Virginia—people who are not mental patients—can testify that Mr. Dolan is alive and well and living in a house in Danville. That seems fairly conclusive."

Elizabeth nodded. "That's what Bill said."

"This person who says Dolan is dead may be mistaken. He's an old man. He's talking about events that took place forty years ago. I don't say he's lying or trying to deceive you. I'm sure he means well. I simply think his memory is faulty."

"That does seem to be the logical conclusion," said Elizabeth meekly.

"Well, good! I'm glad we've cleared that up. Now let's talk about me. When they told you someone was here to see you, did they simply say 'a young man'? Not a distinguished young man, or a handsome young man?" He fingered his silk rep tie, wondering what error in fashion had caused him to be so slighted.

Elizabeth did not reply. She sat silently staring at the oatmeal-colored carpet, looking, Geoffrey thought, like someone waiting for a bus. He allowed a few more minutes for her to say something. Elizabeth always filled silences if you gave her

----

enough time. She considered it a form of courtesy. This time, however, no remarks were forthcoming.

"You don't buy it, do you?" he said at last.

"No."

"You actually think someone is impersonating a ninety-year-old man. Are you cra—"

"Yes!" said Elizabeth a shade too loudly. "Yes, I am. Crazy. Officially. A certified resident of the Cherry Hill Psychiatric Hospital. Quite demented."

"Well, don't be touchy about it, Cousin. Some of my best friends are crazy."

"All of your best friends are crazy, Geoffrey. It is the chief requirement for the position. Never mind my feelings, though. Sane or crazy, what if I'm right? What if the old man in the house in Danville isn't Jack Dolan?"

Geoffrey shrugged. "He's ninety. Pretty soon the problem will solve itself."

"But Jack Dolan owned that house. Or he did until his children lost it in a land deal. At least that's what Bill was told. Suppose it isn't true. Does that mean Bill doesn't own the house? Could he lose all his money in the deal? And then there's the real Mr. Dolan. What happened to him, and when? Was he swindled out of the house? Murdered for it? Is he dead?"

Geoffrey tried again. "Have you thought of calling the Danville police? It sounds like their business, not yours. Surely they could root around in the courthouse records and come up with something."

"Of course I can't call the police, Geoffrey! What could I say?" She mimicked speaking into the receiver. "Hello, I'm Elizabeth MacPherson. I'm a mental patient, and I was wondering if you'd check out a statement about a crime made to me by another mental patient. . . ."

"I see your point. Of course, you could investigate it yourself."

"I'm in here, Geoffrey."

"Ah."

"Voluntary commitment. Mandatory stay of one month, to be extended upon the recommendation of the attending physician. Now if I start babbling about wanting to investigate geriatric impersonators in Danville, Virginia, how likely is it that they're going to turn me loose at the end of the month?"

"Did you tell Bill about this? It is his house, after all. And his little old man."

Elizabeth frowned. "Of course I told him! He made soothing noises to humor me. He would have agreed to anything I said, but he doesn't really believe a word of it. He won't even think it over. He'll just think they need to adjust my medication."

"I don't suppose—"

"I am not delusional! It's just that at present I have no credibility."

"But you thought that I might believe you?"

She waved aside the implied compliment. "Oh, you! You don't care. You don't set any great store on normal, or plausible, or even ethical, as far as I can tell. You'd probably investigate Jack Dolan for the novelty of it. Or to test your acting skills. Or to have a tale to dine out on. But at least you would do something besides humor me. And in your own twisted way, you are undeniably clever, so while you were larking about, you just might find out the truth."

"What fulsome praise!" said Geoffrey, smirking. "When

the time comes for my eulogy, I must leave instructions that you be the one to deliver it."

"Oh, shut up. Will you do this for me or not?"

Geoffrey appeared to consider the matter. Actually, he was reflecting on the fact that a number of minutes had gone by without any discussion of the late Cameron Dawson. This new obsession of Elizabeth's was surely nonsense, but it might also be therapeutic. As an amateur psychologist, he thought her interest in so trivial a matter was a classic case of displacement: Elizabeth's brain was focusing on an inconsequential puzzle to distract her from the real source of her misery. A psychiatrist might try to talk her out of her obsession and urge her to focus on working through her grief instead, but Geoffrey, who was a firm believer in the avoidance of pain, thought that distraction was about all the healing that most people could ever expect. Anyhow, it was worth a try.

"All right," he said at last. "Since you cannot persuade anyone else to take this tale seriously, you are left with me: humanity's professional gadfly. And you want me to do . . . what?"

Elizabeth opened her mouth and shut it again. "I hadn't thought that far ahead," she said. "I concentrated all my efforts on convincing you to do something, without concerning myself at all about what that something ought to be."

"You realize that I think this whole thing is a mare's nest?"

"Yes, but you will look into it, won't you? With an open mind?"

Geoffrey sighed. "In lieu of sending you flowers, I suppose I could give it a couple of days."

"Good. Now . . . what should you do? You might begin by

finding out everything you can about Jack Dolan, and trying to get an accurate description of him as a young man. We can find out his eye color, the shape of the ears—things like that."

Geoffrey shook his head. "You know, with all due respect for Jeremy Brett, I have never had any desire to play Sherlock Holmes."

"Good," said Elizabeth. "Because if you go prancing around Danville in a cape and a deerstalker, you'll be back in here before you know it, and then I'll have to get somebody else to do the research."

A. P. Hill was back in her hotel room by six forty-five, enough time to check her messages, shower, change clothes, and order a salad from room service before she sat down to review her notes and to wait for the arrival of Lewis Paine. She had one less thing to worry about now. The court case that had brought her to Richmond was now on hold, if not permanently abandoned. The two sides had wearied of the legal battle, and now they were going to take a break for a week or so, presumably to catch up on all the business matters that had been let slide while they whiled away the hours in the courtroom. After that, they wanted to meet to try to reach an out-of-court settlement. That was fine with A. P. Hill. She had already cleared a few days' absence with the office, and now she would make the most of them.

When Lieutenant Lewis Paine knocked on the door at 8:57, A. P. Hill was ready. She was calm and composed, cell phone switched off, and a manila folder of photocopied pages was tucked away out of sight in the bedroom of the suite.

129

"Hello," she said with a perfunctory smile. She motioned for him to sit down on the sofa next to the window. "Would you like a drink? There's a soda machine down the hall."

He shook his head. "I'm fine. I think I should tell you that I'm not officially on duty at this time. Let's just say that I dropped by for a friendly chat. Strictly off the record."

Powell Hill nodded. She sat down in the desk chair and stared past him at the lights of the city. Off the record and out of your jurisdiction, she thought, but she smiled encouragingly, because only very stupid people were rude to law enforcement officers.

"I was just wondering about our conversation the other night. The one about the lady lawyer and her fugitive girlfriend. I seem to recall your asking me how I'd go about catching them—if they happened into my territory, I believe we said."

Powell shrugged. "Just making conversation."

"Well, that's what I thought. Right up until the time that the police inquiry came in from northeast Arkansas, asking if we have any information on a Virginia attorney named A. P. Hill. They say their suspect is a small, blonde, well-spoken woman in her late twenties. Imagine my surprise," he said in a sarcastic drawl. "In fact, the only reason I'm not falling all over myself to fill out your extradition papers for those good people in Arkansas is because you have such a damned good alibi: me."

Powell nodded.

"It seems that at the time Mr. Jenkins the banker was being fleeced by the two classy ladies at his country club, you were at dinner in Richmond with Katy DeBruhl and me. Or did you already know that?"

"No, Lewis. I really didn't. What did they do?"

He shrugged. "The usual. You know about the previous cases?"

"Yes, but only from what was printed in the newspapers."

"Well, it's pretty much the same, except that this time they went after a better class of victim. I guess they figured he'd have more money on him than their previous marks." He smiled. "It sounds like the banker told the police a highly edited version of the truth, but the upshot is that the two women sweet-talked the old goat into going off to a motel with them. He dances pretty lightly over the sex part, of course. Claims they'd got to talking about investments, and that they invited him back to their place for drinks so that they could continue their discussion of the stock market. Very cozy."

"It sounds plausible," A. P. Hill conceded.

"Except that the banker is the one who rented the motel room. The night clerk not only remembers him, she has the credit card slip to prove it. Besides, the next morning the chambermaid found the victim handcuffed to the bathroom sink pipe, and, believe me, he wasn't dressed for a sober financial discussion."

"He's from a small town, isn't he? He'll have a hard time living that down."

"I thought of that," said Paine. "Has it occurred to you that these outlaw pranksters seem to delight in embarrassing people? Sure, they take the victim's money and his car, both of which they need to stay on the run, but they seem to derive a lot of pleasure out of humiliating their victims. I thought that fact might lead somewhere, which is why we need to talk to people who knew them before the crime spree began. People like you."

A. P. Hill felt her face redden. "I know you think I was being evasive," she said at last. "But I knew I couldn't be of any help to you. Believe me, if I had told you that I knew P. J. Purdue, it would have misled you in the opposite direction. You would have thought I knew more than I actually did. In fact, I haven't seen Purdue since we left law school at William and Mary. We were never close. All I know about her present circumstances I read in a supermarket tabloid."

"Then why after all these years did she suddenly start using your name as an alias?"

A. P. Hill considered the matter. She blushed a little as she spoke. This was delicate ground. "Oh . . . spite, I think."

"Spite? Really? After all these years?"

A. P. Hill sighed. "My friends may be a fickle bunch," she said, "but apparently when I irritate someone, they remember me forever."

"I see. And what did you do to annoy Patricia Purdue?"

"Nothing that I recall. I suppose my very existence was enough to enrage her. I was the good little girl. I studied all the time, turned my assignments in early, and I never participated much in the social life on our hall. Purdue was a great one for parties and pranks, and I just didn't go in for that kind of thing."

"What kind of pranks?"

"Oh, sometimes it was simple ones like fake phone messages leaving a number and telling you to call, say, Mr. Lyon, and the number would turn out to be the zoo. But every so often she'd outdo herself and spend hours on some elaborate scheme just for the hell of it. She liked to pick on the people who would be the most annoyed by it."

"Can you give me an example of one of her elaborate pranks? Were any of them directed against men?"

"Not that I recall." A. P. Hill frowned at the memory of

college life, trying to choose an accurate but neutral recollection. "Well, she did make a list of bad blind dates and post it by the hall telephone to warn the other girls."

"Fair enough," said Paine. "I wouldn't call that a prank, though. More of a public service really. Anything else?"

She nodded. "I was on the receiving end of one of her major efforts. My term paper got the only A in our lit class, and Purdue was pretty annoyed about it. She wrote brilliantly, but she never turned in anything except a first draft. Her intellect probably got her through high school with straight A's despite her laziness, but at the university, there is too much competition to get away with that. So she got a C."

"Not your fault."

"No. But I got the A by spending two days in the library and rewriting my paper three times. By Purdue's lights, such behavior was unsporting. So she decided to take me down a peg. She must have worked all night."

"What did she do?"

"I woke up the next morning about six, and when I opened the door to my room to stumble out to the bathroom, there was no way out. The doorway was blocked by a thin wall of newspaper sheets taped to the door frame from top to bottom. I couldn't even see out."

"That's a lot of work for a brief inconvenience." Paine grunted. "You can go through a wall of newspaper in two seconds."

"I did. I took a running start and plunged right through it. The resulting crash woke up everyone on the entire hall. You see, on the outside of the door, behind that curtain of newspaper, Purdue had stacked up a pyramid of Coke cans and glass bottles, most of which broke when they hit the floor. Some of them weren't empty, either. I spent the next hour cleaning up the mess."

"You didn't insist that she do it?"

"No. I had a test that morning, and at six A.M. I had neither the time nor the inclination for a shouting match. Purdue would have protested her innocence, of course. So I cleaned it up myself. She probably thought I was a Goody Two-shoes for that, too."

"Probably," Paine agreed. "I'd say she thought you tried too hard to stay out of trouble, and all these years later she has thought of a way to make your life messy again."

There were several things that A. P. Hill might have told Paine, but she didn't: the phone call from the fugitive Purdue, for one. While she was debating the wisdom of confiding in him, he said, "Well, it's a long way from papering a dorm-room doorway to assault and robbery. I'm still not getting a clear picture of her. That story about the newspaper wall was from your undergraduate days, wasn't it? But weren't you also in law school with Patricia Purdue?"

"Yes. She was brilliant. That C she got on her term paper was an unusual occurrence for her. By the time we were juniors she had learned how to work the system with a minimum of effort, and her grades were excellent. Besides, she made seven hundred on the LSAT. She had no trouble getting into law school."

"Women must have been a minority in law school. Did the two of you band together on account of that?"

A. P. Hill thought before she spoke. How much of what she told him would the detective check? Weighing her words carefully, she said, "I think I assumed at first that we'd be friends because there were so few women in the program, but it didn't turn out that way. We weren't much alike. She thought I was too serious. I thought she was a time bomb."

Lewis Paine smiled. "And you were both right."

He still had the dreams. Sometimes he'd go months without having to relive bits of the past, and he would think that at last he had succeeded in outliving the memories, but then for no apparent reason, the past would come roaring back, indelible in its clarity and just as intense as the experience itself.

The dreams were a part of the depression that had put him in the hospital to begin with. Rage and sorrow at growing old, at opportunities missed, and loved ones lost to time—all these made up the fabric of his despair, but beneath them all lay the dreams. It seemed odd to him to call his condition "depression," as if the old wounds and losses were only a figment of his imagination, an unhealthy state of mind at odds with reality. The mirror told a different story, though. So did the aches of decades' old injuries, and there was nothing imaginary about the fact that he was past seventy, and that his death grew less theoretical with each passing day. Sometimes the notion of oblivion frightened him, but mostly, he thought, what he felt was anger over all that he had left undone. He wondered if he would have the time and the means to remedy any of that before his own demise.

He had hoped that his stay in Cherry Hill might offer new choices in drugs, something that would give him sleep without dreams, but if such a pill existed, he had not yet found it. Each night, though, he took the sedative proffered by the night attendant and hoped that he would wake to sunlight, the rustle of starched cotton, and the sounds of familiar voices. Instead, he would drift into awareness in a darkness remembered in his mind. Darkness and then flames.

He wondered what Jack Dolan's face looked like now—forty-odd years later. It was the photograph of the house that had triggered this latest episode of the nightmare, but in the dream, although he was an old man with his scarred face and his misshapen hand, Jack Dolan had leered back at him unchanged, looking just as he had on that last night.

*"I can't help it. I was born
sneering."*
—W. S. Gilbert, *The Mikado*

Chapter 8

Geoffrey Chandler stood in the open doorway of the Dolan mansion, surveying the hallway with its chipped plaster ceiling, dangling overhead lightbulb, and newly whitened walls.

"I have not come a moment too soon," he announced.

"That is a matter of opinion," said his cousin Bill Mac-Pherson, who was still holding on to the front door as if reluctant to relinquish the option of slamming it. "What brings you here, Geoffrey?"

"Why, family solidarity," said Geoffrey, spreading his hands in his best display of innocence. "I heard about your recent acquisition, so naturally being the one person in the family with taste and an instinctive knowledge of interior design, I came to offer my assistance in this mammoth undertaking of yours." He glanced about him with narrowed eyes. "Although in this case, I believe the mammoth is a white one."

"We do not need your so-called skills in interior design," said Bill, picturing apes and peacocks strutting through the drawing room. "This place just needs a little cosmetic touch-up, that's all. When we finish with it, it will be a showplace."

"As is the site of the Little Big Horn," murmured Geoffrey, easing his way into the hall. He pointed up at the lightbulb dangling on a frayed electrical cord. "This is not what they mean by shabby chic, you know."

"We're going to replace it," muttered Bill. "Several of the light fixtures are faulty. I was just going to the hardware store to buy a new one."

"To the hardware store?" Geoffrey closed his eyes and shuddered dramatically. "Surely you are not planning to purchase furnishings for this house at some local do-it-yourself shop?"

"We don't have much money to spare right now," said Bill. "Maybe later . . ."

"Speaking of money, shouldn't you be practicing law right now, instead of acting as handyman in the House of Usher?"

"The cases I have now are mostly in the paperwork stage," said Bill. "Nothing all that time consuming. And my partner is in Richmond, but she's probably billing her corporate clients for a hefty fee, so, while it's kind of you to worry—"

Geoffrey waved away his excuses. "Never mind. About the renovations of this place, let me see what I can do. Consider it a housewarming gift." He pulled a silver-bound notepad out of the breast pocket of his jacket and scribbled a few words. "Now you may show me the rest of the house."

Elizabeth was not having a good day. She had taken her pills after breakfast, just as she had on every morning since her

----

arrival, but today they might as well have been aspirin, so little effect did they have on the cloud of misery that seemed to envelop her. She sat on the battered sofa in the dayroom, staring at the scuffed tile floor and trying to think of something to do that was better than being dead. So far, nothing qualified.

She knew that she had to be out of the dayroom before the poetry group began its meeting, or risk being bored to death, but so far she could not muster the energy to move, even to escape the perils of amateur poets.

When she saw Emma O. come in carrying a manila folder full of paper, Elizabeth felt a stab of fear. "I thought poetry wasn't meeting until ten," she said, struggling to her feet. "I was just leaving."

Emma O. motioned for her to sit back down. "Relax," she said. "You're safe. This isn't poetry. That group isn't due in here for another half an hour. Plenty of time for both of us to escape. This folder is my therapy project. It's designed to improve my attitude."

"Really?" said Elizabeth. She tried to imagine what sort of papers might improve the personality of Emma O. If a lobotomy was out of the question, Elizabeth would vote for deportation forms, but that probably wasn't it.

"It's Dr. Shokie's idea," Emma O. said, indicating the papers. "He says that I'm so angry and hostile that I'm making him crazy. Two weeks ago he suggested a beauty makeover, but that didn't seem to work."

Elizabeth studied the young woman's scrubbed reddish moon face and her cropped brown hair. Whatever the makeover had consisted of, its effects had surely worn off. No one could be plainer than this.

Emma O. met her gaze with an indifferent shrug. "Anyhow, nobody noticed. So now he has given up trying to make me fit in. Now he wants me to practice random acts of kindness to mellow my attitude toward humanity." She shrugged. "I thought I'd give it a shot to humor him."

"What are you doing?"

"Writing apologies to people."

"Oh, really? Making amends to people you've hurt?" Elizabeth beamed at her encouragingly. "That seems like a very mature and wholesome thing to do." And it will probably take you two hundred years to write to all the people you've annoyed, she added to herself. On the other hand, Emma O. never seemed to notice when people were angry with her, so perhaps by her lights she had relatively few apologies to make.

Emma O. shook her head. "You don't understand. I'm not apologizing to anyone that I've ever offended. All those people were moronic weasels who deserved everything they got from me in the way of invective. My task is a more cosmic approach to restitution. I am apologizing to people who have been mistreated by everyone—by society at large."

"Oh!" said Elizabeth. "And you feel that you can speak for society?"

"Well, somebody has to. But anyone who wants to participate is welcome to sign the letters. Would you like to sign one?"

"It depends. Who on earth are you writing to? The Plains Indians? The Tuskegee Airmen? Bob Dole?"

"I haven't made my list yet, but I've started with Richard Jewell."

Elizabeth turned the name over in her mind until she made

the connection. "The security guard suspected in the bombing at the Atlanta Olympics?"

"The man was a hero," said Emma O. "He was helping people. And despite the fact that he was never charged with a crime, and that he later was completely cleared, everybody acted as if he had been convicted; talk-show hosts made jokes about him, and the press made his life miserable. Do you know why?"

"Well," said Elizabeth, "I think I can guess what you're going to say. Richard Jewell was heavyset and not good-looking. America bullied him because he fit the image of what they thought a bomber should look like. The movies teach us that the pretty people are the heroes and the ugly people are the villains. Right?"

"Exactly!" Emma held up the handwritten draft of her first letter and began to read, "Oliver North, who looks like a movie star, was mixed up in the Iran-Contra scandal and lied to Congress. What happened to him? Ran for the U.S. Senate, got his own talk show, whereas you, Mr. Jewell, unfashionably overweight and not celebrity material, were a hero but still you were trashed by the media for weeks, despite the fact that you weren't even charged, much less convicted!"

"Well," said Elizabeth. "I hope Mr. Jewell takes your letter in the spirit that it was intended." The message of apology wasn't exactly her idea of a compliment, but she realized that flattery was foreign to Emma O.'s nature. In social situations Asperger's people don't lie, which is why you find them so seldom in social situations.

"We owe Mr. Jewell an abject apology for the way society treated him," Emma announced. "So he's getting one from me. Sign here."

Elizabeth shrugged. "Why not?" she said. On a sheet of paper labeled SIGNATURES, she scribbled her name as illegibly as possible under the scrawl of Rose Hanelon and the neat printing of Matt Pennington. She tried again to reason with the author. "But, you know, Emma, Oliver North can't help being handsome, and maybe Mr. Jewell can't help looking the way he does, but it seems to be human nature for people to like and trust pretty people. You can hardly blame them for it."

"Equal under the law. Constitutional right," said Emma, waving away human nature. "Shouldn't matter what a person looks like. The public convicted him without a trial because they didn't like his looks. We should all be ashamed. I wonder if they'll let me use a word processor to print out the final copy?"

I wonder if they'll let you mail it, Elizabeth thought. She tried again. "Emma, are you sure that this is what Dr. Shokie had in mind for your attitude therapy? It doesn't seem to be making you more mellow. If anything, this project is simply channeling your rage and hostility into new outlets."

"Yes, but you can't expect miracles. This is only my first day at it. Anyhow, I am doing good works. Random acts of kindness."

Elizabeth suppressed a mischievous smile. "You know, Emma," she said, "if you want to perform a really noble act of kindness, you ought to stay here for the morning poetry reading. You could listen to everyone's work and then praise all the amateur poets for their efforts."

With a stricken look Emma O. glanced at the dayroom clock and began to edge toward the door. "I'm an Asperger's person, remember?" she said. "My whole social life failed because I couldn't tell lies. Me? Stay for the poetry reading? There is no one in this entire institution who is that crazy."

Carla Larkin was worried. She had been reading the local newspaper's graphic account of the abduction of Mr. Jenkins, a prominent local businessman. The PMS Outlaws had driven over the bridge from Arkansas into Tennessee to lessen their chances of being captured, and now they were staying on the outskirts of Memphis, in an upscale hotel that catered to business travelers. On the room registration they said they were librarians.

The newspaper had been left neatly folded outside the door of their room, a standard amenity for guests. Carla had snatched it up, searching its pages for any mention of their latest exploit. P. J. Purdue, who affected indifference toward their notoriety, ordered the all-American breakfast from room service, then flipped the channels on the television, looking for cartoons, which she said were less stressful than the news and usually more truthful.

That comment certainly applied to the carefully worded news story about the plight of Jenkins the banker, Carla thought. The article implied that Mr. Jenkins had been overpowered while conducting a private business meeting with two prospective investors. Unfortunately, his version of the story would have to go unchallenged. Even his picture was misleading. The file photo that accompanied the story showed the banker at his executive best, in a three-piece suit, staring out at the reader with a silver air of command that put one in mind of a recently retired general. Carla giggled and tapped the picture with her forefinger. "Look, Purdue! There he is, the old stoat. He didn't look nearly that impressive in polka-dot boxer shorts, did he?"

Purdue smiled. "A photo of Jenkins in his polka-dot shorts chained to the sink pipe would have sold a lot more newspapers. Maybe we should start carrying a camera. We could tell the johns: If you describe us to the cops, we'll send your picture to the local paper. I'll bet they'd forget what we look like in a hurry, don't you?"

"The cops already know what we look like," said Carla. "Every time we pull one of these jobs, they know exactly who we are within hours."

"Yes, but you've cut your hair, and I've dyed mine, so that ought to create a little confusion. Besides, by the time the crime has been reported, we're long gone."

"Do you think we ought to change what we're doing?" Carla asked her partner. "I mean, with all the publicity we're getting, the word will eventually get there ahead of us. If we keep trying to pick up guys as a twosome, sooner or later one of them is bound to recognize us. There have been a lot of stories about us in the papers."

"Yeah, but the articles weren't on the sports page," said P. J. Purdue. "So most men will never notice. Besides, I think it adds to the thrill of the hunt to warn the prey. It gives them a sporting chance to escape."

"I thought we were the prey," said Carla. "I thought the whole idea of this was for us to escape, so that we can end up somewhere safe like Canada, with nobody out looking for us. We were going to get jobs, remember? The robberies were just

----

supposed to provide us with money and transportation so that we could get away. But instead of making a straight shot north, you're tooling around the southeast hunting up more victims."

P. J. Purdue shrugged. "It's fun. It's about time somebody taught men a lesson."

Carla glanced at the clock. She had hoped to get an early start, but now it was only two hours until checkout time, and Purdue was showing no inclination to leave. "But don't we have enough money yet, P. J.? I'll bet if we drove nonstop, the banker's car could get us all the way to Canada."

The leering face of a cartoon wolf appeared on the television screen, and three determined-looking pigs prepared to hit him over the head with a mallet. Purdue set down the remote, and leaned back on her pillow to watch. "Canada?" she said. "Oh, we'll get there, but I have a few more scores to settle on the way."

Geoffrey's progress through the downstairs rooms of the Dolan mansion had been slow, and largely conducted in an ominous silence, broken only by the scratching of the pen in his silver notepad. His cousin Bill had confined his remarks to announcements on the order of, "And this is the dining room," but as a conversational gambit, it was not a success.

After three rooms of frosty forbearance, Bill finally burst out, "I'm sure you don't approve, Geoffrey, but Powell and I don't want to be poster children for *Southern Living*, which is just as well because we couldn't afford it. We just want a halfway decent law office so that we can attract a better class of client. Why are you peering up that fireplace?"

"Checking for loose bricks," said Geoffrey patiently. "If there's any deterioration of the chimney brickwork, the fire won't draw, and you could end up with a room full of smoke—or worse. However, if you have a body stuffed up a fireplace somewhere, and you don't want me to discover it, you have only to say so."

"No. No," muttered Bill. "Feel free. Just don't blame me if you get bats in your hair. Though I doubt that they'd do such a thing to you. Professional courtesy."

Geoffrey strolled away without dignifying that remark with so much as a glance. Bill called out after him. "Well, what do you think?"

"I think it's a pity that you bought it," said Geoffrey.

"Oh."

"Because in the right hands, this house could be a masterpiece."

Bill brightened a bit. "Well, maybe someday, when we get on our feet financially, we can put some money into renovations."

"Oh, money!" Geoffrey waved aside financial considerations. "That's hardly the issue here. Would you carpet the entrance hall?"

"Uh—I guess so."

"What about the walls? Photographs?"

Bill considered it. "Well, maybe a couple to set the tone. We have one of A. P. shaking hands with Senator Robb at a banquet, and I have an autographed picture of Meg Ryan. Bought it on the Internet. Somebody might steal that one, though."

Geoffrey's eyes sparkled. "You'll have waiting room furniture. Sofas and whatnot. What sort of upholstery were you thinking of getting?"

"Something sturdy," said Bill promptly. "Something that doesn't show dirt. We don't want to have to replace it every six months. Maybe some rough fabric with metallic threads."

Geoffrey closed his eyes dramatically. "Of course," he said. "Anything else? Don't spare me. Plants? Plastic, of course. Bowling trophies?"

"Well, in my office I have a stuffed groundhog wearing judge's robes. He's a real conversation piece."

"I don't doubt it," said Geoffrey with feeling. "And you want to attract well-to-do clients. I have made my point."

"What point?"

"You have scored absolute zero on the test for style and good taste. In fact, you owe points in that category. This has nothing to do with money. It is your judgment that is faulty. Large amounts of money would only make it worse. Then you might gild the groundhog statue and carpet the walls."

Bill blinked. "Well," he said, "I had thought of asking Mother to give me a few pointers, but as long as you're here, if you want to make any suggestions, go ahead."

"Suggestions? It is past that. Drastic measures are called for. I shall direct the entire project." Geoffrey shuddered. "Someone must save you from yourself before you turn this house into an eight-thousand-square-foot double-wide."

Edith came into the room in time to hear this last speech. "He saw the groundhog, didn't he?" she asked Bill.

Bill nodded. Belatedly remembering his manners, he added, "Edith Creech, this is Geoffrey Chandler. You'll probably be seeing more of him."

Edith looked appraisingly at the tall young man in an impeccably cut blazer with a silk tie knotted over a Turnbull &

Asser shirt. "Pleased to meet you," she said. "Are you a decorator or a defendant?" she asked.

Geoffrey smiled. "I'm sure I deserve to be both," he said.

"Geoffrey is my cousin. He is not the black sheep of the family: He's the Judas goat. Was there something you wanted, Edith?" Bill had noticed that she was carrying the large earthenware jar that usually sat on the kitchen counter.

"Yes. Where's the sugar? I could have sworn this thing was full."

"I put some in my tea this morning," said Bill.

"I bought five pounds on Monday," said Edith. "And I can't find a single spoonful in that kitchen. I thought you might be lining the cat box with it."

Bill shrugged. "The bag probably got put away somewhere. It will turn up. Anyhow, Geoffrey is going to help us decorate the place, so why don't you show him the upstairs while I return a few phone calls." The only calls all morning had been two wrong numbers, but if it meant getting away from Geoffrey, Bill would return them.

A. P. Hill had left Richmond, heading south on I-85, and for a few miles she actually thought about going home. If she stayed on 85 until it intersected with Highway 58 west in Emporia, Virginia, it would be a straight shot home, and she would reach Danville in less than two hours. She ought to be back there helping Bill and Edith fix up the new offices. She was sure that Bill had been hurt by her apparent indifference to his cherished project, but she couldn't very well explain her preoccupation. A. P. Hill had never been a person to shirk her responsibilities, and her present dereliction of duty was costing her sleep and worry, but she reminded herself how important it was to settle this business with Purdue before circumstances got beyond her control and made a mess of her life. The real reason that the thought of returning to Danville was so appealing to her, though, was the fact that she dreaded the visit she was about to make.

She tried to remember everything she had ever known about Patricia Purdue.

"Hey, Am-eee, whatcha gonna do? It's Saturday night." She pictured the scene in her mind. Williamsburg. A Saturday night in early fall. A. P. Hill had been a sophomore in college, spending the evening of a football weekend alone in her dorm room when suddenly the little chicken hawk body had appeared in the doorway, jaw set, eyes narrowed, with a drill sergeant's scowl— the customary expression of P. J. Purdue.

"It's A. P., Patty," Amy Powell Hill had replied without looking up from her book. "My family calls me Powell. Either one will do."

She was sitting on the bed in her dorm room, savoring the silence that meant everyone else had gone out for the evening. It must have been obvious that she had no plans: she was wearing an X-large T-shirt that came down to her knees and the ballet shoes she wore as bedroom slippers. As always, Purdue was wearing her customary black sweatshirt and sweatpants, a terrorist organization of one.

Uninvited, Purdue came in and perched on the end of the bed. "You know, if you were going to keep your nose in a book for four years, you could have gone to correspondence school."

"Inferior degree," muttered Powell Hill, turning a page. "I want to go to law school."

"I intend to go to law school," said Purdue. "I come from a line of Virginia lawyers that goes all the way back to the House of Burgesses."

"Probably what prompted Patrick Henry to say, 'Give me liberty or give me death.' "

Purdue ignored the remark and the frown that accompanied it. "My grandfather is a judge."

"What about your father?"

"He was a pilot. Killed in a training mission at Cherry Point. My mother is dead, too. So the judge raised me to be a Purdue." She grinned. "He didn't set much store by Southern belles. I was the last of the Purdues, and by damn, I had to amount to something more than a pretty face. Just as well."

Powell Hill nodded. Just as well because Purdue wasn't a pretty face. She was short and solid and pugnacious in an era when sex symbols were tall and willowy.

"I've got a bottle of Jack Daniel's in my room," said Purdue. "You do know how to drink, don't you?"

With a sigh A. P. Hill closed the book. If Purdue was in a sociable mood, she wasn't going to get much studying done anyway. Besides, although she would never have admitted it, she was tired of spending her evenings alone. Without another word she followed Purdue down the hall to a spartan single room whose outstanding feature was the fifth of bourbon on the desk. Purdue poured a generous measure into two plastic William & Mary cups, topping it up with Coke.

"To law school," said Purdue, raising the cup.

"Law school," echoed A. P. Hill. She took a small sip of her drink and held her breath to keep from coughing. Purdue mixed drinks with a heavy hand.

"You're not bad-looking for the elf type, U. P. S. Hill," Purdue was saying, studying her with a clinical eye. "Some makeup would fix that washed-out-blonde look, but you really ought to spend more than five dollars on a haircut, you know. I don't bother, but if I had your potential, I might make the effort. So . . . why don't you?"

"I have an agenda," said Powell Hill. "Right now, dating has no part in my plans." She held up a lank strand of short, straw-colored hair. "This keeps it simple. It's like saying no before anybody even asks you."

"You're descended from some general, aren't you?"

"Yes. A. P. Hill. The initials are kind of a family tradition. My brother's name was Andrew. When I was a child they called me Amy at home, but I hated it, so I use my initials."

"So, what about your family? Don't they want their little blonde elf to be a cheerleader?"

"Maybe." When they can be bothered to notice me, thought A. P. Hill. It was probably the effect of the Jack Daniel's. Powell Hill made a point of never talking about her personal life with anyone, but Purdue seemed to be a kindred spirit, and suddenly the urge to air her thoughts was irresistible. She leaned back in the plastic chair by Purdue's study desk and moved her cup in time to her words.

"My folks had a boy to pin their hopes on, so I was pretty much an afterthought. They shunted me off to ballet when I was little, and they bought me a canopy bed and a lot of stuffed animals without really trying to see who I was at all. I might have been a doll out of a catalog. Then when I was ten, my brother died in a car wreck. My folks split up, and I didn't see much of my dad after that."

"Yeah," said Purdue. "Sometimes I think your dad dying isn't the worst thing that can happen to a kid. What if he lives and he doesn't want to see you? That's rough."

"I started getting interested in grades and careers after my brother died. I guess I thought if I took over the boy's role, and became what he was supposed to be, my father would love me."

"Did it work?"

"No. When Dad remarried, his new wife came with a pretty, giggly daughter in tow. She's a year younger than I am, and she might as well be a Barbie doll. He's always talking about Kim. When I made valedictorian, he wrote back to say that Kim had been asked to do a commercial for the local car dealership." She sighed. "Apparently, that outranked my four-point-oh grade point average."

"No," said Purdue. "It's never that easy with sick bastards like him. He's probably driving Kim crazy by bragging to her about what a brilliant scholar you are. So he makes sure that you're both miserable."

"You know what?" A. P. Hill took another swallow of bourbon and giggled. "Secretly, I used to pretend that Jimmy Stewart was my dad."

Purdue nodded. "Yes, I can see how a girl with a lousy dad could fantasize about that. Were you thinking of *It's a Wonderful Life*?"

"Mostly that one, I guess. I watched all his old films on the movie channel. Every picture he was ever in. Bought the videos of my favorites. *Broken Arrow. Mr. Smith Goes to Washington.* That's when I decided to be a lawyer."

"Ummm . . . he wasn't a lawyer in that one," said Purdue. "He was just a congressman. He was a lawyer in something else, though, wasn't he?"

"*Anatomy of a Murder.* That was sad, though. I hope practicing law isn't really like that."

"Maybe. I guess it depends on your practice."

"Well, I want to do courtroom scenes. Like Jimmy Stewart in *Mr. Smith Goes to Washington*, only in court. He inspired me."

"Did you ever write to him?"

"To the real Mr. Stewart?" A. P. Hill blushed. "No—I can't believe I'm telling you this—I was afraid that the real James Stewart might ignore me, or that he might say something that would spoil the fantasy. It's stupid, I know. But I really needed my image of him. Sometimes it's like I can hear him talking to me."

"Jimmy Stewart?"

"Yeah. I've seen the movies so often that I can just hear him talking, you know, in that voice of his that all the comedians used to imitate. And sometimes when I'm not sure what I should do, I close my eyes and listen to hear what he'll say."

Purdue smiled. "So—ask him now! What does he say about you being holed up in your room with a book on Saturday night?"

A. P. Hill took another swallow of her drink, leaned back, and closed her eyes. "He says . . . 'Waal, Powell, it's important to work hard, but you shouldn't forget to be happy every once in a while along the way.' "

"Good advice," said Purdue, emptying her cup. "Why don't

we go out on the town and see if we can pick up a couple of . . . lawyers?"

They burst out laughing.

"Hey, it beats spending Saturday night in a dorm," said Purdue.

A. P. Hill shrugged. "Sure. Why not?" she said.

They trooped off together a bit unsteadily, in the direction of town, but it began to rain, so instead of barhopping, they ended up in a movie. The pact had been made, though, and not very many Saturdays later, they did something a bit more daring, and something happened.

It was a memory that A. P. Hill had been walling out of her consciousness for nearly ten years. She shook off the memory and focused on the road ahead, glad that she had left Williamsburg behind, both past and present.

Geoffrey Chandler, the self-appointed interior designer of the new headquarters of MacPherson & Hill, had dutifully followed Edith on a tour of the upstairs bedrooms of the Dolan mansion, springing ahead of her to open doors and listening to her room descriptions with rapt attention. He was chattier with his new guide than he had been on the downstairs leg of the tour, and he contrived to express polite interest in his surroundings, but privately he thought he had wasted enough time on questions of decorating schemes. The upstairs wasn't particularly important anyway. The clients of MacPherson & Hill would see only the downstairs, and Geoffrey thought it would be presumptuous of him to try to decorate A. P. Hill's rooms, and hopeless to try to decorate Cousin Bill's. Still, he smiled and nodded, and scribbled on his notepad as they walked from room to room.

When Edith showed signs of tiring of her role as guide, he said, "I thought that the original owner of the house was still in residence here. I haven't seen him."

Edith nodded. "Oh, Mr. Jack is around someplace. It worried me, too, for the first couple of days when he would disappear like that. I was afraid that he'd crawled off somewhere and died of old age. But he always turns up about four-thirty, when I put the teakettle on. I always have a brownie or an apple turnover set aside for him. He's a sweet old fellow."

"And quite old, I hear."

"Past ninety. He's like an old turtle these days, creeping about the house in slow motion, but he's still as sharp as ever if you take the time to hear him out. He likes to talk about the old days."

Geoffrey's interest quickened. "How wonderful!" he said. "Quite an inspiration to us all. What does he talk about?"

"I don't know," said Edith. "Things that happened before I was born, I'll tell you that. He tends to mumble a lot, so I just nod and smile."

Geoffrey nodded sympathetically. "Does he ever drag out the old photo albums?" he asked.

"No, I can't say I've been subjected to that."

"It would be interesting to talk to him about the house," said Geoffrey. "I'm sure I would find him quite fascinating. And I'd love to see old photographs. It would tell us how the house was originally furnished."

"Well, you can ask him," said Edith. "In fact, you're

welcome to have him for a tour guide, if you can stand the pace, which is about one hundred yards an hour. I'm sure he could tell you more about this place than I can."

Geoffrey smiled. "I shall be delighted to ask him."

A. P. Hill had made better time than she wanted to on the journey, which had been made longer by her mind's refusal to concentrate on anything but the coming interview. Once in a while she would remember to glance in her rearview mirror to see if anyone was following her, but she never noticed any particular car trying to keep pace with her. Apparently, Lewis Paine was not concerned enough to have her watched, or else the city of Richmond had much more to worry about in the way of criminals than an evasive witness. Given the city's high annual murder rate, this was the likeliest explanation.

A few miles north of Emporia, A. P. Hill left the interstate and followed a two-lane blacktop west into the rural area of Dinwiddie County. She had looked up the address in the alumni records at William & Mary, and then in Richmond she had consulted maps to determine the route. She had considered telephoning ahead to announce her visit and perhaps to receive more specific directions, but it was just as likely that she would be told not to come. A. P. Hill could think of too many reasons not to let them know she was coming, so in the end she had set out on what was probably a wild-goose chase.

She managed to get within a few miles of her destination before narrowing country lanes and a dearth of road signs forced her to stop at a country store and gas station to ask for direc-

----

tions. She bought a sports drink in order to be a customer rather than a supplicant, and the weary-looking woman behind the counter told her which road to take, without even a question about why she was going there. Sometimes, thought A. P. Hill, it helps to be blonde and petite.

A few minutes later, she was headed up a long gravel driveway that was only marginally smaller than the road that led to it. The drive was bounded on both sides by horse pastures and freshly painted white board fences. Ahead of her, a white-columned house shone out from a grove of spreading oaks. This was the ancestral home of Patricia J. Purdue. It would be. With a flicker of annoyance A. P. Hill wondered why some rich kids seemed to be born arrogant. They seemed to feel that rules were only suggestions, or at best strictures that were a good idea for civilization in general, but that did not apply to them in particular. Maybe it's because they're working with a net, she thought. No matter what happens to them in life, Daddy's money will make it all better. Did Purdue still think that?

A. P. Hill parked the car near the front porch and prepared to enter the lion's den. She straightened her skirt when she got out of the car. Linen wrinkles the minute you put it on. After a two-hour drive, she looked as if she had slept in it. Still, she supposed she looked all right, by which she meant that she had dressed to be taken seriously. She was in lawyer mode: navy linen coat and skirt, low-heeled shoes, and slung over her shoulder was the strap of her white Coach bag for summer.

There was a leering gargoyle door knocker on the massive

front door. As A. P. Hill struck the ring against the sounding brass, she heard it echo through the hallway beyond and she closed her eyes to concentrate on her carefully rehearsed words of introduction. When she opened them again, she saw in the doorway a heavyset old woman with an apron over her faded housedress. She was peering out at A. P. Hill with an expression of deep suspicion. "We don't want to buy your magazines or visit your heathen church," she announced.

A. P. Hill said, "That's not why I'm here. I'm a friend of P. J. Is the judge at home?"

The woman looked at her appraisingly. "I expect he would be for you," she said with a harsh laugh. "But he tires mighty easy. Remember that."

Without another word the woman turned and stalked down the hall toward the back of the house. A. P. Hill took this to be an invitation to follow her, and she hurried to catch up, with her sensible shoes beating a muffled tattoo on the marble tiles. She barely glanced at her surroundings, except to wonder briefly if the new headquarters of MacPherson & Hill would ever achieve this degree of staid elegance. She thought not. Even if they hired the most exclusive decorator in Richmond (which they could not for one minute afford), Bill would probably insist on dragging his mascot, that dreadful stuffed groundhog from the flea market, out into the foyer, or he would put up framed baseball cards instead of Stubbs horse prints on the oak-paneled walls. But she had neither the time nor the inclination to stop him. Their legal expertise would speak for itself, and perhaps Bill's eccentric ideas of decoration would be taken as a sign of power and creativity—at least by people who hadn't met the rest of his family.

The door to the study was ajar, and Powell Hill went in quietly, wondering if the old gentleman might be sleeping. The room smelled of tobacco, wood fires, and leather upholstery. In the dim light from the partially curtained French windows, she could see a wood-paneled room lined with bookcases. "Judge Purdue?" said A. P. Hill, walking toward the armchair by the dark fireplace.

"I'm not asleep, young woman." The voice from the chair was reedy with age, but it had lost none of its ring of authority. "Do I know you?"

"No, sir. I went to law school with your granddaughter. My name is A. P. Hill."

"Ha! She beat you out, though, didn't she? Top of her class, she was. She's a Purdue, through and through."

"Yes, sir. Have you seen her lately, Judge?"

"Oh, some time back, I guess," said the old man. "Why? Are you trying to get in touch with her? Job hunting, are you?"

"I would like to find her, sir," said A. P. Hill. The conversation reminded her of a turn on the witness stand, and here, too, it seemed best not to elaborate on one's answers.

"I suppose we have her address around somewhere. She's practicing out of state, you know. Wanted to make her own way. Stubborn. All the Purdues are stubborn."

"She hasn't been to see you in the last couple of weeks?" asked A. P. Hill. She already knew the answer to that one. If the name A. P. Hill did not immediately register with the judge as his granddaughter's most recently assumed alias, it meant that the police had not kept him apprised of Purdue's latest escapades.

"We haven't heard from P. J. for a good while," the old man muttered. "I always keep meaning to give her a call."

"Have you been to see her since she started her out-of-state practice?"

The judge considered this. "Can't say I have. Health's not what it was. Not up to much in the way of travel."

Powell Hill's eyes strayed to the end table beside the judge's leather chair, where a stack of travel brochures heralded the charms of Paris and Amsterdam. She wondered if Purdue had planned to skip the country, and if the judge was part of her escape plan. She tapped the top brochure with her forefinger. "Paris," she said. "I went there for a couple of weeks one summer."

"Too hot in the summer," said the judge. "Too many tourists. I always go in September when things have simmered down a bit. Go every year. The wine does wonders for my digestion."

A. P. Hill nodded. "Did Patricia ever go with you?" she asked. "I don't remember her ever mentioning it."

"I go alone," the old man said. "This year, though, I may take Mrs. Rampling with me." He nodded toward the open doorway, where the housekeeper hovered, arms crossed, glaring at A. P. Hill. "She can keep me out of trouble. Make sure I take my pills, don't you know?"

A. P. Hill thought she did know. So you're too ill to visit your granddaughter three states away, but you go to Paris every fall. She thanked the judge and turned to go. She had learned something after all. Wherever P. J. Purdue decided to go, it would not be here.

MacPherson & Hill
Attorneys-at-Law

TO: Elizabeth MacPherson
FROM: Geoffrey Chandler
SUBJECT: News from home

Is that you, Elizabeth? I seem to recall that patients at Cherry Hill could receive faxes, provided that
they were not of an inflammatory nature. You know,
things like: "Go and save France. Signed, God." or
"The lab report came back. You are a teakettle."
However, let me take this first paragraph to assure
whatever medical personnel are reading this missive
that I have no desire to contribute to the delusions of
anyone. I merely wish to convey cheery messages to
my ailing relative in hopes that the comfort and support of her loved ones will sustain her in her time of
sorrow.

Note: Elizabeth. If the preceding paragraph actually made you retch, you may consider yourself en
route to recovery. I nearly gagged while writing it.

Well, typing it, actually. I am composing this
on your brother's office word processor because
I thought it would look more official that way. I
did consider writing it out in my most illegible
handwriting—slanting all the letters to the left,
perhaps—but in the interests of time, I plumped for
the easy way. (Surely anyone reading this would be
too bored by now to continue. . . .)

I have arrived safely in Danville, as I suppose you have surmised from the letterhead on the writing paper. Your dear brother was, of course, touchingly glad to see me. He practically begged me to take over the entire project of decorating this house of theirs, and with some reluctance, I finally allowed myself to be prevailed upon to oversee the renovations.

At this point in a normal correspondence, I would be tempted to set down my thoughts regarding paint selection, wallpaper choices, and a general outline of the design concept that I have in mind for the office area, contrasted for emphasis with the ludicrous suggestions made by the occupant himself: your brother, the owner of a stuffed groundhog, which he seems to consider an objet d'art. But I digress. . . . And I suppose that if I spend many more words discussing aesthetic considerations, you will begin to scream—you are so impatient, dear. You really should see if they can give you something for that. . . . Anyhow, I must get to the point, because if burly guards had to come and sedate you, they would probably confiscate this letter, and then I would have wasted all this effort trying to remember which letters on the keyboard are on which row. Thank God for Spell Check.

Where was I? Oh, yes . . . Lafayette, we are here. (An American general said that. In Paris, I believe. He had just arrived to fight a war, so I feel the quotation is not inappropriate in this case.) I suspect that

Bill may put up some sort of feeble resistance to my more daring experiments in interior design, but I shall be firm. Fortunately, I think, his clever partner, Miss A. P. Hill, is away from Danville at the moment. She might resort to restraining orders if she were displeased with my work, but I'm sure I can manage Cousin Bill.

I took an exhaustive tour of the house, and I must say that it does have possibilities, particularly if you are fond of the Georgian style. However, the chief object of our interest was not in evidence this afternoon. Apparently Mr. Dolan spends a good part of the day napping in some secluded garden spot, or at least otherwise engaged out of sight, because he was nowhere to be seen, and his housemates did not seem to know where he was. Edith promises that if I will turn up for tea and pastry at four-thirty, the old man will come toddling in, and then I'll see what I can do about extracting information from him. I have already asked about photo albums and stories of Jack Dolan's youth. I plan to be the best audience a garrulous old man ever had.

Meanwhile, you must see what further bits of information you can elicit from your fellow patient there in Cherry Hill. I suggest that you try to get a description of the youthful Dolan that I could compare to old photographs. I suppose I'll have to go to the library sooner or later to see what sort of information is available on the house and its occupant. I shall probably know more when I have actually met our quarry, but I must tell you that in terms of urgency, I think your brother's decorating crisis is the greater of the two emergencies.

Yours in haste,
Cousin Geoffrey

"I never met anybody
who learned by talking."
—Elvis Presley

Chapter 9

Since the day was fine, the members of the Cherry Hill afternoon group therapy session had decided to meet outside. They
were seated on borrowed cafeteria chairs in the dappled shade
of a broad-limbed maple tree, enjoying the sunshine, perhaps
more than they enjoyed the recitals of their fellow patients. Clifford Allen, seated as far back in shadow as he could get, was
anointing every visible part of his body with sunscreen.

After the usual preliminaries had been conducted by the
brisk and hearty Warburton, Emma O. indicated that she would
like to begin the discussion. "I've been making a list of my
friends," she announced. "Or trying to. It's hard to know if you
have any, isn't it?"

Someone had to break the ensuing awkward silence. Matt
Pennington, who prided himself on his charity, spoke the obvious,

expected line, "Well, we're all your friends, Emma." He turned to Elizabeth. "I don't believe I know you, though."

"Shut up, Matt," said Elizabeth. "You had ECT this morning. You forgot me again."

"Oh." He looked doubtful and peered at her more closely, waiting for a spark of recognition that was evidently not forthcoming.

Emma O.'s impatient scowl suggested that Matt's well-meaning, if insincere, offer of friendship had failed to impress her. The others in the group remained silent, reflecting on the fact that it isn't easy to tell comforting lies to someone suffering from depression. As Emma O. was fond of pointing out, depressed people believe the worst, and so often they are right.

"No," Emma told them. "You people are not my friends. At this point you are all fellow travelers in neurosis, but I'm not sure that the attachment will last after our present circumstances change. It probably won't. My friends never do seem to carry over from one situation to the next. They drift away."

"Well, you can always make new friends," said Beulah. "Church is an excellent place to meet people."

"It isn't easy for everybody to make friends," said Clifford Allen. He looked around defiantly, daring anyone to challenge his statement. Nobody did.

"People come and go," said Emma, who did not sound overly concerned about it. "I suppose that the people in the books I read are my friends. The characters on *Star Trek* are my friends. Maybe I should list them."

"But those aren't real people," Warburton reminded her.

Emma shrugged. "They've been in my life longer than any-one else has stuck around."

"Friendship is one of those tests you can't study for," said Rose Hanelon. She had picked up a maple leaf from the lawn beside her chair and was tearing it into narrow strips, but her abstracted gaze suggested that she was not thinking about the leaf. "When I was in the eighth grade, our health teacher did an exercise on friendship that has haunted me ever since," she said. "Can I talk about that?"

Warburton remembered to change her shrug into an encouraging smile. "Go on, Rose."

"Eighth-grade health was an all-girls class. Two days a week it alternated with gym class. We were at the giggly stage of friendship, just before boys and status begin to matter. Anyhow, one day Miss Sharp asked us to list our friends. Who in the class would we want to go on a picnic with? Go to a movie with? Tell a secret to? Sit next to in class? She took up the papers and tabulated the results. The next day in class she drew a diagram on the board—without using any names—showing us the patterns of friendship in the room.

"There were popular girls and unpopular girls. The teacher called them 'Stars' and 'Isolates.' The Stars were the girls who got the most votes, of course. The circles representing them were surrounded by other little circles of their friends and admirers. They were the pretty, self-assured girls who everyone wanted to be friends with. Some of the Isolates only got one vote. What was interesting about our class, according to Miss Sharp, was that sometimes the Stars picked the Isolates for friends. Often the Isolate's only vote came from a Star. And the Isolates usually chose a Star. No Isolate picked another Isolate, which I guess proves that not even misery loves its own company."

"And you never found out which you were?" asked Elizabeth

"No. Miss Sharp wouldn't tell any of us. Ever. I'll bet no one else in the class even remembers doing that exercise, but for thirty years I've wondered if I was a Star or an Isolate."

"Why do you still care?" asked Clifford Allen, to whom relationships were either profitable or cumbersome.

"I don't know," said Rose. "Perhaps I think that I could learn some fundamental truth about myself from that exercise. I don't think the pattern of personality changes much after eighth grade for most people. I think we remained whatever we were— Stars or Isolates—forever." She shivered.

"You were probably an Isolate," said Richard Petress, striking a pose. " 'Cause, honey, let me tell you, the Stars know who they are."

Warburton considered Petress's remark contentious enough to require her intervention before a shouting match began. Since Rose apparently had nothing to add to her story, and the others were looking around uneasily as if they were pondering the results of such a quiz among themselves, the group leader decided to provide a distraction. "Emma, I believe you introduced this topic," she said with a plaster smile. "Perhaps you'd like to tell us why you are making a list of your friends?"

"You're not writing your will, are you?" asked Clifford.

"No. No real reason. I just wanted to list my friends to see if I had any."

Before she could develop this theme, with possibly unpleasant results, Elizabeth saw a chance of using the discussion to her advantage. Turning to Hillman Randolph, she said, "What about you, Mr. Randolph? Did you keep in touch with any of your friends from your days in law enforcement?"

Hillman Randolph's eyes widened. It was unusual for a patient to solicit another's opinion on a topic neither of them had commented on, but after a moment of startled silence, the old man shook his head. "After this," he said, touching a tentative hand to the roughened skin on the side of his face. "After the accident . . . I had to quit working, you know. It took so many operations to get me put back together to where I could go out without making small children cry. . . ." He broke off for a moment as he struggled with the memory. "And my hands . . . Well, some of the fellows came to see me when I was in the hospital—at first—but I was so depressed by what had happened to me that I wasn't much company. I hardly spoke to them. And I reckon pity is no basis for a friendship. So they stopped coming, and I never looked them up. That life was all behind me. It was time to make a clean start."

"So you weren't curious to find out what happened in the cases you had been working on?"

He shook his head. "Maybe they told me. I've forgotten. When you're in a burn unit, young lady, your mind is not apt to be concerned with much of anything beyond the next dose of pain medicine. Pray that you never find that out the hard way."

Before Elizabeth could pursue the matter, Emma O. took the floor again. "You have more friends than I do, Rose," she declared. "You have visitors from the newspaper just about every day, bringing you magazines and wanting to tell you all the gossip from work. Everybody is terribly worried about you for being an alcoholic, and about Seraphin because she's beautiful and she won't eat. But when you have Asperger's, people never much like you in the first place, so you're on your own, because nobody cares if you get well or not."

Warburton saw a chance to insert therapy into the discussion. "Emma, we are trying to treat your depression, but you know that Asperger's syndrome is a developmental disorder. You can't just take a pill and make it go away, but you might be able to modify your behavior. How do you think you can change yourself to make people like you?"

Emma O. shrugged. "I have no idea what makes people like other people, except for the beauty thing, and in my case I don't think there's much chance of that. I can't do crowds and parties like Rose does. I just don't see the point of parties, and I can only focus on one person at a time, which means that even when I attend parties I always bore one person to death and antagonize the rest."

"What's so hard about parties?" said Rose. "If you're nervous, just have a few drinks to loosen yourself up."

"Rose loves parties," said Emma. "She's fun, even when she's dead drunk, but I can't do it. I can be clever with words, even occasionally funny, but I guess it isn't the same. Anyhow, when people start to get tired of me, I just go away and I never bother them again."

"Oh, honey, that goes double for me," said Richard Petress. "When relationships start to cause me more pain than gain, I just walk right on off, and I do not look back."

"Is that a good way to be?" asked Warburton.

Hillman Randolph said, "Sometimes you don't have any choice."

A. P. Hill glanced at the directions scribbled on today's page of her planner. Third house on the left. She was driving along the tree-lined streets of an old neighborhood of Colonial-style houses. She looked out approvingly at the well-kept yards and the neatly tended flower beds. The houses were not identical, but they all blended into a harmonious unit, giving the area character without the cookie-cutter effect. So this is where Sally Gee had ended up.

Even if today's inquiry turned out to be a dead end, thought Powell, the trip would be worth it just to find out how Sally was doing.

It looked like a comfortable, happy neighborhood, thought Powell Hill, nodding at a couple of boys on bicycles who stopped to let her pass. She was glad. She had wanted Sally Gee to live happily ever after, and from the looks of the neighborhood, she had as good a chance at succeeding as most people could ever hope for. Sally was a good person, though. She would always carry happiness with her, and that counted for a lot. Still, there had been times when the other girls in the dormitory had feared that Sally's crusading personality might lead to a shallow grave in a war zone or to a tent hospital at some jungle outpost. Sally Gee had such a terrible combination of innocence and social conscience that she could have ended up anywhere.

A. P. Hill had spent the half-hour drive from her hotel to the suburbs of Richmond remembering her student days on campus, when Sally Gee had been dorm president and general guardian angel to the immediate world. She was only two years older than the incoming freshmen, but somehow she seemed to stand midway between them and the remote adult authority figures who controlled their lives. Sally, self-appointed foster mother of the third floor, dispensed tea and advice at all hours, advised her charges on course selection and relationship problems, and generally kept an eye out for those likely to find trouble in one way or another. For A. P. Hill, who studied too much and laughed too little, Sally would prescribe a movie every couple of weeks. She always asked Powell to go with her as a favor. "Please," she would say, "Jim has football practice [or a golf game, or a term paper to write], and he can't go with me. Would you come along? I hate to see movies alone." The film was always a comedy; the outing was always fun. A. P. Hill was well into her junior year before she realized, thinking back, that she had received the favor, not granted it. Sally Gee cared about everybody. Anyone's unhappiness diminished her. She was beloved, the girls told one another, but so vulnerable. They worried.

Sally had been enshrined in campus legend as the girl who had received an obscene phone call and didn't know it. She had been on her own in the residence hall one afternoon when the pay telephone rang. Sally, ever the good citizen, ran to answer it, ready to deliver a message to whichever of her hallmates the caller wanted, but when she said, "Hello. Third floor," a hoarse male voice had replied, "I'm going to jack off now."

After a moment of shocked silence, Sally said earnestly, "Oh, no, you mustn't! Think how upset your parents would be!"

On the other end of the line the heavy breathing ended in a gasp. "What?"

"If you killed yourself. Think how devastated your folks would be. I'm sure they'd blame themselves. Whatever is troubling you, I'm sure it will pass."

Sally and the caller had continued to have a lovely conversation, with her assuring him of all the joys of living, until at length the young man averred that he did indeed feel . . . relieved.

"Can I call you again?" he asked after another pause.

"Oh, yes!" said his ministering angel. "Any time you are feeling this way again, just call Third and ask for Sally."

She had spent the rest of the afternoon in the afterglow of good works, and that evening when Jim, her fiancé, came to pick her up for the evening, she could not resist regaling him with her triumph. They were walking out side by side that evening, tiny sweet-faced Sally Gee and big Jim Klingenschmitt, a linebacker who was built like a thumb. As they neared the front door Sally looked up at Jim and said, "Oh, Jim, I must tell you: the saddest thing happened today. A boy called the third floor and he was so depressed about life that he was going to jack off."

Several minutes later, after Jim Klingenschmitt had stopped waving his arms and shouting, and after the threat of the fire extinguisher and the campus police had dissuaded him from charging upstairs and ripping the third-floor pay phone off the wall, he sat Sally down on a secluded sofa in the long parlor and carefully explained to her that the phrase "jacking off" was not a euphemism for suicide.

Sally took the news philosophically. Her intentions had been good, after all, and this one unpleasant setback did not deter her from being a mother hen to the rest of the residents. Her one concession to reality after that incident was that for the next month all male callers for Sally Gee were first routed past P. J. Purdue.

Purdue and Sally had been the yin and yang of their residence hall community. They lived at opposite ends of the hall. Purdue dispensed cigarettes in lieu of tea, and her advice tended to be more terrorist than motherly, but they balanced college life well between them. In order to survive college, sometimes you need guerrilla tactics and sometimes you need tea and sympathy. As A. P. Hill pulled into the driveway of the green-shuttered Williamsburg colonial, she found herself wondering for the first time if Sally and Purdue, the saint and the terrorist, had ever sought advice from each other.

Sally G. Klingenschmitt, as she had been known ever since the Sunday after graduation, had not changed much. She was still small and slender enough to pass at a distance for a teenager. Her silky dark hair showed only a trace of gray at the temples, and her earnest brown eyes were as warm and intense as ever. She hugged Powell Hill at the door and ushered her into a snug living room, replete with chintz and polished mahogany. It smelled of lemon polish and fresh-brewed coffee. Above the mantlepiece hung an oil painting of a radiant Sally, blue gowned, sitting formally erect in a leather wing chair while Jim hovered protectively behind her. It was, thought A. P. Hill, a good likeness of the couple spiritually as well as physically.

By the time Powell had been settled in on the rose-patterned sofa and plied with coffee and raisin cookies, she felt eighteen again, ready to put herself and her problems into the capable hands of the dorm president.

"It's good to see you again," she said, suddenly loath to come to the point. "How's Jim?"

"He's great!" said Sally, beaming. "He's head coach this

----

year at the new junior high school, so I get a lot of chances to try out new cookie recipes. But it's wonderful to see you, too, Powell. I teach kindergarten now, which is a joy, of course, but sometimes it's so nice to talk to a grown woman for a change. And you're a lawyer now! I always knew you would be, Powell. Never doubted it for a minute."

A. P. Hill smiled her thanks. The fact that Sally G. had probably never for a minute doubted the Tooth Fairy, either, did not take the shine off her good wishes. "I came to talk to you about Purdue," she said at last. "You've heard?"

Sally shook her head, her eyes wide with apprehension. "No. She's not dead, is she?" Her voice was a horrified whisper. "Poor Purdue! She was always such a wild one. Brilliant, of course, but so wild. So doomed."

"She's still alive," said A. P. Hill. "And I'm trying to see that she stays that way. I need to find her quickly." She opened her purse and took out a tabloid clipping about the PMS Outlaws. The accompanying photo, unflattering but definitely P. J. Purdue, said it all.

Sally read the article, wide-eyed with astonishment. When she finished, she looked up at Powell Hill and shook her head. "I'd heard she became a lawyer, and so I thought surely she had outgrown her rebel phase."

"Apparently not."

"No," Sally agreed. "Purdue always was like a terrier with a rat about her hates. She'd never let go of an insult or an injury."

"I know. She may think this is about rescuing her client from prison, but I'm beginning to think that the fugitive part is just an excuse. Otherwise, they'd be keeping a lower profile on the run. She called me to say that this was more fun than practicing law. Then a few days ago in Tennessee, she used my name as an alias."

"So she's determined to drag you into it."

"It looks that way. I just wondered who else she's contacted. You?"

"No. I wish she would. Maybe I could talk her into getting some help."

"Think back. Is there anyone whom she was close to, or anyplace she might want to go to hide or to get help?"

Sally traced the rose pattern on the sofa with one slender forefinger as she considered the question. "Her parents are dead, aren't they? And she lived somewhere in southside Virginia with her grandfather."

"The judge. I spoke to him. He's very old and frail, and he doesn't seem to know about any of this. Since the crimes all happened outside Virginia, nobody in law enforcement has been to see him about it. I didn't tell him. Anyhow, I don't think she'll go there."

"Seeing his disappointment would be worse than jail for Purdue," said Sally. "I remember thinking how much was expected of Purdue academically, and how little she ever achieved socially. Nobody seemed to care about that. As long as her grade point average was first rate, the judge seemed to think she was fine."

"Well," said Powell Hill, "she might have been fine if she were male. With women, though, academic achievement is never enough."

"No. I suppose it isn't." Sally tapped the tabloid article. "I can just feel Purdue's hostility bubbling through this. It's rage—but directed at whom?"

A. P. Hill shrugged. "Men, I guess. That's nothing new. Remember the blind-date rating chart beside the hall phone? The time she met the flasher in the quad and critiqued his performance?"

"Poor Pat Purdue. She was such an idealist. I know she sounded like a tough little cynic back in college, but think about it. She wouldn't have been so angry at men if her expectations for them had not been so high. You know . . . 'Someday my prince will come.' "

"Well, she didn't find him," said A. P. Hill, glancing again at the tabloid photo of P. J. Purdue and Carla Larkin. "Now she is him. And I need to find her, before she tries to change from Prince Charming into Steven Seagal and gets herself blown away by the police."

Sally Gee nodded thoughtfully. "How can I help?"

"You haven't heard from her, have you?"

"No. A couple of Christmas cards. Purdue manages to send out cards about every other year. Once we got one in March. But really I haven't seen or spoken to her in years. I saw her a couple of times for lunch while I was working on my master's and you two were in law school, but you were her classmate in law school. Surely there are more recent friends you could ask?"

"Not that I know of," said Powell Hill. "She lived in an apartment. Alone. She antagonized most of the men in the class at one time or another, and she wasn't attractive enough for them to forgive her for it. I guess I was her friend—or as close as she got to having one. She tolerated me because she considered me smart enough to be a worthy opponent."

"That seems to be what you are now," said Sally. "A worthy opponent. Catch me if you can."

"I don't know that I want to catch her. I'd like to keep her from throwing her life away, but it may already be too late for that. At least, I'd like a chance to talk to her. That's why I'm trying to figure out where she's headed. I thought you might remember something that would help me to find her."

"It's been a long time," said Sally. "And if anyone else had come asking for a lead to Patricia Purdue, I'd have told them to go and find you."

"We didn't keep in touch."

"How about her coworkers? Wasn't she in a law firm before . . ." Sally tapped the page of the tabloid. "Before all this?"

"I called them first thing. Nobody's talking. They're afraid that they'll be implicated in whatever lawsuits her victims manage to bring before the court." A. P. Hill shrugged. "They're right. I probably wouldn't talk either, if my law partner went off the rails."

"You said you've heard from her, though, since she became a fugitive?"

"She called my office. Yes."

Sally Gee looked thoughtful. "Why?"

"To gloat, I guess. She claims she's having fun. Why?"

"Well, I was just thinking that maybe you won't have to find P. J. after all. Maybe she's going to find you."

A. P. Hill nodded, thinking, *That's what I'm afraid of.*

"If I were you, Powell, I'd keep an open line, and I'd think very hard about what I was going to say to her."

Bill MacPherson put a plastic Realtor key chain on Edith's desk. "Spoils of war," he told her. "The paperwork is finally to the point that the sellers consider it a done deal. They mean that they can sue me for all I've got plus a kidney if I suddenly come to my senses and try to back out of this deal."

Edith looked up at him suspiciously. "You're not going to change your mind, are you?"

"Can't afford to. Besides, everyone keeps telling me what a brilliant investment I'm making. Anyhow, according to Holly the Realtor, it's okay for us to start moving into the house now. I stopped by the liquor store for some cardboard boxes, and I thought we could start packing up the office today. If we can manage to be out by the end of the month, we'll save on rent."

He looked around at the shabby secondhand furniture, the battered file cabinets, and the threadbare area rug. "We'll need all the paperwork, of course, but some of this furniture can go straight to the dump."

"Right," said Edith. "I'd say that decision was long over-due. Have you given notice to the building manager?"

Bill reddened. "I wish Powell Hill were here. She'd handle him without batting an eye. I'll tell you what: You type it and I'll sign it."

"The man won't bite you," said Edith. "He looks like a pit bull, but he doesn't bite. I will type the letter though. We want the departure to be legal. I'll tell you what I won't do, though."

"What's that?"

"Tell your mother. You're on your own there."

Bill smiled. "I'm not worried about her reaction. She'll love it. She'll probably try to hold her book-club meetings in the parlor. I just want to wait until we're settled in, that's all. Knowing my crazy relatives, more of them will descend on us to try to help us decorate."

Edith's gaze rested on the stuffed groundhog that graced the bookcase in Bill's office. "Heaven forbid," she murmured.

"I think we can haul everything in my car. It might take a few trips, but we can manage."

"Are you paying me overtime for this?"

"Sure," said Bill. "Just keep track of your hours."

"In that case, I'll get my cousin to bring over his pickup truck. We ought to be able to get the desks and file cabinets over there in two loads."

"How much should I pay him?"

"Don't be silly," said Edith. "You've got house payments, remember? Just offer him gas money."

Chapter 10

MacPherson & Hill
Attorneys-at-Law

TO: Elizabeth MacPherson, Patient
Cherry Hill Psychiatric Hospital
FROM: Geoffrey Chandler, Interior Designer
Danville, Virginia

Dear Cousin Elizabeth:

Isn't it a good thing that technology is so silent? I mention this because it is quite late at night—three A.M. to be exact—and here I am tapping away on the word processor in Bill's unlit office. The computer keyboard is quiet enough not to call attention to my presence. On an old typewriter, people would be able to hear me crashing and dinging two floors away.

When I finish composing this, I shall fax a printout to you at Cherry Hill, and since it is the middle of the night, I am struck by how pleasant and convenient it is that fax machines, too, are relatively quiet devices. A ringing phone would certainly cause complaint at this hour on your end, but I can slip a few pages of text to you on little cat feet, as it were. It's too bad that you don't have e-mail, which is quieter still, and even less obtrusive, but I quite see why mental hospitals might frown upon their patients having quite so much access to the world at large.

I didn't mean you, dear. I'm sure you wouldn't send threatening letters to the vice president or try to tap into the country's nuclear launch codes, but somewhere there is probably an undermedicated soul in custody who would. So, all right, I shall word process and fax: a small price to pay for the safety of the planet, I am sure.

I finally did have the pleasure of making Mr. Dolan's acquaintance. As Edith suggested, I turned up in the kitchen for late-afternoon tea and pastry, and sure enough, there he was, tucking into a plate of brownies as if it were his first meal in weeks. I accepted a cup of tea, which, fortunately, I take without sugar, because there wasn't any. I wisely decided against trying to reach for one of the brownies. As Mr. Dolan ate, I introduced myself and received a nod in return. It was evident that as a point of interest, I came a distant second to the works of Betty Crocker.

"What a lovely house this is!" I said to him

when the brownies began to disappear at a slower rate. "Have you lived here all your life?"

"Nope," said Mr. Dolan between swigs of milk. "Born poor. Outran it, though."

"Well done, sir! The American dream. The poor but honest youth makes his fortune."

He grunted and reached for the milk jug. "That is a dream, son."

Edith smiled at us. "I'll leave you two to get acquainted," she said. "I have some office work to do. Tidy up the kitchen when you're through, boys."

I don't know where Bill was. Gainfully employed in the practice of law, I hope. He's going to need all the money he can bilk from clients before I'm through setting this house to rights. Anyhow, I told Mr. Dolan that I would be staying for a while because I was in charge of the renovations, and that I'd welcome information from him about the original state of the interior. Paint colors, light fixtures, and so on."

He peered at me with interest. "You're a carpenter?"

I nearly went over backward when he said that, but I managed to regain my wits in time to murmur, "Something of the sort. Do you have any old photographs of the house that I could see to give me an idea of how it ought to look?"

He gave me a canny leer. "There may be one or two around someplace," he said. "You have a car, don't you?"

I said I did, still trying to figure out where this was going.

"Good!" he said. "You can take me out to the grocery store."

And off we went.

I suppose I ought to describe Jack Dolan for you, so that you can run the description past your fellow patient, though I do see that an interval of forty years or so would make a great difference in anyone's appearance. Still, as it is best to be thorough, here goes: Jack Dolan is probably in pretty good shape for a man in his nineties. He walks unassisted. He can see where he's going, and he still has reasonably good hearing. (Apparently he can hear a brownie fall on a plate from a hundred yards away.) His eyes are a watery blue, and his hair—what there is of it—is white, so that won't be particularly helpful. Judging from his pale to pinkish skin tone, I'd say his hair would have been a brownish color in his salad days. He's less than six feet tall, judging by my own height, but I've heard that people tend to lose an inch or two of height as they age. Still, he was never a lanky fellow, I'd say. Just average. He's slender now. Fat people don't tend to reach advanced old age, have you noticed? Let that be a lesson to us all. I am going to surmise that he was never obese. He seems to have the metabolism of a chipmunk, anyhow.

I hope this is helpful. The old fellow hasn't told me very much about his past, but I'm reasonably certain that his mental faculties are quite intact. He man-

----

aged not only to get me to take him to the grocery store, but also to make me pay for his groceries and carry them for him! If I have to lug many more ten-pound bags of sugar across a two-acre parking lot, I'll be the one needing a walker!

It is now so late that it's early. More news when I have some.

Your man in Havana, er—Danville (with apologies to Graham Greenc),

Geoffrey

The dinner hour was over, and since quiz shows were playing on the television in the common room, Rose had invited "the girls," as she called her hallmates, to come to her room for an impromptu party of bring-your-own soft drinks and crackers from the vending machines. Emma O., despite her earlier profession of loathing parties, was persuaded to come anyhow, as a therapeutic exercise in socializing. She sat on the floor with her back to one of the twin beds and watched the others laugh and talk as if they were a play and she was the audience. She had brought her legal pad and a stack of envelopes, so that she could work on her correspondence while she listened.

"Still writing letters of apology to society's victims?" Elizabeth asked her. "Who is it this time?"

"Tonya Harding," said Emma O., still scribbling.

"The ice skater? Because . . . ?"

"Well," said Emma O. "Tonya Harding may or may not have conspired with her husband to break that other ice skater's leg before the Olympic tryouts, but a year or so after that incident the other ice skater definitely did break up some other woman's marriage. In fact, after the divorce became final, she married the guy. So if it's a question of which of the two skaters inflicted the more lasting injury to someone, I'd say that the answer is: Not Tonya."

"Okay . . ."

"Also, I think Tonya was hooted out of skating because she wasn't the willowy well-bred ice princess that people expect to see in the sport. She was a scrappy working-class kid from a trailer, and skating was her one chance to make it out, but nobody cared. They threw her out of amateur skating permanently for something she was never convicted of doing."

"Yes, Emma, but athletes are role models. They are held to a higher standard."

"Oh, please!" said Emma O., waving her pen. "Mike Tyson went to prison for rape and got back in the boxing ring, where he promptly bit part of his opponent's ear off. Darryl Strawberry continued to play professional baseball after his drug convictions—and Tonya can't skate. Why?"

"Well, if you put it that way . . ."

"Damn right I do. Tonya Harding got a raw deal. On behalf of the planet, I'm begging her pardon. Anybody want to sign this one?"

Three hands went up.

"Being crazy is so damned liberating," said Emma O., passing the letter around the group. "I wish I'd cracked up sooner."

"I wish I could get all the way to delusional," Elizabeth said. "Then maybe I could forget Cameron." She thought for a moment. "Am I the only person who ever talks about why I came here?"

Seraphin, whose weight on the bedspread caused scarcely

a wrinkle, looked up. "Sometimes people talk about it," she said softly. "I don't mind telling you. I came because my parents insisted. I just hope my marriage can survive it."

"Oh, but surely your husband understands that you're ill. . . ."

Rose Hanelon, who had overheard the conversation, laughed. "That creep! He refuses to believe that there's anything wrong with her!"

Elizabeth looked at Sarah Findlay's hollow eyes and the childlike body with its pipe stem arms and legs. "But surely . . ."

Seraphin smiled. "Philip loves the way I look. Like a greyhound, he says."

"Can't he afford to buy food?"

Rose laughed again. "Interesting that you should say that, Elizabeth. Sarah's husband has more money than God. He comes from one of those old blue-blood families who haven't had to buy any silver in a hundred years. It's quite a Cinderella story—which should make you think twice about fairy tales."

"I wasn't poor," said Seraphin. "Just middle class. My father was a bank president and my mother's a nurse. We even belonged to the local country club—but I wasn't in Philip's league. We met in college, when it's hard to tell what class anybody is. He was majoring in philosophy, but that didn't tell me much. I thought he might become a minister."

"What did he become?" asked Elizabeth.

"Philip didn't exactly become anything," said Seraphin. With one bony finger, she traced a pattern on the untouched can of diet soda on her lap. "He just went on being himself. I mean, we moved to one of the family homes near Savannah, and Philip serves on the board of a few of the family's companies, but that still leaves him most of the week to play golf, and lunch at the club, and sometimes we go sailing. But mostly we go to parties. I didn't fit in terribly well. I kept making mistakes that I didn't even know were mistakes, like saying 'couch' instead of 'sofa,' or 'drapes' for 'curtains.' And all the women were so terribly thin. They used to make catty remarks, in their well-bred tones, about my 'healthy appetite,' and my 'buxom' figure. Then Philip started to make 'helpful' suggestions, like, 'Do you really need a whole baked potato, darling?' So one day I just decided that if I wanted the marriage to last, I'd better slim down. A lot."

"I wish you could teach me how to do that," Emma O. remarked.

"There's no trick to it that I know," said Seraphin. "As a teenager I was always rather thin, and of course we all dieted, because it was a social thing to do, whether one needed to or not. So I may have had a tendency to skip meals a bit too much. Anyhow, after the day I resolved to become as thin as I could get, I just wasn't hungry any more. And I felt very powerful, because my body was the one thing in my life that I could control. Everyone there thinks I look marvelous in clothes now. Philip is pleased."

"But your parents weren't?"

"No. I went home for a visit, and I had a silly fainting spell, and my mother, who's a nurse, put me in the hospital. The doctors insisted I come here, but Philip is furious. He says that a corn-fed hick may be my parents' idea of normal, but it isn't his."

Everyone was silent, because there didn't seem to be anything to say that wouldn't make things worse. Seraphin was going to die or she was going to lose her husband, or possibly both.

"Too bad therapy can't fix what's really wrong with the world," said Emma O. "But it can't, which is why it's so tempting to try to kill yourself."

"It was tempting," said Rose. "I know just what you mean. I got up one morning, and I was just sick of trying. Sick of being ugly. It's wearisome for a woman, being ugly. You always have to watch your man, because you know that no matter how good you are, or how successful you are—" She nodded toward Emma when she said "successful."

"Are you successful, Emma?" Elizabeth was surprised. Somehow she had imagined Emma O. living in her parents' basement and spending her days watching *Star Trek* videos.

Lisa Lynn, Emma's roommate, laughed. "Are you kidding? Emma O. is a whiz with computers. Companies were fighting to get her, and throwing stock options at her left and right. She made her first million at twenty-eight."

Emma O. shrugged. "Money didn't help. The software industry is practically a sheltered workshop for Asperger's people, but they're mostly guys, so it's all right. Allowances are made for them. Women are expected to be the grease between the wheels for all these loners—and I was just as bad as they were. Nobody wants to work with me."

"Maybe money would help for a while," said Rose. "I'd sure love to find out. But I think that in the long run, nothing would change. Like I said, no matter how good you are, or how successful—"

"What?"

"You know what. The relationship." She drawled the word with a mocking smile. "He'll leave you for anybody. Anybody. And every year the pool of anybodies gets a few thousand girls larger, and you get older and wrinklier."

Elizabeth realized that they had come round to the subject of loss. "So you lost a loved one, too?" she said.

"Of course, I did. Loved one may be putting it a bit too strongly, but he was pretty important to me. He was a photographer at the paper. He wasn't much, but I did think we got along pretty well together. He was forty-seven and unmarried, not particularly good-looking, practically no social skills, and he barely made minimum wage, and so I thought, 'Well, this is a nice, safe little relationship. Who else could possibly want him?' Ha! Some twenty-something blonde in Classifieds got her hooks into him, though God only knows what she saw in him. I guess that's when my drinking really got out of hand. Being ugly is like an automatic twenty points off in the quiz of life."

"You know, they shouldn't send women to crazy houses," said Emma O., waving a candy bar for emphasis. "They should send them to spas and plastic surgeons. Because there's almost nothing ever wrong with a woman that being thin and pretty wouldn't cure."

"You're not going to start that again are you?" Elizabeth sighed. "There are lots of people worse off than you are, Emma. Look at poor Mr. Randolph with his scarred face."

"Hillman Randolph is a man. I'll bet there are people who say that his scars give him character. Catch them saying that about a woman!"

"I think he's just as unhappy as the rest of us, though. Does anybody ever visit him?"

"Not that I've noticed," said Rose. "He doesn't hang out with anybody much. Why are you so interested all of a sudden?"

Elizabeth shrugged. "He seems lonely," she said. She patted the pocket of her sweater, where her cousin Geoffrey's fax lay carefully hidden. It seemed that to make any progress, she would have to befriend Hillman Randolph.

P.J. Purdue liked to drive. Under ordinary circumstances she was inclined to go well above the speed limit, but just now she was driving a stolen car, and even though they had taken the precaution of swapping license plates with an unsuspecting fellow hotel guest the night before, she knew that it would be dangerous to call attention to herself on the highway. She drove the speed limit and stayed in the right-hand lane as much as she could. Carla, who was already worried because they were not making a beeline for Canada, had made Purdue promise to stop using any credit cards, her own or stolen ones, because charged purchases left a paper trail, thus increasing their chances of being caught.

She glanced over at Carla, asleep in the passenger seat, with only her nose visible through a tangle of corn-colored hair. Carla wasn't really a daredevil. Her crimes had been committed out of poverty and desperation, not for the thrill of exacting revenge on an unjust system. Purdue's unholy glee at finding more victims for their rampage had left her confused and frightened. She kept saying, "But the point is to get away, isn't it?"

Purdue would always solemnly agree that the point was to

escape and to live happily ever after—ultimately—but she had business to take care of first, and now that the roads were beginning to look familiar again, she felt her pulse quickening with excitement.

They were on I-81 now, headed east, and a large blue-and-gold sign had just welcomed them to Virginia. Now she was six hours from her alma mater in Williamsburg, three from A. P. Hill's law practice in Danville, and somewhere in between lay the ancestral home of the Purdues, where her grandfather lived, but she had no plans to visit him unless she had nowhere else to go. She wondered if A. P. Hill had got in trouble when her name turned up in Banker Jenkins's complaint to the Arkansas police. She had probably been questioned, which meant that she would be annoyed, but A. P. Hill needed to be shaken out of that good-little-girl complacency that enveloped her like a cocoon.

She pulled into the VIRGINIA WELCOME CENTER AND REST AREA. "Bathroom break," she told Carla, turning off the engine. "Are you coming?"

"No," came a sleepy voice from within the tangle of hair. "You go ahead."

Purdue grabbed her purse and headed for an empty pay phone. The cops were probably monitoring her telephone calling card number, but perhaps they had overlooked that detail in tracing her. Besides, this was a public area far from their destination. It didn't seem like much of a risk. She pulled a piece of paper out of her billfold to refresh her memory, and then punched in 0, the 804 area code for southeast Virginia, and then the number. When the mechanical voice asked for her calling card number, she punched that in, too. Live dangerously, she thought.

After three rings, a brisk voice said, "MacPherson and Hill, attorneys-at-law. Edith speaking."

"Hello, Edith!" said Purdue in her best imitation of a social voice. With any luck she'd be mistaken for someone else. "Is Powell there? I really need to chat with her for a minute."

There was a moment's pause, during which Purdue could picture the secretary trying to place her voice. Finally she said, "A. P. Hill is out of the office this week. Would you like to leave a message?"

Purdue laughed and did her best imitation of a socialite. "Goodness, no! It isn't business. It's girl stuff. Can you give me her cell phone number? My address book went to the cleaners in my raincoat, and all the numbers got smudged."

The idea of the driven and humorless A. P. Hill having any girl stuff to talk about was entirely beyond Edith's powers of comprehension, but hers was not to reason why, she thought. The voice on the phone obviously wasn't a salesman, an old boyfriend, or a bill collector, so there didn't seem to be any reason not to give out the cell phone number. She recited it slowly so that the caller could write it down. "Now what did you say your name was?" asked Edith, in a belated attempt to document the call.

She heard a gurgle of laughter on the other end of the line. "Tell her it's about Milo. She'll know. Thanks, Edith!" said the young woman's voice. Then a click.

Purdue hung up the phone and glanced at her watch. She had been on the line less than a minute and a half—not that anybody would be trying to trace her from A. P. Hill's number, but still it was reassuring to know that they couldn't. Besides, in another couple of minutes they'd be miles away down I-81. She

---

headed into the mock-colonial building that served as the state's welcome center. She might as well pick up a free road map while she was here. Later on they might need to take a few detours if the cops did pick up their trail. She grinned at the thought of careening down Virginia back roads with sirens wailing behind them. It was an exciting thought, but it didn't fit into her plans, and she knew for a fact that Carla would be too scared to enjoy the experience. She'd better keep driving sixty-three miles per hour and not take any chances. Well, maybe a couple more chances. They were going to need more cash pretty soon. She'd have to talk Carla into doing one more job—one more, that is, before the one that counted.

The house had been dark and silent for hours now. Soundlessly, he swung open the door to the sunporch. He kept its hinges well oiled. Of course, the young fellow upstairs probably wouldn't have heard it, anyway. The young are sound sleepers. He, on the other hand, could switch from deep sleep to full consciousness in a heartbeat. The barest sound or change of light was enough to jerk him back into wakefulness. Sometimes he felt that he never really slept any more, and he wondered if this was his old body's protest against wasting any of the little time that was left to him. Why sleep now when someday soon death would put an end to waking? More likely, though, his light sleeping was a habit from the old days, when his life—or at least his freedom—had depended on his vigilance.

He stepped out into the soft darkness of the garden, wondering if he was hearing crickets or if his ears were manufacturing noises to fill the silence. He wished that he still had the night vision of his youth, when he could have read the fine print of a newspaper by moonlight. Now he'd be doing well to read one at high noon, reading glasses and all. Fortunately, though, he knew where he was going, and the flagstone path kept him from losing his way. No need to switch on the flashlight until he reached the outbuildings. There was a slim chance that someone could be glancing out an upstairs window, and he didn't want to take any chances on being spotted.

Not that they showed much interest in him, anyhow. He supposed they meant well, though; and if they had written him off as a harmless old man, he had never given them any reason to think otherwise. He wondered what they would say if he really talked about his past, instead of giving them garrulous tales about Model T Fords and Tom Mix movie matinees. He didn't intend to find out, though. Old age inflicted many indignities on its victims: dimmed vision, impaired hearing, loss of mobility. But to his mind, the worst indignity of all was the lack of privacy and freedom.

His carpet slippers swished against the flagstones, but he barely heard them. He had reached the little cluster of outbuildings now, one hundred yards behind the house. Now he could rest for a moment and catch his breath before he went inside. The new owners had not inspected the outbuildings. Neither had Bill and his crew when they took over. They had been so busy trying to fix up the downstairs that they'd barely noticed there was even a lawn around the house, much less sheds and a garage, so for now he had the place to himself. He patted the flashlight in the pocket of his flannel dressing gown. He would need it in the windowless darkness of the shed.

It had taken him several minutes to work his way across the flagstones to the door of the shed. His bones were brittle with age, and he could not risk falling in the dark. Another stay in a nursing home would probably finish him off. He hated confinement—always had. Even worse was the prospect of one of the children being summoned. They didn't want him—nor he them. They were far from Danville, deep into their own busy lives, and they had lost the thread of kinship with him many years before. All right, he had pushed them away. But he didn't regret it. He was an embarrassment to them now, and he'd be damned if he'd live under house arrest on the charity of one snooty daughter-in-law or the other. Might as well be dead as that.

He pushed open the door to the shed and switched on the flashlight. It looked like a perfectly ordinary storage building, which mostly it was. There were bags of fertilizer stacked against the back wall, with various rakes and other gardening tools hanging from pegs above them, all festooned with cobwebs. The air smelled of loam and must, with a faint whiff of gasoline from the ancient lawn mower. There was nothing clean or new or valuable here. Nothing to make anyone want to linger. And no electric lights to help anyone to investigate the premises.

He turned his attention to the plain wooden wall to the right of the door. It was splintery and unpainted. There was nothing about it to attract anyone's attention. Unless you knew where to push. Just at shoulder level, about five feet from the back wall. His flashlight wobbled a bit as he tried to find the spot with the beam of light. It was a good join—to his old eyes there was no seam to give away the secret. But he had made this wall himself a long time ago, and he knew where to push.

Tucking the flashlight under his arm, he put both hands flat against the wall and gave it a gentle shove. He was careful not to push too hard, lest he fall forward and down when the door swung inward. With barely a squeak of protest the door moved, and he let the light play on the flight of crude wooden steps that led to the earth-banked room below. After a moment's rest to catch his breath again, he shuffled forward and gripped the rough wooden railing to the stairs. He was glad he'd put a railing on the stairs all those years ago. Of course, in those days he could run up and down the steps two at a time, but he'd installed the handrail as a precaution, in case anybody lost his balance carrying heavy objects up or down the stairs. There had certainly been a lot of lifting and carrying heavy objects in those days. Now it was all he could do to get himself and a plastic grocery bag down those ten steps.

Why was he doing this again? he asked himself as he rested on the fifth step. Because the fellas were counting on him, and some of them acted like they didn't believe he could do it any more. Besides, he had to go on being himself. He'd have died years ago, if he hadn't.

Chapter 11

At breakfast the next morning, Elizabeth broke ranks with the sex-segregated seating arrangement and set her tray down at a nearly empty table, across from Hillman Randolph's cup of black coffee.

The old man sat by himself at one end of the six-person table. At the other end, Clifford Allen and Charles Petress were passing sections of newspaper back and forth as they shoveled in their respective breakfasts. Neither of them looked up to acknowledge her presence. Elizabeth noticed that Clifford, in deference to his sports car body, had limited his morning meal to slices of grapefruit and half a piece of dry toast. As he ate, he eyed each forkful as if he were looking for traces of poison, or worse, butter and sugar. Elizabeth looked down at her own helping of eggs and bacon with a twinge of guilt. She sat down opposite Hillman Randolph, who did not seem pleased to have company.

"Good morning," she said, with the best smile she could muster before nine A.M. "I thought I'd get out of the rut and talk to someone different at mealtimes for a change. How are you?"

He favored her with his usual scowl. "I don't sleep well," he said. "Before my second cup of coffee, I'm not fit company."

Elizabeth nodded. "Well, at least you won't talk about how men have ruined your life and made you go insane," she said. "That's the usual topic of conversation at the ladies' table."

The old man grunted. "Insane is not a word they like people to use around here. Though, of course, I do, whenever I feel like it. However, as to the ladies' topic of conversation, I thought you'd been singing along on that tune yourself."

Elizabeth took a deep breath. She had resolved not to think about her own problems for a while, and now to have them tossed back at her as breakfast banter stopped her cold for an instant, but she had taken her pill when she first woke up, so her feelings were packed in cotton wool for the day. "I suppose I have," she said calmly. She would not give him the satisfaction of seeing her cry. Perhaps the only way to handle a ruthless old investigator would be to give back as good as you got. She was glad she had found something else to think about.

She took a sip of bitter coffee while she considered her opening gambit. After a while she said, "Let's talk about your past, not mine. You mentioned the other day that Jack Dolan died in a car wreck. Is that where you got your injuries?"

He touched the side of his face with his good hand. "That

----

was a long time ago," he said. "Nothing to be gained by rehashing about it."

"Well, it's just that I happen to be interested in Jack Dolan," Elizabeth said, changing her tack.

"Why?"

"I told you. Because my brother bought his house. You saw the photograph the other day in art class, remember?"

"That was Jack Dolan's house, all right, but since he's been dead for forty years, none of it matters now. Certainly not to you. Besides, I never talk about my accident."

"But isn't that why we're all here?" asked Elizabeth. "To learn to confront the things we avoid talking about?"

"I don't know," said Hillman Randolph. "I came here to keep from eating my gun. If they give me enough happy pills to keep me going, I don't have to work through squat. As for you, I haven't noticed you being too eager in group to talk about your problems."

"I don't have any problems," said Elizabeth. "My husband is missing. I'm only here to deal with the stress of that."

Randolph took a bite of his toast and looked at her reflectively. "So your husband is missing. Do you want to talk about that?"

Elizabeth blinked. "Not particularly. No. I don't see the point of it."

"Really?" He grinned at her over his coffee cup. "I thought you were eager to discuss dead men."

He's baiting you, Elizabeth told herself. He's good at it because he was in law enforcement. He interrogated people for a living. Do not take it personally. Do not lose your temper. After a few more deep breaths, she said carefully, "I wanted to talk about Jack Dolan, who may or may not be dead. You said you knew him."

"All right, missy. I'll make a deal with you. Get me some more coffee. Then for as long as it takes me to drink it, I'll talk about Jack and about how I came to look this way, and you talk about this missing husband you claim to have."

Elizabeth's eyebrows rose. "Claim to have?"

"You could be delusional." He grinned at her. "Could have just made him up. You know, we used to have Mel Gibson's ex-wife in here."

"But I don't think Mel Gibson has an ex-wi—Oh. I see what you mean." She sighed. The clock said 8:45. In less than half an hour the day schedule would begin, routing them to therapy sessions, doctors visits, and other commitments of time. This might be her best chance to talk to him. Later, he might change his mind. She thought of Matt Pennington and his ECT sessions. If Mr. Randolph happened to be scheduled for ECT, he might not even remember later. "All right," she said. "You're on. I'll talk to you about my husband. I'll even show you a picture of him, if that will convince you he's real. . . . No, I suppose it wouldn't. I'm sure 'Mrs. Gibson' had lots of photos of Mel."

Mr. Randolph nodded. "Sally Ann? She sure did. Thanks to *People* magazine. It's a deal, then. We'll talk. You go first."

"Is this an investigator's trick?" Elizabeth glared across the table at the old man, unconvinced by his look of studied innocence. "Somehow, sir, I don't trust you. I think we should do this in turns, so that nobody welshes on the agreement."

"I could give you my word," said Hillman Randolph with a trace of a smile.

"Mr. Randolph, we're both certifiably crazy. Our word is useless these days. Now put up or shut up."

"All right." His eyes twinkled. He actually seemed pleased at her shrewdness. He pointed to his empty cup. "Coffee?"

With a sigh of resignation, Elizabeth went to the beverage table and refilled both mugs of coffee. She set them down with a thump on the table between them, and sat with folded arms and a look of exasperation, waiting to see if the old man would keep his word.

He tasted his coffee. "Question for question then," he said. "I'll ask first. Tell me about your husband."

"His name is . . ." She had vowed to keep saying is. Her use of the present tense was an expression of hope, or perhaps of defiance. She would not give up. ". . . Cameron Dawson. He's tall and thin with brown eyes and light brown hair. He has an offbeat sense of humor, and he played football—actually, it's soccer to us—at university."

Elizabeth paused to see if her answer was sufficient, but Hillman Randolph nodded for her to go on. She found that she wanted to. For weeks now people had looked embarrassed when she tried to talk about Cameron. They would always change the subject or stop her reminiscences with platitudes. She found herself glad that someone actually wanted to hear her talk about her missing husband.

"Cameron is a marine biologist from Scotland," she said. "He was raised in Edinburgh, and he has a younger brother named Ian. We've been married nearly two years. We had a lovely Scottish-themed wedding at my aunt's house in Georgia, and on our honeymoon we attended the Queen's garden party at the Palace of Holyroodhouse." She looked around. Richard

Petress and Clifford Allen had vanished, leaving behind on the table a crumpled pile of newspaper pages. Most of the other people in the cafeteria were going back for last cups of coffee now. Their trays were pushed aside, ready to be returned to the kitchen. "My turn, Mr. Randolph," Elizabeth said, before he could take another sip of coffee. "When did you know Jack Dolan?"

He shrugged. "A lifetime ago. Early nineteen fifties, near Danville, Virginia. He'd made a small fortune in the Forties. That's when he built that big house of his. Since he was a farm boy who had no heritage to speak of and even less education, a lot of us wondered how he had managed to become so prosperous. Certain sections of the government thought he might bear watching."

Elizabeth gasped. "Jack Dolan was a gangster?"

"Is that your next question? It isn't your turn."

"I'm sorry. I merely want you to clarify your answer about how you came to know him."

"I was one of those government agents assigned to keep an eye on him. I think it's my turn for a question now."

"Go ahead."

"All right. So, how did you meet this biologist fellow?"

Elizabeth took a sip of cold coffee. "Cameron came to Virginia on a visiting professorship. He was doing seal research. On his first weekend here his hosts decided to take him to the Highland Games. It was very silly of them, really, because the Highland Games is to Scotland what the rodeo is to most of America these days—that is, a historical footnote. But they meant well. Anyhow, to be polite, he went to the games, and I was there with the Chattan Confederation, which is the clan

203

- -

the MacPhersons belong to. I had charge of the bobcat for the weekend. 'Touch not the cat' is our motto." She smiled, thinking of happy memories for the first time in many weeks. "Cameron was Clan Chattan, too, but he didn't know it. He was hopeless on Scottish folkways. His idea of Scottish music is Sheena Easton, not bagpipes."

"You're off the subject," said Hillman Randolph, glancing up at the clock.

Her smiled faded. For a little while there she had managed to forget. "Cameron. Yes. Well, I suppose you could say I liked the look of him, so I appointed myself his guide for the weekend event. That was in my Scottish culture phase," she added. "And I thought I might learn something from a real Scot. Ha! I knew more Gaelic than he did. Anyhow, we hit it off rather well, despite the fact that my cousin Geoffrey nearly got us thrown out of the festival park for sabotaging the herding ducks. I know! I'm digressing again. Now it's my turn to ask a question."

"Shoot."

"So forty-odd years ago you were a cop watching Jack Dolan. What was he up to?"

The old man sighed. "I was not a cop. At least not a local one. I was federal. But, yes, my job was to keep him under long-term surveillance. What was Dolan up to? Nothing that anybody ever proved. They had planted informants around him, and he was being pretty closely watched for those last few weeks. I don't know if he realized that or not. It was all supposed to come down on the night of the accident, and that was the end of it. They started out wanting him for tax evasion, but they would have settled for murder."

"Murder? Who did he— Sorry. Your turn again. Ask away."

"You said that this husband of yours is missing. Now what is that supposed to mean? Did he run off and leave you a note, or what?"

"No. He didn't run off. I stood on the dock and waved goodbye when he sailed away." Elizabeth concentrated on viewing the scene as if it were a film and not part of her life. She thought that if she could recite the facts, and keep her distance from the emotions involved, she might just be able to get through this conversation. She looked away, paying careful attention to the procession of patients who were depositing their silverware and garbage in the proper receptacles, and handing in their trays at the stainless-steel counter that divided the kitchen from the dining room.

She heard one of the heavyset women ask Seraphin, "How much weight do I have to lose before I can stop smiling all the time?"

Elizabeth strained to hear Seraphin's reply, but her words were lost in the clatter of silverware hitting metal trays and the clunk of crockery on the counter. Hillman Randolph, sipping his coffee, was watching her with interest. "Where was I?" she said. "Oh. The question. You wanted me to explain about Cameron being missing. He went off by himself on that stupid little boat of his, to do a bit of observation out in the open sea. I can't remember what. Measure the water temperature, check the currents, watch for seals? It doesn't matter, I suppose."

"He went out in a rowboat?" Seeing Elizabeth's mutinous look, Hillman Randolph added quickly, "I'm not throwing in more questions. In your words, I am clarifying an answer."

"Oh, all right," she muttered. "It doesn't matter anyhow. If I have to talk about it, you might as well understand what I'm trying to tell you. A rowboat? No, of course not. It was a . . . well, in Georgia we'd call it a cabin cruiser, though that's not quite it. It looked big enough at the dock on a bright summer day with a calm sea, but given the size of the ocean, and the unpredictable harshness of the Scottish weather, it was not big enough."

"Scottish weather?"

"Yes. I'm sure I mentioned that. We were living in Edinburgh, and that's where he sailed from. Well, not sailed. The boat had an engine. I think one says sailed anyhow, though. So he went off by himself that morning, and by midmorning it was turning out to be a gray day, but nothing unusual. A couple of hours later, though, a storm hit with a vengeance. And I waited, but I hadn't really begun to worry yet. Do you know what expression they use over there when they mean to be worried? They say to get the wind up. The wind was up, all right, and I should have been worried. Well, he didn't come back, and I thought he was going to be late, of course, but I supposed he had put in at the nearest port, somewhere up the coast, perhaps. I was sure that soon he'd be calling me to come and fetch him in the car." Her voiced trailed away, becalmed on despair. "But . . . the call never came . . . and the boat wasn't found. And since that day he's just . . . gone."

"In the North Atlantic," said Hillman Randolph in a flat voice. "Off the coast of Scotland."

"Yes. They searched, of course. But with the wind and the currents, there's no telling where he could have ended up. I've thought of chartering a boat and conducting the search myself, but everyone says . . . Anyhow, there are so many places to look. There are islands. There's Norway . . ." She heard the rising note of panic in her voice, and for distraction she glanced up at the clock. Ten past nine. Old Mrs. Nicholson was tottering out of the cafeteria, and she was always the last to leave. Focus, Elizabeth thought. "All right, Mr. Randolph. I believe I've answered your question, and time is short. Now I want to know what happened on the night Jack Dolan died and you were so badly injured."

"You will have to trust me to tell you later," said Hillman Randolph, setting her empty coffee cup on his tray as he stood up. "I have music therapy this morning. But I don't go back on my word. When there's time today to tell you, I will. Meanwhile, I have one last question for you. It may sound irrelevant. I hope you'll indulge an old man."

Elizabeth scowled at him. "Well? What is it?"

He was watching her carefully. "Did you see the movie *Titanic*?"

Her jaw dropped. The question was miles away from anything she had expected. "*Titanic*? Yes, of course. But what on earth does that have to do with anything?"

When he did not answer, Elizabeth searched her memory for some connection between the film and the topics covered in their previous conversation. Shipwreck, she thought. Missing loved one. Of course. "*Titanic*—I see. You are referring to the heroine's dreadful fiancé thinking she is dead when he cannot locate her after the ship goes down. He thinks she's dead, but really she has changed her name and started a new life to escape from him." Elizabeth gave the old man a pitying smile. "No, Mr. Randolph. It's a romantic theory, but I don't think my husband was anxious to get away from me, and even if he were, he would never change his identity because that would force him

----

to abandon his life's work. He loved marine biology, and his name was becoming very well known in scholarly circles. He had too much to lose to disappear and try to start over. And if he did try to turn up in, say, Hawaii or Sweden, he would be recognized sooner or later. A scientific discipline is like a small town—everybody either knows you or knows of you. You can't stay in the field and pretend to be someone else. So your theory is just not on, Mr. Randolph, but I'm sure it would make an exciting premise for a movie. You ought to write it as a screenplay. As for my question about Jack Dolan, we're out of time. I'll see you later, so don't you try to disappear."

Elizabeth swept away without a backward glance, and Hillman Randolph watched her go with an uncharacteristic expression of sadness on his ravaged face. As he shambled off to turn his tray in, he reflected on the fact that he was relieved that he had not had to explain his question to her. Her interpretation of it was not what he had meant at all.

A. P. Hill had turned the living area of her hotel suite into a war room. On the wall a map of the United States, scored with felt-tip marker lines, traced the route of the PMS Outlaws from their initial escape up to the last reported sighting in west Tennessee. On the desk were stacks of newspaper clippings, mostly from the less-reputable tabloids, who were enamored of the story. A grainy photocopied enlargement of a recent shot of Purdue was taped over the insipid framed print on the wall above the desk.

"Why don't you go home?" Lewis Paine sat on the sofa, hunched over a soda machine can of iced tea and staring into it as if he were planning to read her fortune in its nonexistent tea leaves.

"I can't," said A. P. Hill as she paced.

Paine squinted at the rate chart posted on the back of the door. "This place has to be costing you over a hundred a day."

She shrugged. "Yeah, well, they gave me a weekly rate."

He shook his head. "Great. And you are accomplishing—what? Do you think fugitives make special trips to the Embassy Suites to turn themselves in? Do you think you can find her sitting around here when a computer-linked network of law enforcement units has failed? I told you: I'm monitoring everything we get on the case. I'll fax you if I hear anything. Go home and practice law. Stop sitting around here."

"I'm not sitting around here, Lewis. Every day I go out and talk to people, or check the archives in Williamsburg, or make calls to mutual acquaintances to see if I can uncover anything that will help us find her. I know I can't do the phone traces, or the credit card checks, or any of the other high-tech stuff you people do to find fugitives, but sometimes talking to the suspect's circle of friends gives you some insight into what stops the fugitive might make, who might help them along the way, and ultimately where they might be headed."

Paine shook his head, wondering what had happened to A. P. Hill's usually flawless logic. "And you couldn't do all that from Danville?"

"No!" She sank down beside him on the sofa and put her head in her hands. "Most of Purdue's acquaintances are within an hour of Richmond. Danville is too far away, and I think I'll learn more in face-to-face interviews than I would over the phone. Besides, I don't want Purdue to go to Danville looking for me."

"Why? The only weapon the ladies have used so far is a stun gun, which packed a temporary wallop, but the guy didn't even have to go to the hospital afterward. The worst injury has been from too-tight handcuffs. Purdue and Larkin have made no threats that I have any reports on. And going after a young woman attorney does not fit their current M.O. So I ask you again—what's the deal here, Powell?"

Paine studied A. P. Hill as if she were a reluctant witness. She looked tired. There was none of the buoyant enthusiasm of people who like to play cop and to second-guess the real detectives on a case. In his experience only friends of the suspect and relatives of the victim displayed this weary tenacity in an investigation, a dogged intensity that you could almost describe as obsession without interest. What Paine could not see in Powell Hill was where the interest lay. Surely she was overreacting to the troubles of an old school friend.

"Look," he said, "You're a trial lawyer. You consort with criminals for a living. And while I'll deny this if you ever put me on the stand, this Outlaws case is not that big a deal with us. It's not even in Virginia's jurisdiction. Purdue and Larkin haven't killed anybody. In the department it's a running joke. So, I have to ask myself why it's bothering the hell out of you."

She shrugged, turning away from him so that he could read nothing in her expression.

Lewis Paine tried again. "Look, Powell, I know that people aren't exactly eager to confide in somebody who carries a badge in his jacket, but—"

The telephone rang, and A. P. Hill lunged for it. "Yes? . . . Oh, hello, Edith. Fine. I'm fine. How's the house going? . . . Good. Bill's okay?" There was a long pause here while A. P. Hill held the phone in silence, her face settling into a worried frown as she listened. At last she said, "Okay, when? Just now. Okay, did you happen to look at the Caller I.D. box? Oh. Out of area. I see. And she said what? . . . Are you sure? . . . No, Edith, it's all right. It's okay that you gave her my cell phone number. No, it isn't anything important. Yeah. Yeah. I'm fine. Of course I'm eating!" She cast a guilty look at the cellophane wrappings of peanut-butter crackers on the end of the coffee table. At least she remembered to take vitamin supplements. Well, most of the time. "Soon, Edith. I'll be back soon. Tell Bill not to worry. Tell him . . . tell him hello."

She hung up and sank back down on the sofa next to Paine.

"That was your office, right?"

Her fingers ruffled her hair. She nodded. "Yes. That was Edith. Someone just called the office asking for me. Edith thinks it was Purdue."

"But the Caller I.D. showed no traceable number. Probably a pay phone somewhere," said Paine. "Patricia Purdue isn't stupid. Crazy, maybe, but not stupid. Did she leave a message?"

A. P. Hill hesitated. "No."

"Look, Powell, why you? Maybe you were pals in college and law school, but you certainly haven't kept up with each other in the years since you graduated. Now all of a sudden, Patricia Purdue is a wanted fugitive, and after all this time, she's started making phone calls to you. Why?"

A. P. Hill's hands covered her face, muffling her voice. "I think she wants me to join them. Because originally it was my idea."

The main public library in Danville, Virginia, is a large, multistoried modern building on a hill in the downtown area. Geoffrey took its imposing size as a sign that it might contain enough information to help him with his investigation of Jack Dolan. He resolved not to be tempted by the shelves devoted to art and interior design.

He had spent most of the day in decorator mode, making phone calls to various friends in Atlanta who were purveyors of upholstery fabric, lighting fixtures, and other items necessary for the refurbishment of an old house. He had faxed them sketches and solicited second and third opinions about wallpaper and crown molding. He was enjoying himself hugely.

Now that the really important tasks had been taken care of, he felt that he could in good conscience spare an hour or so in pursuit of Elizabeth's wild goose. So far today, Mr. Dolan had not made an appearance, but Geoffrey planned to be back by four-thirty, bearing gifts from the bakery, in hopes of learning more from the old man himself. First, though, he would pay a visit to the library so that he could collect some background material. Then, when he did get a chance to talk to Jack Dolan, he might know what sorts of things to ask about.

Where does one look for a man who is reputed to be dead? The obituary pages?

"Excuse me," Geoffrey said to the young woman at the information desk. "I wonder if you could help me? I'm looking for back issues of local newspapers."

"Well, it depends on how far back you need to go," the librarian told him. "We have actual copies of the newspapers for the last couple of weeks, or so, but since they deteriorate very badly with age, older issues are stored on microfilm, and that would be in the special collections section."

Armed with directions, Geoffrey went to the special collections room, where he repeated his request to yet another earnest librarian, this time a personable but harassed-looking young man whose name tag said Rob. "Old newspapers?" he said. "What year?"

"Nineteen fifties, I think."

"Ah, 'return with us now to those thrilling days of yesteryear ' " Rob the librarian waited for Geoffrey to recognize the Lone Ranger quote, and when no reaction from him was forthcoming, he sighed at yet another instance of inappreciation. His wit and charm were quite wasted in Special Collections—pearls before swine, really. Wearily he motioned Geoffrey toward a large gray filing cabinet. He slid out the top drawer to reveal half a dozen rows of small white cardboard boxes, each labeled with the name of a newspaper and the dates of the issues contained on that particular roll of microfilm. "The whole cabinet is filled with rolls of microfilm. We have documents going back more than a hundred years. Census records all the way back to the very first one, which was in 1800. What'll it be?"

Geoffrey considered his next move. He was pretty sure what he wasn't going to say, which was something along the lines of: "My cousin, who is a charming girl, but currently in a mental institution, seems to think that the ninety-some-year-old man in her brother's new house is an imposter. How would you suggest I go about verifying that?" No, that definitely would not do. Geoffrey's motto, insofar as he had one, was Emily Dickinson's maxim: "Tell the truth, but tell it slant." He decided to try another variant of the facts.

"Actually," he said, "I'm really not sure what year I need, or even what source. My cousin Bill has bought a grand old house on the outskirts of town, and I'm helping him restore it, so we thought it might be helpful to do a bit of research about who built the house, and so on."

"House research." The librarian looked thoughtful. "Shouldn't you go to the courthouse for that? The Registrar of Deeds has records about property and ownership, and tax bills. Probate records. Wouldn't that be faster than reading old newspapers?"

Yes, thought Geoffrey, but the courthouse won't have any of the gossip, and the newspapers might. "It's a wonderful suggestion," he admitted with an apologetic smile. "Silly of me not to have thought of it. But, you know, as long as I'm here, perhaps I'll just take a look at a few of these films. The early nineteen fifties, I think. You never know what may turn up."

"All right," said the librarian. "You're welcome to look. I do think research is fascinating. You never know what you'll find. Don't be surprised if you find yourself led astray by topics that have nothing to do with your original search."

Geoffrey touched his well-chosen silk tie. "I should be astonished to learn that Yves St. Laurent had visited Danville."

The young man laughed. "So would I! Well, let's get you started. Do you know how to use the microfilm reader?"

"No, of course not," said Geoffrey. "I am determined to be the major nuisance of your afternoon."

"You'd have to take a number," said Rob. "At least you

look like you can be taught to use the machine. That will make a nice change from the blue-haired old dears who are trying to trace their ancestors back to King Arthur—or, as one of them spells it, King Author." He smirked. "I told her to check the census records for Maine. Come on then. I'll show you how it works, but do pay attention so that you can do it yourself, because I'm on my own today, and I have hours of paperwork left to do before we close."

After a few minutes of brisk instruction, in which Geoffrey endeavored to give the machine his complete attention, the reel for 1950 was loaded, and he was ready to begin. Sitting in front of the microfilm reader and peering at the dark screen, he attempted to read the fine print of a newspaper page greatly reduced in size. This would take some getting used to, but at least he wasn't going to get his hands dirty with old newsprint. He scanned the headlines of the first newspaper, found nothing of interest, and turned the knob to view the next page. Read, scroll, read, scroll. The exercise was tedious and time-consuming, but not difficult.

Occasionally, as the librarian had predicted, he would become sidetracked by an interesting bit of half-a-century-old news. When Geoffrey read the article about Britain's young toddler Prince Charles and his new baby sister, Anne, he had the smug feeling of superiority over the original readers of the 1950 story: after all, he knew how it would all turn out. He did not allow his attention to wander too much, however, because his time was limited, and he was by no means sure that he was in the correct year to begin with. It might be necessary to scroll through many more reels of microfilm before he found anything useful.

An hour later, Geoffrey had skimmed through two years' worth of news, and all he had to show for his efforts was a certain proficiency in loading microfilm machines. This new skill had proved useful when a well-dressed elderly woman came in and, perhaps mistaking him for a library employee, asked him to help her load a reel of census records into one of the other machines. She knew how to thread the microfilm, she explained with an apologetic smile, but her arthritis prevented her from doing so. Geoffrey managed to set up the film for her on the second try, but aside from doing good deeds and gaining technological competence, he had not made any progress in his own investigation—or rather, in his cousin Elizabeth's investigation, blast her.

"This could take forever," he said aloud, after a particularly dull succession of newspapers. He could feel the beginnings of a headache coming on, probably the result of having years of Danville trivia seeping into his brain.

When he spoke, the silver-haired woman looked up from the next machine with a smile of commiseration. "It is tedious at times, isn't it?" she said. "It makes my eyes water. You ought to get up and stretch every now and then, too. Otherwise your back will be quite stiff by tomorrow morning."

Geoffrey yawned and stretched. "I could put up with the physical discomfort if I thought I was getting anywhere," he said. "It's the futility that makes it all so maddening."

"Perhaps I could help?" she said. "I need to rest my hands for a bit, anyhow. Not to mention my brain. What family names are you looking for?"

"Oh, I'm—"Geoffrey had intended to say "not doing genealogical research," but just as his mouth began to form the words, it occurred to him that barking up one's own family tree would be the perfect excuse to root around in the past history of any of Danville's citizens. While Geoffrey considered his fellow researcher's offer of help, he studied her with the practiced eye of a socialite. The silver-haired woman had carefully styled hair and a strand of baroque pearls that seemed quite genuine. In Geoffrey Chandler's sphere of life, her name was legion. If anybody knew the history of this part of Virginia, surely it was she.

Thankful that he had not denied an interest in genealogy, Geoffrey took a deep breath and began again. "It's very kind of you. I'm so new at this that I'm completely hopeless, but I did promise Mother, you know. . . . Well, I'm trying to find information about the Dolans."

The woman's encouraging smile turned to a look of bewilderment. "Dolan." She stared upward at nothing, the way people do when they are searching their memories for some elusive bit of information. "Dolan . . ." she said again. "Now, that is odd. I thought from the look of you that you would certainly have family connections here. . . ."

Geoffrey nodded complacently. She had spotted the look by which the gentry know one another, much as he had recognized her. She noted that he was tall and thin, with an aquiline nose, long narrow feet, and aristocratically high cheekbones. He was expensively dressed and shod, but without any ostentation in his appearance. Geoffrey Chandler knew that he would look like a somebody in any Anglo-Norman outpost of civilization, and therefore he would be treated with respect and accorded the presumption of wealth and position. How very reassuring, he thought smugly.

"There must be two dozen family names I was waiting to hear you say, but do you know, you have me quite buffaloed!" She shook her head, still puzzled. "Dolan."

"Oh, well," said Geoffrey, turning back to his microfilm reader. "It was very kind of you to offer, anyhow."

"I wish I could help," she said. "But really, there's no family of that name in the county." She laughed. "Except the notorious Jack Dolan, of course. But you'd hardly be related to him."

Old Miss Nicholson, who was nearer ninety than eighty, sat in a soft, high-backed chair in front of the bay window, staring out happily at the well-tended flower gardens of Cherry Hill. The leaf colors and the flower variations seemed to change every day of the growing season, and the weather was always interesting. So changeable, such a range of temperature and patterns of sun and cloud. Sometimes she thought it was as if the fifty-two weeks of the year were a deck of cards that someone had thoroughly shuffled, so that instead of getting all the weeks of one season in order, you got them randomly: spring, spring, summer, fall, winter, fall, fall, spring. She didn't mind the variables of temperature; the novelty, she thought, was worth it.

She seldom spoke to anyone, but she gave no trouble. She just sat there with a vague, secretive smile, which made people wonder what this ancient being with no close relatives could possibly have to be pleased about. It was this: Miss Nicholson quite liked her new home. She had been planning for it all her life.

When Caroline Nicholson was a little girl, she'd always dreamed of the day that she would grow up to marry some capitalist version of the handsome prince, and go off to live in a beautiful white-columned mansion on a hill. The prince never came, but Miss Nicholson never stopped planning for the day when she would be the lady of the manor. She began a hope chest as a teenager, putting in linens and tablecloths that she meticulously embroidered in the evenings as she sat alone in front of her small black-and-white television. Later on, her parents' legacies and then her job at the local library had enabled her to purchase more accoutrements for her someday home. She would drive to estate sales in the better part of town and to auctions in the surrounding counties, using what money she could spare to buy beautiful things for the house: a set of Limoges game plates, a sterling silver tea set, enough crystal stemware to serve a hundred guests at the lawn party she never had.

The years seemed to slide by in a haze of tag sales and silver polishing, as she sketched room plans for her perfect house, while scarcely bothering to dust the one she currently occupied. It didn't matter. It was only a way station to her true home—the one she would have someday, the one that all her silver and linen belonged in. She grew quite knowledgeable about antiques—one year she caught herself putting the Batemans, the Burrows, and the Chawners on her Christmas card list, before she remembered that those renowned silversmiths of Georgian London had been dead for well over a century. Although her knowledge of fine things increased with endless study, she seemed oblivious to the passing of time.

Her retirement from the library came, but a few weeks later Social Security checks began to arrive in her mailbox, so that was all right. Now she had more free time to go to the auctions, and to wait for her real life to begin. She was blessed with good health for many years, and indeed, her body was still remarkably fit when her mind began to show the signs of age. The house became more of an untidy wilderness, and Miss Nicholson, absorbed in her decorator magazines, could no longer be bothered to shop for groceries.

At last the neighbors notified a nephew, an elderly man himself, who scarcely remembered Aunt Caroline from his boyhood visits. Still, he was the one living relative she had in the world, and it was clearly his duty to see that she was cared for. So one day, having finished all the legal formalities with the lawyers and county officials, the nephew came for Miss Nicholson in his large, gray car. She thought him a very nice looking man, although a trifle old, but he was obviously well-to-do, and she went with him happily.

After a longish but pleasant drive through the country, they came to a large tree-shaded drive that curved for nearly a quarter mile before it ended in a circle in front of a large, white-columned mansion. Caroline Nicholson was enchanted. It was perfect.

Her escort seemed a bit nervous as he stopped the car, as if he wondered whether the place would meet with her approval, but she nodded and smiled, eager to inspect her new home and to meet the servants.

That had been many months ago, and Miss Nicholson couldn't remember seeing the man lately, but she supposed he was busy in the city, earning the money to keep up such a splendid estate. She settled in happily, planning for new curtains and a rearrangement of furniture, but really, she seemed so tired nowadays that she had never managed to make the effort. Still, it was a lovely place. The home she had always dreamed of. She gathered that the place was called Cherry Hill, such a nice, elegant name for a country place. She was quite content.

For his part, the nephew was relieved that matters had been settled with a minimum of fuss, and that the old lady seemed genuinely pleased with her new place of residence. Money was no problem, either. When he auctioned off all his aunt's possessions, the money raised amounted to more than enough to pay for her care.

Chapter 12

"You seem a little anxious today," said kindly old Dr. Dunkenburger, observing his fidgeting patient.

Of course I am, thought Elizabeth. You're interrupting my investigation. Just when she had managed to muffle the pain of Cameron's disappearance behind a regimen of possibly meaningless—but nonetheless interesting—activity, Dr. Dunkenburger hauled her in for another excruciating analysis of the nature of grief.

"Are you sleeping well?" he asked, making a little note on his legal pad.

She barely glanced at him. "How could I not be? The pills I'm given would stop an elephant in its tracks."

Dr. Dunkenburger looked at her thoughtfully. "Do you feel ready to do without them? You will have to reach that point sooner or later, you know."

Elizabeth hesitated, and then shook her head. She had almost forgotten the intensity of emotion that she had felt without them, but she was quite clear on the fact that she never wanted to feel it again. "Let's keep things as they are for a while longer," she said.

He scribbled another note. "I think we'll try you on a different medication. See if that helps. And how are you feeling otherwise? Settled in all right?"

"Never a dull moment," said Elizabeth. "Emma O. may be lengthening everyone else's stay, though. Last night in the common room she reduced half of us to tears by asking if we had any friends who were substantially thinner, prettier, or richer than we considered ourselves to be. Of course everyone's answer was no, and Emma grinned and said, 'See? The cliques go on. Junior high school is forever.' "

Dr. Dunkenburger nodded. "I'll ask Dr. Skokie to have a word with her. Everything all right otherwise?"

Elizabeth shrugged. "It's interesting. Sometimes I feel like I'm attending an evening of experimental theatre."

"These people's problems are very real, I assure you," he said gently. "And so are yours. Trouble won't go away because you ignore it. It might manifest itself as depression, or a sleep disorder, or irritability, or a series of aches and pains, but either you deal with it on its own terms, or it will sabotage you from now on in a dozen little ways."

"My problem isn't me," said Elizabeth. "If Cameron gets found, I'll be well in a heartbeat."

"That sort of thinking postpones healing, doesn't it?"

"How do you heal if your problems are real? How does Mr. Randolph come to terms with being disfigured? That isn't all in his mind."

Dr. Dunkenburger gave her that uneasy look that meant she had strayed into unsound topics. "Well," he said. "Staying angry won't solve anything, will it?"

Just after lunch an orderly had delivered to Elizabeth the latest fax from Cousin Geoffrey. Elizabeth walked into the meeting room for group therapy ten minutes early in order to read it before the session began. Emma O. was there already, hunched over a legal pad, composing a new letter of apology on behalf of society. Elizabeth could not resist peeking at the salutation, which read, "Dear Ms. Reno . . ."

Emma looked up at her and grinned. "I think I can get Warburton to sign this one."

Elizabeth nodded. "I expect you can." She took a seat near the window, pulled out the fax from Geoffrey, and began to read.

MacPherson & Hill
Attorneys-at-Law

TO: Elizabeth MacPherson, Patient
      Cherry Hill Treatment Center
FROM: Geoffrey Chandler, President & Founder,
      Geoffrey Chandler Design Inc.
      (What do you think? Has a ring to it, n'est-ce pas?)
      Danville, Virginia
NOTE: Attachments

Dear Cousin Elizabeth:

I trust that you are well. Hmm. I suppose the conventional pleasantries do not work when one is

addressing the—what is the word? Not "incarcer-
ated," which means to be in prison. And you are not
precisely "hospitalized." . . . "Facilitated"? Perhaps
not. Well, anyhow, I hope progress is being made, or
that little chemical miracles are taking place in your
cranial cells so that you can come up here and do
your own dirty work.

Not that I lack entertainment here. I always con-
trive to enjoy myself hugely. Nothing annoys other
people quite so much, you know. Anyhow, the chance
to annoy Cousin Bill is in itself a vacation. I have
taken over a sunny south-facing bedroom upstairs,
just across the hall from him, and we are currently
conducting a war of attrition to see who can occupy
the bathroom for the longest time morning and evening, while the other one paces the hall, muttering
imprecations under his breath. Also, I occasionally
drag in fabric swatches designed to spike his blood
pressure. You should have seen him when I suggested
purple tubular neon artwork for the walls.

But I do need to work seriously on this renovation plan.

I'm on Bill's computer again, and I plan to
do a little hardware shopping on-line as soon as I finish this progress report to you. It is nearly eleven
here. Mr. Jack is on the sunporch sleeping the sleep
of the just (well, perhaps not the just, but anyhow,
he's snoring quite soundly). Bill is upstairs running
virtual road races on his Nintendo. Today he moved
some more belongings from his apartment to his

room upstairs. I told him that he could put things in the closets without disrupting my renovation plans. He insisted on hauling in his television and his electronic game system as well. In fact, I believe his clothes were an afterthought. Nevertheless, he is busy and happy, and I have taken advantage of his absence to use his computer, about which he is inordinately possessive.

Normally, I would at this point share with you the details of my efforts at transforming the house, but I can sense your growing impatience boring right through the page like the glare of an oncoming train. I am happy to report that I have been successful in my quest. I found out just the sort of thing you wanted to know.

Libraries really are the most wonderful repositories of knowledge. Particularly the archive room containing newspapers and census records, which is the place they have set aside for people who want to do local historical research. All one has to do to find out about some point in local scandalmongering is to hang about in the local archives room looking personable and helpless. Sooner or later, some chatty biddy will come along, strike up a pleasant conversation, and Bob's your uncle! Or your second cousin once-removed on your mother's side, anyhow. Ask the right leading questions, and the biddy will proceed to tell you everything you wanted to know, thus saving you from having to do any work at all. Wonderful, I call it.

After a twenty-minute conversation with a Mrs. Verger, whose family apparently has been in Danville since neolithic times—No, that can't be right. They had to take time off after the Crusades to be kings of France and whatnot—but anyhow, Mrs. V. reckons herself a member of one of the area's first families, and I wisely did not bring up the subject of certain indigenous tribes of Native Americans or the buffalo that preceded them. . . . With her talk of "first families," I believe she was speaking euphemistically. What she meant was: we the people who do not have to buy our silver. We understood each other perfectly. And as Mrs. Verger could talk the hind leg off a donkey, I learned a great deal in a comparatively short time, without having to fiddle any more with those tiresome microfilm machines, or whatever they're called. I had been at it for most of the afternoon until my brain was beginning to glaze over, so I was no end grateful to the old dear when she began to natter away about Jack Dolan.

You probably want to know what she told me, and the answer is: nothing that would be news to any of the old-timers around here. The trouble with you and Bill is that you grew up too far out in the suburbs to know Danville, and you were born too late to catch the gossip of the Truman era. Fortunately, Mrs. V. is qualified on both counts to dish the local dirt, and she did so at length.

Jack Dolan is much more interesting than one would think to see him today: a stooped old man with

skin like the cover of a Bible, tottering around looking sweet and fragile. According to Mrs. Verger, fifty
years ago, Jack Dolan was the Butch Cassidy of Danville, Virginia.

An outlaw, I mean. He did not precisely rob
trains or banks, but he did manage to stay afoul of the
law on a regular basis. (Note: I was able to document
much of this gossip via the old newspapers on microfilm once I knew what—and when—I was looking
for. I photocopied a few choice articles and will fax
them to you along with this letter.)

I even think I know why your inmate—er,
patient—might have believed Jack Dolan was dead.
At least if he got his injuries when I think he did. May
1953, right? The story stayed on the front page for
most of the week. The "feds," as we in the detective
business call them, had been keeping Jack Dolan under surveillance for a couple of months, apparently,
and that particular night in May was the time for the
big bust. Dolan was moving a shipment out that night,
and there was to be an ambush outside Danville to
catch him red-handed with the goods. Unfortunately,
the plan turned out to be a disaster. Instead of stop-
ping at the roadblock, the car plowed through one of
the government agent's cars, and they ended up with
a fiery two-car wreck, an officer burned into an un-
recognizable crisp, and the driver and passenger of
Dolan's car incinerated. So for the first couple of
weeks of the story, the newspapers were all proclaim-
ing Jack Dolan dead. I guess that's the last news your

guy had on the matter. If he was in a burn unit, I'm sure he had a lot of other things to think about, and after he recovered, it never occurred to him to ask for an update. Or did you tell me that he quit his job after that? I guess he would have, because of his injuries.

Anyhow, then one night a couple of months later, Jack Dolan got arrested for speeding on a country road outside Danville. The trooper was a local man who knew Dolan on sight. So now they're wondering who died in the fire. The driver on the night of the wreck was a fellow called Larry Garrison, but as far as I can tell, the second passenger was never identified. Probably doesn't matter after forty-something years. Dolan spent a couple of years in prison for a smorgasbord of charges. When he was stopped for speeding, the trooper found "controlled substances" in his vehicle. In the Fifties, I'm guessing alcohol, not drugs. As far as I can tell, though, Jack Dolan is not a wanted fugitive these days. He's just an ancient old man haunting a house, even though he hasn't quite died.

Your fellow patient appears to be simply the victim of incomplete information—not an unusual occurrence when one's source is local newspapers. Sometimes you could go over their articles with a divining rod and not find any facts. But I digress. . . .

Shall I broach the subject of Mr. Dolan's checkered past? Do you want to know more? What if he tries to beat me up with his walker? Aside from that, would it be in good taste to inquire about his criminal history? I cannot find anything in Miss Manners on Etiquette Regarding Felons. Please advise, but be quick about it. I have done all I can in the way of decorating advice at this stage of Bill's patience and budget, so I am coming back to Georgia tomorrow. As it is on my way home, I will stop by and see you for an hour or so: a ray of sunshine in your somber existence. But I warn you: I will not be undertaking any more errands in the way of grief therapy. This is merely a social call.

> Until tomorrow then . . .
> Your man in Danville,
> G.C.

It was nearly nine o'clock before Jack Dolan managed to make it to the local Hardee's for his regular breakfast of black coffee and an egg-and-sausage biscuit. That Edith girl meant well with her bran flakes and grapefruit, talking nineteen to the dozen about vitamins and fiber (whatever that was), but he was too old to reform his habits now. He had made it past ninety on sausage biscuits and black coffee, and he reckoned if his diet was going to kill him, it would have done so by now. He'd had to eat some of Edith's health muck to get a minute's peace out of her, and then the lawyer and his arty cousin had come down and insisted on joining him at the table. They hadn't liked Edith's idea of a healthy breakfast any more than he had, and he'd almost offered to bring them back sausage biscuits from his breakfast run, but it occurred to him that if he mentioned his plan to go to Hardee's, one of them might insist on accompanying him. Company would cramp his style, so the minute they wandered out of the kitchen in search of the newspaper, he'd snatched up his hat and jacket, hobbled out the back door, and lit out through the shortcut in the tall shrubbery that lined the property. His morning trip to the fast-food palace wasn't just for mealtimes. He had business to conduct.

He settled into an orange-upholstered booth, out of the line of sight of the workers behind the counter, and sipped his coffee. He was a regular, and with the privilege of his great age, he could sit there all morning if he wanted to and nobody would bother him. The most they would do was come out and take a look at him every now and then, just to make sure he was still breathing. Mr. Jack began to unwrap his sausage biscuit, with an approving smile at the film of grease oozing from within. That ought to counteract the health muck he'd been forced to eat back at the house.

After a few pleasant moments of solitude and sausage grease, another elderly man approached the booth. "Mornin', Jack," he said in a hoarse voice that was trying to be a whisper. He slid into the booth opposite Jack Dolan, glancing around to see if anyone was watching. "I hear that you're back in business."

Mr. Jack took another swig of black coffee. He'd known the man for years, and the damn fool never did have any manners to speak of. Not so much as a how are you? Or nice weather we're having . . . Straight to business . . . Mr. Jack didn't bother to wonder how the fellow had known he was back in business. Small towns are always full of rumors. It stood to reason that occasionally one of them would be true.

"Just to keep my hand in," he said, doing his best to sound

----

indifferent. "Not really what you'd call business. Not at my age."

"Well, there's people that might want to lend a hand, Jack. Know-how like yours doesn't come along every day."

"Or even every decade," grunted Jack Dolan. "I am the last."

"You are that. But I'd need a sample to take to these fellows. To show them that you haven't lost your touch."

Mr. Jack turned his head like an old turtle and surveyed the restaurant with narrowed, unblinking eyes. Satisfied that they were unobserved, he reached into the pocket of his coat and drew out a pint-size glass bottle. It was filled with an amber-colored liquid. "That ought to show them," he grunted.

"And there's more where that came from?"

"There could be."

Sometimes we are as unlike ourselves as we are unlike other people. Who had said that? La Rouchefoucald? A. P. Hill had found the phrase in a translation exercise in her fourth-year French text, and while she had forgotten exactly which French philosopher had made the statement, she never forgot the phrase itself. She had found it shortly after the incident, which Purdue called their finest hour. Powell Hill never called it anything. She contrived never to think of the incident at all, but when it did cross her mind, she banished it with that phrase from her French book. She had been unlike herself that night. But, if present circumstances were any indication, Purdue must have been more like herself than ever before.

They had not done it out of pity. She was sure of that.

Otherwise, the motives eluded Powell Hill. It had begun with the sound of crying. A Saturday night in October on the third floor. Late. Everyone else either out on a date or away for the weekend. Even Sally Gee had left the fold, probably out with Klingenschmitt, which meant an all-you-can-eat buffet followed by Clint Eastwood or a no-cover-charge dance. One of the great advantages of going steady was that it removed the necessity of spending large amounts of money to impress one's date.

A. P. Hill had been in her dorm room alone, filling up index cards with footnotes, a preliminary step in a term paper for an anal-retentive history prof. She sat cross-legged on her bed, glancing out the window from time to time at the full moon that was shining through the branches of the oak tree. From the other end of the hall she could hear the thud of notes from Purdue's CD player, even through the closed door. A male singer's voice, something about "leaving her by the river." Purdue played it a lot. Then in the moment of silence between one song and the next, A. P. Hill had heard it: a hiccuping sob, a wail, then a slammed door. Not Purdue's. This side of the hall. Couple of doors down.

A. P. Hill listened for a moment. Nothing. Perhaps she had imagined it. She waited for the music to begin again, but all was quiet. With a weary sigh, she tossed the index cards onto a stack of library books and went to her door. When she looked out into the hall, she saw P. J. Purdue, in her customary uniform of black T-shirt and sweatpants, peering out of her own doorway just past the water fountain.

"What's the matter with you?" Purdue called out, squinting into the empty hallway.

A. P. Hill shook her head. "That wasn't me." She put a finger to her lips, and together they waited for the sounds to come again.

Together they walked up the hall, creeping up to the door of each room, listening for noises from within. In the deserted hallway past the stairwell they saw a crack of light under a closed door. Purdue motioned her forward, and together they crept closer. The muffled sobbing was just audible now.

A. P. Hill glanced at the high school calling cards taped to the door: Sandra Terrell; Pamela Bullington. Easy enough to guess which one of the roommates was in there now. Terrell's parents lived in Richmond; her boyfriend since high school went to Richmond, Virginia's Commonwealth University, and so every Friday afternoon at four o'clock pretty Sandi Terrell and her dirty laundry went home to mother and to Tim. She wouldn't be back until Sunday night.

Bullington, on the other hand, an aptly named bovine chem major from Pennsylvania, was either shy or surly—nobody much cared which. Anyhow, she barely had acquaintances on the hall, much less friends. Terrell was reportedly polite to her roommate, but looking to change partners next term.

With her ear pressed against the door, P. J. Purdue listened for a few seconds to the ragged bouts of weeping. "Where the hell is Sally Gee?" she muttered. "Ministering angel is her gig."

A. P. Hill shrugged. "House mother?"

"Be your age." Purdue rolled her eyes. "Talk about making things worse. They might even call her parents."

"So leave her alone then?"

The third-floor cynic considered this. "Nah," she said at last. "Too risky. If she jumps out the window, we're screwed. Do you want to go through life haunted by the hulking shade of Bullington?" Without waiting for a reply, Purdue turned the doorknob and went in.

The lights were off, but the moonlight from the window outlined a lumpish form under a quilt on one twin bed, head under the pillow, still emitting muffled sounds of distress.

"Yo, Bullington," said Purdue, flipping the light switch. "You got a cat in here?"

The crying stopped in midgulp, and a red, tear-blotched moon face emerged from under the pillow, blinking at the sudden burst of light. "A c-c-cat?"

"Yeah. We thought we heard one. Sounded like somebody was stringing a violin with it." Purdue's expression was one of bright interest. She strolled over to the desk and sat down in the straight-backed chair, giving every indication that she planned to make herself at home.

A. P. Hill, still hovering in the doorway, cringed, wishing that she could turn and run, but Bullington was clearly distraught about something. Leaving her at the mercy of P. J. Purdue was probably more cruelty than the girl could bear just now. She cleared her throat. "Umm . . . is there anything we can do, Pam?"

"Coke machine," said Purdue, before the weeping girl could answer. She peered into the metal wastebasket beside the desk. "Bullington here seems to be a Cherry Coke fan, so why don't you bring her one? I'll take a Diet, myself." Purdue waved her away without even a glance at the girl on the bed.

As A. P. Hill fled back down in the hall to retrieve her change purse, she heard Purdue's voice bellowing after her. "Bring chocolate, too!" The snack machines were in the basement next to the laundry room: four flights of concrete stairs that echoed her footfalls like drumbeats in the emptiness. She did not hurry. The errand of retrieving soft drinks and chocolate gave her a mission of charity without requiring her to be where she did not want to be: in the same room with a hysterical Pamela Bullington. She thought it might be easier for Bullington to tell her troubles to just one listener, even if it was the third-floor terrorist in black. Perhaps Purdue had thought that, and that was why she had dispatched her to the basement for refreshments. Ten minutes, thought A. P. Hill. That ought to give them enough time to talk over whatever it is that's freaking her out.

Powell Hill took her time descending the stairs, and she emptied the contents of her change purse on a laundry table to count out just the right amount of coins for the soda machine— in nickels. She dawdled further while she debated the comfort value of each packaged item in the snack machine. Was a Snickers bar more soothing than a chocolate cupcake? She got one of each. She had absolutely no idea which snack foods Pamela Bullington favored. Judging by the bulk of her, probably all of them—often. Finally A. P. Hill had wasted all the time she could on the fine points of her errand of mercy. She gathered up what little change she had left, tucked the soda cans in the crook of her arm, and made her way back up the stairs to the deserted corridor on the third floor, wondering what sort of problem could have driven Bullington to tears. Surely not man trouble. Bullington? Surely not.

As she turned the corner into the third-floor hall, she saw
P. J. Purdue leaning against the doorjamb, waiting for her return.
"Here she comes!" she called back to Bullington in a cheery
voice. "About damn time, right?"

As A. P. Hill handed over the soda cans and chocolate, she
saw the grim look on Purdue's face, an expression completely
at odds with the jaunty tone of her voice. She gave A. P. Hill
a look that said "Later," and carried the food into the room.
Bullington was sitting up now, wiping her swollen eyes with a
wet washcloth.

"Well," said Purdue, still brisk and calm, "I'm not going to
tell you not to be upset, Bullington. I personally would be homi-
cidal in your place. And I'm incapable of dispensing soothing
words of encouragement—if you want that sort of help, try Sally
Gee's room in a couple of hours. But, if it's any consolation to
you, we will take care of this. You don't need to know how. You
don't need to know when. It will happen. Got that?"

Bullington reddened as if another storm of weeping was
imminent, but she nodded and reached for the Cherry Coke.
Purdue tossed the cupcake and candy bar on the bed. "We'll
be back to check on you later," she said as she headed for the
door. "Why don't you study or something? Why let your evening be wasted by people you hate, huh? Read, sleep, or study.
Don't brood. Don't go home. Don't throw yourself out the
window. We'll be back. And you'll want to hear what we did,
won't you?"

Pamela Bullington nodded again, still leaking size-sixteen
tears.

"Of course you do. Stay tuned. Save me some chocolate."

Purdue's voice had been calm and unconcerned. She

gave the girl a casual wave, and sauntered out of Bullington's room, smiling as if she had just made a casual visit to an acquaintance. Once the door closed behind her, though, Purdue's smile vanished and she jerked her head in the direction of her room. "Move!" she muttered to A. P. Hill. She stalked off down the hall, and A. P. Hill hurried after her, still wondering what was going on.

When they were safely ensconced behind the closed door of Purdue's room, A. P. Hill said, "So what's the matter with Bullington? Trouble at home?"

"No. Trouble here." Purdue was perched on the window ledge, looking out at the dark shapes of trees outlined against a sky bleached by the lights of the city. She sighed. "The poor beast took a blind date. Fraternity party. Guy called up on the house phone a couple of hours ago, trolling for meat. Bullington was feeling bored and sorry for herself, and she decided to accept the offer. They will do it, these stupid girls. I blame the Brothers Grimm, myself. Maybe Barbara Cartland. These girls really think Prince Charming is going to turn up in the lobby of the dorm as a blind date, and that he will love them for their beautiful souls. Five thousand years of collective human behavior fails to convince them otherwise."

"True, but not very enlightening so far, Purdue. Could you just tell me what happened?"

Purdue scowled. "Oh, the usual," she said, but there was a bitterness in her voice that A. P. Hill had never heard before. "Some jerk asked Bullington to go to a party at his frat house, and she went, and she thought she was having a pretty good time. Bright lights. Loud band. Cute guy. Then she went to find

the bathroom, and on her way there she overheard a couple
of the guys talking about the 'pig party,' and wondering who
would win the prize for bringing the ugliest girl. She slipped out
the back door and ran back to the dorm. She's been crying ever
since."

A. P. Hill winced. She wasn't particularly fond of Bullington, but she wouldn't have wished that experience on anyone.
She found it hard to believe that civilized people could be capable of so much casual cruelty. She would concede that war or
famine might drive people to commit ignoble acts out of rage or
desperation, but she would never understand why young men
on a supposedly enlightened college campus would make a sport
of it. Then she remembered Purdue telling Bullington that the
matter would be taken care of. As usual, A. P. Hill thought of
legal redress. "So, are you going to ask your grandfather about
taking the case?"

"What case?"

"Bullington's. You told her you'd take care of things. Are
you going to sue the guys who gave the party?"

Purdue scowled at her. "Will you listen to yourself? Sue
the guys who gave the party? For what? Something Bullington
overheard but can't prove?"

"It isn't a good case," Powell conceded. "It may not even
be illegal. I'm not sure the discrimination laws cover that. I'd go
for a civil suit on the grounds of emotional damage."

"You would, would you, Tinkerbell? And what would happen if she did sue those creeps? Media coverage most likely. Is
that going to make Pamela Bullington feel any better, do you
think? Becoming famous as the disgruntled guest at a fraternity

----

pig party? She'd never live it down. She'd probably drop out of school from the humiliation of it, and the story would follow her for the rest of her life."

"Well, I don't see what else you can do," said A. P. Hill. "You could try throwing an ugly-guy party, but it probably wouldn't faze them. I suppose it's theoretically possible to hurt a guy's self-esteem, but I've never actually seen it done."

"Maybe nobody ever tried hard enough before."

"What, the whole fraternity? No way, Purdue. I wish you hadn't promised Bullington some action on this, because there's nothing we can do."

"Not the whole fraternity. Just one guy. She told me the name of the guy who picked her up here in the lobby. I say we go after him. Make an example of him. That ought to make the rest of those cretins think twice about what they're doing."

"Go . . . after . . . him?" A. P. Hill's eyes widened. "You'll end up in jail, Purdue."

P. J. stopped pacing and flopped down on the bed. "There ought to be some way to teach him a lesson. Something he couldn't—or wouldn't—report to the authorities."

Powell Hill looked thoughtful. "Maybe there is."

Elizabeth's day had been uneventful, which is a primary goal of treatment facilities. She had not tried to kill herself, or stared off into space brooding over her loss, or even given way to a brief storm of weeping. The pills saw to that. She had wandered quietly from art to group to lunch, with the vague suspicion beneath the chemical haze that this monotonous regimen was an empty waste of one's youth. She must do something about that, she thought, but her resolve floated away before she could formulate a course of action. This must be one of her bad days. Dr. Dunkenburger said that her moods would zigzag from almost normal to despair. There were pills for the latter, if she cared to request them. Elizabeth thought not. Not yet.

Finally, after an afternoon that seemed to last for weeks, it was dinnertime. She wasn't sure that she was hungry, but at least dinner was a semblance of society, a break in the monotony of watching the clock hands. She could sleep through it, of course. She felt that she could sleep twenty hours a day if they left her alone. But of course they wouldn't. That was the whole point. Go through the motions of living until you find that once again you mean it. She wondered if that worked.

First you swallow the pills, and then the pills swallow you, she thought.

She went through the cafeteria line without even noticing what was put on her plate. From force of habit she wandered over to her usual table. Emma O. was surrounded by chattering women. Elizabeth heard one of them say, "Dan Quayle! He can't be as stupid as the media makes him out to be. He has a law degree, for God's sake!" Another one said, "Kato—oh, never mind."

Tomorrow's letter in the making, Elizabeth thought. At the last moment she turned aside, and headed for the table near the door, where Hillman Randolph sat alone.

"You!" he said with an unwelcoming grunt. "I suppose you want to keep on playing twenty questions with me."

Elizabeth stared down at her plate. "No."

She thought she heard an intake of breath. Then the sound of a fork being set down on the plastic tray. "We had a deal," he said. "I may be crazy—though I doubt it—but I do keep my word."

"It doesn't matter any more," said Elizabeth. "You were wrong, that's all." She began to push the mashed potatoes around, trying to obliterate the soggy green peas.

"What do you mean I was wrong?"

She shrugged. "Mistaken, then. There were developments in the case after you were injured. Apparently nobody bothered to inform you. Here. See for yourself." From the pocket of her sweater, she pulled out the fax from Geoffrey. She had crumpled it up in her pocket during therapy and had never bothered to take it out again. She hadn't felt the need to reply to it.

Hillman Randolph scanned the pages with the scowl of impatience that Geoffrey's prose style usually evoked in the estrogen-challenged. Elizabeth found that Mr. Randolph's reaction interested her no more than the tasteless food congealing on her plate. She took a sip of iced tea, wondering if anybody would check to see how much she'd eaten. Well, let them. She was a voluntary patient. And since she was nobody's idea of too-skinny, she thought it might even help if she skipped a meal every now and then. If she had to be around for another fifty years or so, she might as well look good.

Hillman Randolph looked up from the fax message. "He is still alive," he whispered.

"Apparently so," said Elizabeth. "But I think he got put in jail a while back, so your efforts weren't altogether wasted.

Anyhow, I have no more questions for you, but if you'd like my Jell-O, you're welcome to it. I'm going to my room." Without waiting for a reply, she swept out of the dining room without a backward glance.

Hillman Randolph sat still for a long time, staring at the last page of the fax message while his untouched coffee grew cold.

*"Successful and fortunate
crime is called virtue."*
—Seneca

Chapter 13

The young man in the campus snack bar took deep breaths and tried not to appear nervous. He could feel cold sweat in his armpits. They say that dogs can smell fear. What about foxy ladies? He looked at the two small blondes who had positioned themselves on either side of his bar stool. There probably wasn't any scent of fear attached to them, but it would be hard to tell anyway under all that perfume. Two of them. He had no pick-up lines equal to that situation, but then he didn't appear to need one. He couldn't believe his luck. He'd stopped in at the local watering hole after the fraternity party to take a pre-study break, with no further plans for the evening beyond two beers and a chapter of anthropology, when suddenly these two young ladies had cut him out of the herd like a couple of Border Collies after a lamb. He wondered if he could find out—in a roundabout way, of course—just what it was that attracted them to him. His haircut? His blue shirt? Was he wearing aftershave? He had managed to down two beers in five minutes, more or less in shock, and their effects were not doing anything to enhance his powers of deduction. Women had never appeared to find him irresistible before, more's the pity. Why now?

An unpleasant thought crossed his mind. "Um . . . no offense, ladies, but, you two aren't . . . um . . . professionals, are you? I mean, not that you look it. . . ."

They didn't look it. They looked like a couple of undergraduates from upper-middle-class homes, but that was the whole point, wasn't it? Couldn't hookers assume whatever persona the customer required? And presumably in a college hangout . . .

"Are we professional?" The sturdy-looking one with the boyish features laughed softly. "Experienced, yes. Professional, no."

"Good, because I haven't got much money." He blushed at having to mention such a delicate subject. Money. "I could stand a round of drinks, though."

The pretty one, who smiled like she had to be reminded to, shook her head. "Nothing alcoholic for me," she murmured. "Do they have bottled water here?"

"Probably." Trust a woman to make a drink of water expensive, he thought. But who was he to argue? He was being picked up by two nubile young blondes, when most nights he couldn't even get the time of day from the snack bar's resident cat. Go figure.

"Nice ring," cooed the other one. "Fraternity letters, hmmm?"

"Oh. Yeah. I'm an anthropology major, really. I never thought I was the fraternity type, but . . ."

The two women looked at each other. He caught only a glimpse of the look, but it wasn't the mellow, wide-eyed gaze they had directed at him for the last ten minutes. This look carried more words in it than a microchip. In a remote corner of his skull a few brain cells flashed him a warning signal, but by the time that thought had threaded its way through a cerebral swamp of alcohol-fueled lust, the warning had all the urgency of a lightning bug in a thunderstorm. The young man dodged the cautionary flare from his higher brain, and went right back to thinking with quite a different part of his anatomy, an organ which was presently contemplating the etiquette of the threesome.

"I hear your fraternity has interesting parties," said the sharp-eyed one, tracing the Greek letters on the onyx stone of his class ring.

He shrugged. "Just a bunch of guys out to have a good time," he mumbled. "They're a little coarse sometimes. Typical coming-of-age tribal rituals, male bonding . . ." In his nervousness, he found that he was quoting his anthropology textbook. He gulped and began again. "I mean, the socializing makes a nice change from studying until your eyes glaze over."

"Oh, don't be modest," said the solemn one. "A girl we know attended one of those parties recently. She said it was absolutely unforgettable."

They looked at each other again. That odd look, that seemed to say more than their sentences did.

He felt that he had somehow lost the thread of the conversation. Something was being said between the lines, and he wasn't getting it. It was like being hard of hearing at a Jonathan Demme movie—good luck figuring out what was going on in the film. But maybe men were always hard of hearing when women talked. He wished he hadn't added beer to the spiked punch he'd already had at the party.

"What do you say we get out of here?" said one of the women. "Go someplace more private?"

"A bonding ritual," said the quiet one, with a smile that looked genuine for a change.

Oh boy. Now what? He took a deep breath, blinked a few times, and tried to focus on something less abstract. "What did you ladies say your names were?"

"You can call me Trish," said P. J. Purdue, taking his arm in a firm grasp. "And my friend here is Amy."

For once in her life, A. P. Hill did not object to the use of her first name.

W̲e are going to try something rather different in therapy today," Warburton announced. "Elizabeth, you still are not coming to terms with your problem."

"That's what pills are for," said Elizabeth, with a little sigh of contentment. She had just taken her new medication and was waiting for it to kick in. "Reality-lite. Skimmed. All of life's fat emotional content has been eliminated for . . . your . . . prot-tec-tion. Innit marvelous?"

"We'll see about that," muttered Clifford Allen.

Warburton knew a good opening for group discussion when she saw one. "Are pills and sedatives the answer, ladies and gentlemen?"

"Depends on the question," said Richard Petress, smirking at the nurse.

"We should not become chemically dependent on drugs to solve our problems. They are a crutch." Lisa Lynn was into being the Good Child that day. The word was that she was due to be released soon. She basked in Warburton's beam of approval.

"But crutches are fine for temporary problems," said Elizabeth, with a note of irritation creeping into her mellow mood. "Broken legs, for example. Then you heal, and you throw the crutch away. Same with pills. So, when Cameron comes back . . ."

"I'd like to say something about that," said Clifford Allen.

"Clifford, hush!" said Rose Hanelon, shaking her head.

"Let him talk," said Emma O. "That's what we're here for, isn't it? To clean out our wounds?"

"You cannot possibly know anything about marine biology," said Elizabeth. "You are a burglar."

"That's right," said Clifford, tipping his chair back on two legs. "I'm a burglar." His slouch became less pronounced, and his smile less pleasant. "In fact, I'm not just a burglar, I'm a certified nut case. I use other people's living rooms for a litter box, and I can't stop, and I don't know why. I'm crazy, all right. But at least I'm not stupid."

Elizabeth gasped. "What do you mean by that?"

Several other members of the group tried to silence Clifford. They all began to talk at once, in an effort to drown him out, but raising his voice as loud as you could get before the orderlies came bursting in, he called out, "Have you seen the movie *Titanic*?"

Elizabeth emerged from her grief with a snarl. "That again?

Why does everybody keep asking me what movies I've seen lately?"

Clifford Allen smirked at her. "And you're the Ph.D.," he said. "In science, yet. So answer the question. Did you see it? Surely you cannot be the only person in North America who did not see *Titanic*?"

"Of course I saw it. So what? What on earth does that movie have to do with anything?"

"Quite a lot, judging by what you've told us of your husband's disappearance. His boat went down off the coast of Scotland, you said. Now, think about that movie. Ship goes down in the North Atlantic. Handsome young man is pitched into the cold sea. And he survives how long?"

Elizabeth hung her head.

The rest of the room fell silent.

"How long?"

"Less than an hour," whispered Elizabeth at last.

She heard her friends—Rose, and Lisa Lynn, and Seraphin, and even Emma O. let out a collective sigh.

She shook herself as if she felt the coldness of the water. "But . . . the other character in the film . . . the girl who climbed onto the floating debris . . . survived."

"And she was rescued after how long?"

"Couple of hours," said Emma O. As emotionless as ever. "I read a book once on World War Two. It said pilots who were shot down in the North Sea only survived for a matter of minutes because of the low water temperature. Sorry, Elizabeth."

She didn't look sorry. She looked pleased with herself for being able to trot out a few relevant facts. Emma O. would always love trivia more than people, but at least she had remembered to proffer an apology when she said something devastating. It was progress.

Clifford Allen nodded. "I've heard that story about the pilots, too," he said. "So, Elizabeth, since *Titanic* was only a movie, it is just within the bounds of possibility that Leonardo DiCaprio, the actor, might drop in on you here some afternoon. *People* magazine claims he's a charitable guy who sometimes visits the sick in hospitals. Leo is alive and well, because his North Atlantic was a tank of warm water on a soundstage. However, you cannot reasonably assume that someone who actually did meet that fate in the real North Atlantic could survive to come back to you, no matter how much you might wish it would happen. People don't come back out of the North Atlantic. The film was quite specific about that. Everybody knows it."

There was pity on the circle of faces around her, but not one look of surprise. Everybody did know it.

Elizabeth had covered her face with her hands. She waited for the other members of the group to go on talking. Self-centered creatures that they were, it was usually only a matter of seconds before one of them hijacked any given conversation, and turned it into an examination of his or her own concerns. Not this time, though. Now, when she would have paid Richard Petress to launch into a discussion of the symbolism of nail polish colors, or for Emma O. to prattle on about the aristocracy of beauty, all was quiet.

Elizabeth took a deep breath. She knew that everyone in the room was watching her, waiting for a reaction. A cathartic storm of tears, perhaps. But there isn't really any rage to be mined out of a certainty. She had known for a long time now, even while she talked of hope and uncertainty. Or were the new pills simply dulling a pain that she would feel at full force at some later date?

At last she said, "So that's what Hillman Randolph meant when he asked me if I had seen the movie." She looked around, to see if the old man was smiling triumphantly at her through his scarred lips, but she could not find him.

"Where is Hillman?" she asked Warburton, remembering that they were supposed to use first names in group.

"He can't be with us," muttered the nurse, looking away. "Why don't we focus on our problems instead of someone else's?"

Matt Pennington, who remembered everyone today, announced, "Hillman has gone over the wall!"

Elizabeth gasped. "Really? At his age?"

He sighed. "Not literally, dear. I meant he has left the building. Escaped, I guess you could say, except that I'm not sure they had any legal authority to stop him. Anyhow, he took his car keys and drove off without a word to anyone."

"Oh, right." Elizabeth felt somehow that this ought to matter to her, but it all seemed rather far away, like a television movie she had dozed through and couldn't quite recall. "Can you do that in Cherry Hill?"

Matt shrugged. "Who's going to stop you? Unarmed guards making minimum wage? Nobody in here is supposed to be dangerous anyhow. They figure he'll be back."

"Seems kind of funny for a policeman to escape from detention," said Rose Hanelon. "Very ironic."

Clifford Allen gave her his most unpleasant smile. "What makes you think Hillman was a policeman?"

"Well . . . government agent then. Whatever."

"None of the above," said Clifford.

"But he said he was," Lisa Lynn pointed out.

He sneered. "Since when do we take people's word for things in here?"

"Including yours," snapped Rose. "What makes you think Hillman wasn't a cop?"

"I'm a burglar. I know cops. I can smell cops. Did you ever watch him in the TV lounge? Law and order shows didn't interest him. He never questioned any of the police procedure, or reacted to the plot with a personal anecdote. He didn't even seem interested in the shows."

"He's an old man," said Lisa Lynn. "He hasn't been in law enforcement since the Fifties. Maybe the new techniques are so different that he can't relate to them."

"It's more than that," said Clifford. He thought for a moment about how to express a hunch that was more feeling than facts. "Hillman was nice to me."

"So he was a nice guy," said Rose. "With questionable taste."

"You don't get it. He ate his meals with me. He'd talk football with me. He even gave me some change for the drink machine once. And I'm a burglar, remember? Hillman knew it. Everybody knows it. Now no cop—retired, crazy, or dead—ever socializes with a criminal. To them we're scum. We're the element of danger in their low-paying job. We're the cause of their drinking problem, their failed marriage, their nightmares.

Hillman was not a cop, could never have been a cop, because I liked him."

The lawyer who seldom said anything cleared his throat. "Clifford has a point. I see what he's getting at. I know a lot of peace officers, too, in my line of work, and now that I think of it, I have to agree with him. Hillman didn't fit the mold."

The members of group looked at one another, trying to take in the news. "So," said Emma O. "Who was he?"

Richard Petress laughed at her bewilderment. "He was just some crazy old dude, girl. Just like the rest of us."

Elizabeth had been silent throughout this exchange. She was taking it all in, but slowly, as if the sound waves of the discussion had to travel through water to reach her. At last a thought occurred to her. "Did Hillman say where he was going?"

"The word is that he was asking if Virginia had any toll roads," said Matt Pennington. "Nobody knew."

"I know about Virginia roads," said Elizabeth. "I'm from there, and he knew it. I wonder why he didn't ask me." Through a fog of sedatives a voice in her head was shouting, "Because you told him Jack Dolan was still alive! That's where he's going, you dolt!" Elizabeth thought vaguely that she ought to do something about that. Tell somebody, maybe?

"Did it go off all right?" asked P. J. Purdue. The opening of the car door had made her jump. As much as she claimed to be enjoying herself, there were moments when the life of a fugitive took its toll on her nerves. She was sitting in the driver's seat of their latest stolen car in the parking lot of a shopping mall, and trying to read *Newsweek* by peering over the top of her sunglasses. It had taken ten minutes for her partner to emerge from the Uniform Supply Shop, but outside all was quiet. No police cruisers had gone by, and no one seemed to notice her presence. She and Carla might even be able to stay around long enough to have lunch in the Italian restaurant at the end of the row of shops. "Did you get the handcuffs?" she asked, trying to sound casual.

Carla Larkin slid into the passenger seat, smoothing her short skirt and rolling her eyes at such a fatuous question. "Of course, I did. I'm back, aren't I? It was a cinch, same as always." She struck a pose. "I simply told the man in the uniform store that I was buying them as a birthday present for my brother who had just graduated from the police academy. I got the full lecture on brands of handcuffs."

"Which kind did you get?" asked Purdue. "I have become a connoisseur of handcuffs."

Carla shrugged. "I always go for the cheapest. I can't see paying an extra ten bucks for Smith & Wesson's brand name. I mean they're handcuffs, for God's sake. They all open with the exact same key anyhow."

"Well, they work better than wet pantyhose," said Purdue with a grin. "And since we only ever need one key, think of the recycling possibilities." She pushed a strand of hair back from her ear to reveal an earring: a small metal key dangling from a thin gold wire.

"There are some differences in brands, I guess," Larkin said, ignoring her. "I do hate those handcuffs that are jazzed up by putting the bluing on them. That stuff comes off on your skin, your clothes, everything."

"They rust, too."

"Tell me about it," said Carla. "That's what the guards used when they transported us. Ever try to wash off blue dye with powdered soap?" She opened the plastic bag and tilted it toward Purdue. "Matte stainless steel HWC's. Twenty-three bucks apiece. On sale: three pair for sixty."

"So you bought three pair, right?"

"I thought you said we were getting out of the game, P. J."

"Well, we are, but—hey! You never know. Something might come up."

"Like what?"

"I don't know." Purdue fingered the handcuffs. "Maybe we ought to try thumb cuffs some time. I always thought they looked kind of kinky. You know, those little bitty ones that you lock down over each of the thumb joints. A guy would have to tear his thumbs off to get out of those. Besides, they're small enough to carry without a handbag. That's a plus."

Carla rolled her eyes. "Look, given enough time anybody can get out of handcuffs. You could spring the lock with a ball-point pen. A paper clip. I learned that much in prison. If we could get the cuffs that federal agents use—the ones that open with a little round key—they'd be harder to get out of, but we probably can't find any."

"Okay, what about a set of Peerless hinge-plated cuffs? Since there's a hinge plate instead of a chain between the cuffs, the guy would have a harder time getting out of them."

"Eighty bucks," said Carla. "And remember we would use them one time. It's a waste of money. Personally, I could care less what kind we use. All these twenty-dollar wonders do is

----

buy us a little time to get away. After that, who cares? Besides, we are quitting, aren't we?"

"Yes. Of course, we are. But three for sixty. I mean,
come on!"

Carla sighed. "I knew you'd say that. Yeah. Three for sixty.
So I bought 'em. Just in case. It's not like it's our money, really.
That banker sure had a wad of cash on him, didn't he? Guess
he didn't trust his own bank."

"I wish we could find another sucker like him," said Purdue wistfully.

"I don't. You didn't have him slobbering all over your
neck half the night. So where are we headed now?"

"Southeast," said Purdue, handing her the map. "Place
called Danville."

"Elizabeth, you have a visitor." It was Thibodeaux, the
big orderly who had showed her around on her first day. "Do
you feel like seeing him?"

Elizabeth yawned. Group therapy had been over for a
while now. She wasn't sure how long she had been sitting on the
sofa in the dayroom, thinking of taking a nap before dinner, but
perhaps a nice long walk down two corridors to the reception
lounge would do her good. "Whatever," she said, yawning and
stretching as she stood up. Maybe her father or Bill had come to
see how she was getting along. She ambled along the hall beside
the orderly, without much interest in what would happen next,
today or ever.

When the door to the reception room swung open, Elizabeth saw her cousin Geoffrey, impeccably clad in a fawn-

---

colored suit. He was studying the chintz-patterned wallpaper with the practiced eye of one who feels he is entitled to an opinion.

Elizabeth managed a shaky wave and sank down on the sofa. It was soft, and it smelled better than the one in the day-room, but the fact that it did not face a television was a mark against it. "Hi, Geoffrey," she mumbled without looking up at him.

"I was on my way home," said Geoffrey. "I thought I'd just stop by and see you."

"Cameron is dead," said Elizabeth softly.

"Yes. Listen, I've just driven about six hours. Boring road is I-77. I thought we might go out to eat, if you'd like a little fresh air." He frowned at the sight of his cousin. Her unwashed hair and rumpled clothing suggested that she was getting worse instead of better. Despite his misgivings he forced himself to give her an encouraging smile. "The staff person I spoke to said that you could have an evening pass to go out for dinner. Are you hungry?"

Elizabeth sighed. "I mean, really, Geoffrey. Dead."

"Yes."

She blinked up at his impassive face. "You knew it all along?"

He looked embarrassed. "Well, it stood to reason. Terribly cold water. Rough seas. No wreckage ever found. Have you only just worked it out?"

"Had my nose rubbed in it, more like," sighed Elizabeth. "Being crazy means that you get to speak the truth, no matter who it hurts. If you're lucky, you are also too crazy to

257

understand the truth when people tell it to you, but unfortunately, I seem to have a mild case of insanity." She yawned
again. "Sorry. They changed my meds yesterday. These new pills
make life all blurry."

"I liked you better without them." When Elizabeth did
not reply, Geoffrey went on, "Girl zombie is not one of your
more attractive roles. Your brother's new house is shaping up
quite nicely, thanks to me. I brought a few snapshots, if you're
interested. Did you get my faxes about Jack Dolan's shady
past?"

"Yep."

"So you told your policeman friend that he had been
misinformed?"

"Yep."

"Well, in case he didn't believe you—policemen are such a
suspicious lot, don't you find?—I brought some of the articles
pertaining to the case. I thought you might show them to him."

She shook her head. "Can't."

"Why not?"

"He flew the coop. Took his car keys and drove off into
the sunset."

"Really?" Geoffrey raised one expressive eyebrow. "Is that
permitted?"

Elizabeth shrugged. "What can they do? Take away his
dessert privileges? I told him that Jack Dolan was still alive, and
he left. But it turns out that he's not a policeman anyhow. At
least, that's what the burglar says."

He watched her for a moment in silence. Her eyes were
closed, and she seemed to have forgotten that he was there.

"I am beginning to hope that you are delusional," he said at last. "Do you happen to know who this escaped imposter actually is?"

"Just a crazy person, I guess," said Elizabeth, showing very little interest in the discussion. "But I know where he's going."

"Danville?"

"Yep."

"And you'd know him if you saw him?"

Elizabeth's smile turned into a yawn. "So would you if it wasn't Halloween. Scarred face. Burns. Very sad."

That's it, thought Geoffrey. He took hold of her arm and pulled her to her feet. "Come along, dear. You have a dinner pass, and I'm going to take you to a splendid restaurant. March." Without waiting for a reply from Elizabeth, who seemed to be sleepwalking, he half carried her to the door and down the corridor toward the front entrance. As they walked he kept up a flow of bright chatter, laughing occasionally as if responding to something amusing that she had said. When her eyes started to close he tightened his grip on her arm.

After many tense moments, each of which seemed to last a week, Geoffrey succeeded in getting Elizabeth out of the building, into the parking lot, and installing her in the front seat of his car. He fastened her seat belt, and, with a final stretch of his sore muscles, he got back behind the wheel where he had spent the last seven hours.

"What splendid restaurant are we going to?" Elizabeth murmured sleepily.

Geoffrey started the engine. "McDonald's," he said. "In Danville."

It had been a long time ago, A. P. Hill thought as she drove west out of Richmond. She had not called Bill to tell him she was coming back. She thought she'd surprise him. Allow herself to be shown around the new offices of MacPherson & Hill, and then take him out to dinner to celebrate. She hadn't been much of a partner in the last ten days, she thought, and the fact that she'd had a lot on her mind didn't excuse her behavior. After all, what was worrying her had happened a long time ago, too. If a statute of limitations applied to the case, surely it had long since expired. In fact, there might not even be a case. As far as she knew charges had never been filed. Certainly nothing about the incident had ever appeared up in the Williamsburg newspapers.

They had been lucky. The newspapers should have had a field day with the story: LOCAL COLLEGE STUDENT ABDUCTED IN BONDAGE RITUAL BY TWO BLONDES. A. P. Hill shuddered, imagining tabloid headlines, similar to the ones that now featured Purdue's present escapades. Only the stories would have displayed her picture, instead of Carla Larkin's, as the outlaw accomplice.

We must have been crazy, thought Powell Hill for the five hundredth time. They had certainly been angry that night—perhaps there is a point where anger and madness become indistinguishable.

Purdue had called the frat house, asking for Milo, and after long minutes of waiting, while the receiver was laid down on the table, and shouts of "Anybody seen Milo?" filtered back through the line, the same slurred voice came back on and told them that Milo had gone off to study. Try the snack bar, the voice had added. He usually stokes up on coffee and burgers before he hits the stacks.

There wasn't much time for preparation. They had put on a week's worth of makeup from the absent Terrell's supply, and the most provocative clothes they could find in Terrell's closet, completing the look with her largest pairs of dangly earrings. Purdue took a small handbag and emptied everything out of it except her room key, a ten-dollar bill, two pairs of damp panty-hose, and a disposable camera that still had a few shots left on the roll.

"Loaded for bear," said Purdue, tottering a little in Pamela's roommate's platform shoes.

"How will we know this guy if we find him?" asked A. P. Hill, trying to pull down a skirt so short it might have been a dinner napkin.

"I got a description of him," said Purdue. "While you were downstairs at the drink machine, I got Bullington to tell me everything about him that she could remember. If he hasn't changed clothes, I can't miss him. Even if he has, I think I can spot him."

It had been as simple as that. They'd found him in the snack bar, just as the voice on the phone had told them they would, and Purdue had recognized him within seconds. She nudged A. P. Hill. "The dark-haired clown at the counter," she murmured. "Keep smiling if it kills you."

Somehow Powell Hill had got through the next ten minutes, with a plaster smile, and an imitation of a femme fatale that was good enough to fool anyone who wasn't sober. After a few minutes' repartee, which the young man seemed to find bewildering, though of course his macho self-image prevented him from saying so, they led him away to an unlit wooded area that was unlikely to have passersby so late at night. This was the tricky part. Finding somewhere to go. They had discussed this point in hushed, urgent tones on the way to the snack bar. They didn't want him at the dorm, and they couldn't risk going back to his room, so it had to be outside. It was probably a good thing he wasn't sober. He wasn't thinking clearly enough to argue with them.

Working briskly and insistently as they murmured perfunctory endearments, "Trish" and "Amy" had managed to divest the young man of his clothes. As he lurched toward them to return the favor, A. P. Hill caught his wrist. She was surprisingly strong for a slender young woman. Taking martial arts classes instead of ballet had its advantages.

P. J. Purdue took the pantyhose out of her purse. "There's more to the foreplay," she murmured in a sultry voice. "Ever been tied up?"

The anthropology student seemed to be muttering something about South American courtship rituals as Purdue bound his wrists together behind his back with the damp pantyhose, and then tied him to a small tree. With trembling fingers made clumsy by her nervousness, A. P. Hill tied his feet together, trying not to look up as she worked.

In less than two minutes their victim was securely trussed and immobilized. Purdue stepped back and handed A. P. Hill the camera. "Shoot," she said, "but keep me out of the frame. I'm going to tell our boyfriend here why this is happening to him."

"We can't!" hissed her partner in crime. "It will get . . . you-know-who . . . in trouble!"

"Oh, I don't think so," said Purdue, tapping the camera. "Not unless old Studly here wants to see his picture plastered all over campus on homemade posters—WOULD YOU ATTEND AN UGLY-GIRL PARTY WITH THIS MAN?"

The young man stopped struggling with his bonds. "Is that what this is about? Listen, we didn't mean any harm. . . ."

"Oh, tell it to the squirrels, macho man!" Purdue snapped a few more pictures of the captive. "Let's get out of here," she said to A. P. Hill, who was acting as lookout.

As they turned to go, A. P. Hill said, "I'm sure this has been an interesting anthropological experience for you. File it under Revenge Rituals. And tell your Neanderthal buddies that if they don't stop harassing campus women, they'll all find themselves tied to trees!"

Then they ran until the young man's shouts no longer echoed in their ears.

And that had been it, really. Although they read the local and campus newspapers front to back for weeks, there were no articles about a naked man left tied to a tree near the campus of William & Mary. No policemen came to the dorm to question anybody. Perhaps Milo Gordon had escaped on his own, and had slunk back home in the darkness without a word to anybody. It was as if the incident had never taken place.

The next time she went home, Purdue got the photos developed by a friend of hers, probably telling him some plausible lie about the subject matter: a drama class exercise, perhaps. When she came back to campus, she gave Pam Bullington one of the prints and swore her to secrecy. And that was that. Then it was over. Honor satisfied. No repercussions. They soldiered on through the undergraduate year, concentrating on the weightier matters of exams and term papers; gradually the incident faded from Powell Hill's mind until it had the hazy texture of a half-remembered television movie starring a girl who vaguely resembled her.

She had cause to remember it a few years later, when her law partner Bill MacPherson, remarking on his sister's forthcoming wedding, mentioned her old boyfriend, Bill's former roommate, Milo Gordon. When she heard the name, A. P. Hill took a deep breath and willed herself to stay calm, but she'd had to set down her coffee mug because her hand was shaking.

"Where is your old roommate now?" she'd asked Bill, as casually as she could.

"Peru, I think," said Bill, oblivious to her discomfort. "Somewhere in South America anyhow. I get a Christmas card every couple of years. Milo is a forensic anthropologist. Studies bones. I asked him once why he didn't study live people, and he said he didn't much care for them."

A. P. Hill had let out a sigh of relief as she turned the conversation into safer channels. There didn't seem to be any likelihood of her ever meeting Milo Gordon, since he and Bill had lost touch. Even if they did meet, he might not remember her. A. P. Hill wondered if Bill had ever been told about Milo's abduction, and what he had thought about it if he had. What would he think of her?

With P. J. Purdue at large, performing that same old stunt on a succession of strangers, A. P. Hill was very much afraid she was going to find out. Suppose when P. J. Purdue was finally taken into custody, she talked about the first crime of the PMS

Outlaws—the one in which they used pantyhose instead of hand-cuffs, and her accomplice had been A. P. Hill.

Powell Hill eased her foot off the accelerator. She had been doing seventy without realizing it. She was not in that much of a hurry to reach Danville. She still didn't know what she was going to say to Bill when she got there.

Chapter 14

"Did you hear from your cousin Geoffrey yet?" Edith asked Bill as she brought in the mail.

"No," said Bill. "I assume that he made it home to Georgia safely. Why? Are you worried about him?"

"No. I want to make sure he's really gone." Edith's gaze took in the walls of Bill's office, newly papered in chintz; the rowing scull set upright in a corner to serve as a bookcase; and the tartan-matted, gold-framed fox-hunting prints set at tasteful intervals along the walls. "Breaking and entering is a crime, isn't it?" she asked Bill.

"Ye-ees," said Bill, sorting through the letters.

"Well, breaking and decorating ought to be."

"The decorations are probably very nice," said Bill carefully. "I just don't think it's me."

"Looks like a set for a Jane Austen film," said Edith with a sigh. "Still, I suppose he meant well. And he certainly was good company for Mr. Jack. He'd sit and listen to him for hours on end, it seems like."

"I know," said Bill. "I wonder what he was up to."

Edith shook her head. "You know him better than I do," she said. "Well, I haven't got time to stand around here all day talking to you. People keep coming to the back door asking for Mr. Jack. He said I was to tell them he's in the outbuilding. I wonder what he's up to?"

Bill smiled. "At his age? Breathing, I expect. Not much else. Anyhow, I'm going to be busy, too. A woman called a little while ago and said she wanted to talk to me about a lawsuit. Something about her car. I'll let her in if you're busy."

Edith gave him a skeptical look. "Won't that let daylight in on the majesty?"

"That I answer the door myself?" Bill smiled. "I'm hoping that if I let her in after she sees the house, she'll be impressed by my unspoiled humility."

"Oh, right," said Edith. "Unspoiled humility. That's you. Well, if you don't need me to polish your halo, I'll just go back to typing up the bills."

Bill waved her away. "I can handle the clients, but if any more of Geoffrey's workmen show up in coveralls, carrying paint cans or wallpaper rolls, you deal with them!"

Danville had changed a lot in forty-odd years. Hillman Randolph studied the fleeting landscapes as he drove along the road that led to the Dolan place. There were just enough familiar landmarks to reassure him that he wasn't lost. It had been a long drive up from Georgia, and a tiring one for a man his age, but perhaps the most tiring part of the journey had been forcing himself to remember the last time he'd been in Danville: 1953. Try as he might, he couldn't recall that night with any clarity. By the time he woke up days later in the burn center of Duke Hospital in Durham, North Carolina, he was too ill to be questioned, and too consumed with pain for rational thought. He had been fortunate that his accident was south of Danville, only an hour away from Duke University's excellent medical facilities. Otherwise he wouldn't have survived at all. Even with the best treatment available, it had been a near thing, and it had taken all the strength of his young body to pull him through. Sometimes he mused on the irony of the great efforts expended to save him. If the law enforcement people had known who he really was—or more precisely who he wasn't—would they have tried so hard to save him?

Somehow, between the pain, the sedatives, and the reconstructive therapy, he had let himself become the man they mistook him for, and his own past slid away into a blur of confused images. The only thing that stood out with any clarity was the memory of Jack Dolan, who was supposed to be dead, just as he had been presumed dead. In a way he was, he thought. Maybe the real Hillman Randolph had died in Danville that night, but after all, it was his life that continued, even if a stand-in was now playing the part. First fear and then apathy had kept him from returning to Virginia, and soon his old life had become part of the mists. Until now. Whatever happened, whether they arrested him or not, he was going back. Jack Dolan was still alive.

Carla Larkin's pretty face had hardened into a sullen glare. "All right," she told her partner. "I made the phone call like you asked me to, but I still don't see why we're doing this. I mean, what have you got against this guy? It's not like he's some leering old drunk in a roadhouse. The guy I called is just minding his own business, working in his own office, so what's the point of hitting on him?"

P. J. Purdue shrugged. "He's male, isn't he? Besides, he's not important."

"Then why do I have to do it?" asked Carla. "When I bought the handcuffs, you said one more, right? And so when we got gas at that truck stop on I-81, I picked up that big guy in the Kenworth. He was practically drooling into my coffee, and he propositioned me. So, okay, he had it coming, and I'd love to have been a fly on the wall when his buddies found him naked, handcuffed to his steering wheel, but I thought we agreed that we were going to quit. As soon as the cops talk to that trucker, they'll know who we are and what state we're in. Sooner or later they'll track us down."

"Not if we keep moving." Purdue was sitting in the driver's seat, eating a hamburger out of a paper wrapper. She looked tired, and in need of a bath and a change of clothes, but the look in her eyes said that they wouldn't be taking a break yet.

"I don't want to go back to prison," said Carla in a small voice. "You're a rich kid with a law degree. You can probably talk your way into probation, but when they catch me, they'll lock me up for good. Or at least until I'm old and ugly, which is the same thing. After that, no matter where I am, it'll be prison."

P. J. Purdue opened a road map. "This time tomorrow we can be in Canada," she said. "I promise, Carla. I promise."

Geoffrey Chandler never thought that he would owe his life to Louis L'Amour. Ordinarily he was not an admirer of Western novels—he wasn't even sure that he'd ever read one—but this time he had been desperate. He had an eight-hour drive ahead of him, and he was already tired when he started. Elizabeth, under the influence of her sedative, had fallen asleep within a few miles of leaving the parking lot at Cherry Hill, so there was no hope of having conversation to keep him awake.

Geoffrey stopped at a diner to get coffee—although he conceded that coffee could be a time waster on a long drive, since you do not buy coffee, you only rent it. On the counter beside the breath mints was a box of used audio books, a trucker's lending library, he gathered: something to do with your mind when all the roads began to look the same.

After carefully inspecting the tapes on offer and rejecting glitzy love stories and self-help tapes, Geoffrey decided to ride the asphalt trail with Louis L'Amour. He reasoned that forcing himself to concentrate on a spoken narrative would keep him awake, while soothing music from the radio would have the opposite effect. With a bag full of Louies and a couple of candy bars for good measure, Geoffrey climbed back into the car and headed north up I-77.

He thought about calling Bill to warn him of their impending arrival, but after rehearsing several versions of the conversation in his mind, he could think of no explanation that did not make it sound as if he belonged in Cherry Hill as well as Elizabeth. Besides, Bill had been so relieved to see him go that Geoffrey hated to disappoint him by announcing that he was, in fact, returning.

As the car began to pick up speed, Elizabeth stirred in her sleep. "Where are we?" she murmured, stifling a yawn.

Geoffrey sighed and pushed the first tape into the dashboard cassette player. "Back in the saddle again, podnuh."

Bill MacPherson opened the door with a tentative smile, in case he encountered a door-to-door evangelist instead of a prospective client. The smile froze when he saw the scarred face of an elderly man glaring back at him instead of the attractive young woman that the voice on the phone had seemed to promise.

"May I help you?" said Bill when he trusted himself to speak.

"I'm looking for Jack Dolan," the man said, peering past Bill as if he hoped to catch a glimpse of him.

"Well, he's around someplace," said Bill. "Probably in one of the outbuildings, pottering around. He usually turns up at mealtimes, though. Are you a friend of his?"

"We go back a long way," said the scarred man. "The outbuilding, you said? Don't trouble yourself. I can find them. Place hasn't changed much." He turned away before Bill could ask him anything else.

Bill would have caught up with the man, to help him search

----

for the elusive Mr. Jack, but before he could make up his mind to do so, another car swung into the circular drive, and Bill recognized the driver. At least, the long blonde hair and the lovely youthful face certainly matched his impression of the telephone voice of his prospective client. He hurried over to the car.

"Hello!" he said with a much more genuine smile. "I'm Bill MacPherson. Did you call just a little while ago?"

As she slid out of the car, the young woman returned his smile. She was wearing a short skirt with a twinset and a string of pearls, and she might have been anyone from a swimsuit model to a brain surgeon. Bill hardly cared. His instincts for gallantry were roused. She was so lovely that he decided to take her case no matter what. "I did call you," she said. "You just have to do something about my car."

"Umm . . . I'm an attorney," said Bill. He sounded regretful, as if he considered his years in law school a complete waste of time if what this enchanting creature actually needed was an auto mechanic.

"Well, of course you are!" she said, laughing up at him as if that were the wittiest thing anyone had ever said. "And I want you to go after the mechanic that charged me a fortune and then ruined my engine. Did you hear that noise it was making as I drove in?"

Bill shook his head. His senses at the time had been focused on vision rather than sound. "I'm not sure I could tell anything if I did," he admitted. "But that's okay. We can get expert witnesses. Why don't you come inside where I can take notes, and tell me what the problem is?"

She shook her head. "I'd be just hopeless at trying to explain mechanical problems. Let me take you for a spin, and you listen to the engine, and then I'll answer all your questions—if I can, that is." She unsheathed another dazzling smile. "You're not afraid of being kidnapped, are you?"

"Of course not!" said Bill, without putting his brain in gear. As he got into the passenger seat of the woman's car, he found himself thinking about his old roommate Milo Gordon for the first time in months.

There was only one chair in the outbuilding that served as a storage shed for the big house. It was a battered aluminum lawn chair, whose webbing had begun to fray, so that sitting down in it was a form of gambling. When none of his guests expressed an interest in pushing their luck, Jack Dolan himself sat down in it, with his back to the one bare lightbulb dangling from an insulated wire in the rafters. Three men squatted in the dirt in front of him, getting up occasionally to stretch their legs—they weren't what you'd call young, either, but compared to Old Man Dolan, they were teenagers. One of them wore jeans and a plaid shirt, but the other two were in shirts and ties. They looked as if they knew how out of place they were in a storage shed, but nobody spoke. They waited politely while the ancient man in the lawn chair picked up a mason jar full of colorless liquid, unscrewed the lid, and passed it to one of his guests.

Dutifully, the man took a swig, wheezed, and handed it off to the man on his left, who sipped warily and pushed the jar toward his companion. "Well," said the first man, a bit hoarsely. "That'll take the paint off the wall, Mr. Dolan. I can see you haven't lost the touch."

The old man beamed in the half darkness. "Give me a little

backing and a lot of help with the lifting, and there's still a fortune to be made with that stuff. It's the best."

"I'm sure it is, sir."

"Takes a lot of sugar, though," Mr. Jack confided. "More than I can carry."

The three men looked at one another. At last, the man in the plaid shirt said, "I'm sure it's an art form, Mr. Jack, but the fact is, you know, bootlegging just isn't the moneymaker that it was in your day. I mean, even a huge operation—not your little bitty still in the basement there—even a professional concern is just not going to be cost-effective these days. The money, I'm sorry to say, is in drugs, and I know that being a gentleman of the old school, you don't hold with that any more than we do."

"Never could make plants grow," said Mr. Jack. "Especially indoors."

"I expect it's complicated," the spokesman agreed, glancing nervously at his companions. "But what we're trying to explain to you, sir, is that we're not really interested in starting you up in business again. It's still illegal, you know." He softened his words with a chuckle. "If a man can't retire at ninety-two, it's a sad old world, and that's a fact."

The man in the red tie spoke up. "I think my father may have given you the wrong idea about that when he spoke to you in Hardee's the other day."

"What we do want," said his companion, "is to interview you and to see—possibly even to buy—any photographs you may have of your operation in the late nineteen-forties."

Jack Dolan stared at the trio, mistrusting his hearing. "Photee-graphs?"

"And interviews. Tape-recorded interviews. We're doing a project." Having said that, the man felt even more like a teenager, but he hurried on into an explanation. "We have a couple of projects, actually. Jim here—" He indicated the short man in the red tie. "It was his dad who spoke to you at Hardee's—Jim is starting up an exhibit for the history museum: Moonshining in Southside Virginia. He wants to do an oral history project, interviewing some of the old-timers, and he needs to borrow photos of stills that he can enlarge to illustrate the exhibit."

"Museum?" Mr. Jack blinked at them.

After an awkward pause, the spokesman said, "We're history professors, Mr. Jack. I thought you knew that. No? Jim's father didn't mention it? Well, he has a strange sense of humor sometimes. Anyhow, as I said, Jim is doing a moonshining exhibit, and Fred and I are working on a screenplay. It's sort of a Butch Cassidy yarn, set in Virginia in the Forties. We'd like to base the main character on you. Sort of a last-outlaw-stranded-in-the-brave-new-world story. We'd have to make changes, of course, but basically we want to tell your story."

"Hadn't you better wait and see how it ends?" said a voice from the darkness.

Not even on his most competent days would Bill Mac-Pherson ever be mistaken for someone knowledgeable about mechanical devices. Therefore, he was reluctant to tell his beautiful new client that she was wasting her time driving him around and expecting him to detect any engine problems in her car. To Bill, the motor sounded perfectly fine. It usually took

smoke pouring out from under the hood to alert him to any dif-
ficulties in his own car, but he decided not to mention that,
either.

Throughout the drive of five minutes or so down the
tree-lined country road leading away from Danville, the two occupants of the vehicle had maintained an expectant silence,
waiting for the sound of mechanical disaster, but so far the car
had purred along, defying all expectations. Bill glanced at his
watch. It was nearly four o'clock, and if he wanted to take down
the pertinent information about the case from his new client before quitting time, they ought to get back to the office and get
started on the paperwork. He was fairly sure that a longer drive
would not enlighten him in the least, although the scenery—by
which he meant the driver—was not unpleasant.

"We ought to head back," he said. "I'll be happy to take
your word for the car problem until we can get an independent
mechanic. . . ."

Thunk!

Suddenly he did hear it: a dull thunk of metal striking
metal. He started to speak, but the young woman motioned for
him to keep quiet. Scarcely daring to breathe, they listened.

Another thunk.

But it wasn't coming from the engine. It sounded . . . it was
impossible, of course, Bill told himself . . . but it sounded as if it
were coming from behind them. From the trunk.

"Stop the car," said Bill softly.

There was no other traffic on the road, and they were now
on a level straightaway of two-lane blacktop bordered on either
side with fenced-in cow pastures. Moments after Bill had spoken, his companion slowed the car and eased off the road. Just

before she cut the engine, another thunk echoed through the car. Bill sprang out and went around to the back of the car. His mind had just enough time to register "Tennessee license plates. Odd." when the young woman bent forward and put the key in the lock of the trunk. An instant later the lid sprang open, and Bill found himself face-to-face with another blonde, this one pointing a can of Mace directly at his face.

Bill slammed the trunk and spun around just as the driver made a grab for his arm. Part of his brain registered the fact that she was not armed, except with a pair of handcuffs, which she was trying to use like brass knuckles. No problem, thought Bill. He had a sister nearly his own age: He'd had half a lifetime of ex-perience fighting girls, and no compunction about it. He had to admit to himself, though, that perhaps his most useful combat training had been playing the dummy for A. P. Hill's martial arts practice. From time to time Powell Hill would come back from class with a new self-defense move she wanted to demonstrate to Edith, and, in the absence of anyone actually dangerous, Bill would be drafted to play the attacker. These sessions always ended with him dutifully crashing to the floor, but, bruises aside, the experience had been an educational one. His instincts of self-preservation impelled him to learn the moves, and eventu-ally he became so hard to defeat that A. P. Hill had abandoned the demonstrations and enrolled Edith in the class with her instead.

After months of being on the receiving end of A. P. Hill's best moves, and learning to counteract them, the beauti-ful stranger with the handcuffs posed no problem at all. After a minor gash and one resounding blow to his shoulder that would probably turn purple in a couple of hours, Bill managed to subdue his assailant and pin her to the ground. Very considerate of her to provide handcuffs, he thought, fishing them out of the mud. He snapped the handcuffs on one wrist, and dragged her to the back door of the passenger side of the car. She wasn't fighting any longer. Her face was smeared with dirt, and her breath was coming in quick gasps. She had hit the ground with more force than was strictly necessary, but Bill, who had no idea what was going on, was taking no chances.

By the time he had slid the chain of the handcuffs through the door's armrest and handcuffed her other wrist, she was crying softly.

A phrase that A. P. Hill occasionally used rose unbidden to his mind. Testosterone poisoning. An apt diagnosis, he thought ruefully. He had been on the verge of making a possibly fatal mistake just because he had been bewitched by a pretty face. Powell would never let him live it down.

"Don't bother to cry," he told the woman. "I know that trick. I have a kid sister. Now, are you going to tell me what the hell is going on?"

Through a curtain of tangled blonde hair, the young woman looked up at him with a misty, pleading smile. "I just found you so-oo attractive," she murmured. "And I got this crazy idea that we could have some really kinky sex if—"

"Oh, save it," said Bill. "The porn film as documentary? I don't think so. Do you mean to tell me that men actually fall for that line?"

She shrugged philosophically. "In my experience: invariably."

He checked to make sure that the handcuffs were locked,

and that she could not slip the chain out from beneath the armrest. Then he slammed the door and retrieved the car keys from the ground behind the car.

Another thunk came from the depths of the trunk.

"You're staying in there!" Bill yelled, tapping on the lid. "Until I get some answers, whoever you are."

That face looked familiar somehow. On a glimpse of less than five seconds, he couldn't place it, though. With a shrug, Bill climbed into the driver's seat and turned the car back toward the direction of his office. Let the police sort it out, he thought. So much for his beautiful new client, he thought ruefully. On the other hand, he might have grounds for a lawsuit of his own. He brightened considerably at the prospect, and drove back to the house, keeping one eye on the prisoner in the backseat and weighing legal strategies, while the thumping from the trunk grew louder and more insistent.

The three history professors had gone. Mr. Jack, still sitting in his battered aluminum lawn chair, looked up at the shadowy figure silhouetted by the dangling lightbulb. He did not seem particularly upset by the intruder. In ninety-two years, he'd had a lot of time to get used to the idea of death, and he found that it didn't impress him as much as it used to. He had even outlived the threat of jail, because no jury in Virginia was going to send a frail old man of ninety-something to prison, no matter what his crimes. Being ninety was a prison.

"Well?" he said to the man in the shadows. "Were you looking for me?"

"I thought you were dead, Jack."

"Not quite!" snapped the old man. "And I'm not ready to be installed in any damn museum, neither!"

The man knelt down so that the light shone on his face. "Do you know who I am?" he said softly.

Jack Dolan peered into the scarred face of an old man—not as old as he was, but still well past the plump vigor of middle age. "I've no idea," he said flatly.

"I forget myself sometimes," said the man. "It's been decades since I even said the name. I go by Hillman Randolph these days. Most of the time I forget it isn't who I am."

Jack Dolan strained to recognize the voice, but age had changed it beyond anything he would find familiar. The name, though. Hillman Randolph. Just a minute . . .

"The lawman?" he said. "The one in the accident?"

The man nodded.

"Is that how you got those burns?"

"It is."

The old man shook his head. "It's a pity," he said at last. "But you're a tad late to be coming after me, whether it's revenge you want or money. Same thing, I reckon."

Hillman Randolph looked at the shrunken old man in the lawn chair. He'd heard the three professors offer to make a screenplay of the old man's life, as if it were already over. The man was a museum piece. Just because he was alive didn't mean the past wasn't dead.

"I wanted to ask you what happened that night," Randolph said at last. "Just between you and me. I'm retired, you know. No gun. No badge. Man to man. What happened?"

The old man sighed. "You were there—for the end of it,

---

anyhow. I'll bet you wish you hadn't been. The beginning wasn't all that pretty, either. We were sending out a shipment—sort of a sample. A club in Richmond might put a lot of business our way if we could make bourbon good enough to fool their regulars—only cheaper. A whole lot cheaper, because we wouldn't be paying any whiskey tax to Uncle Sam. Well, as we were loading up the car, a fellow showed up here. Never mind his name. He never amounted to much, but he thought it was because I stood in his way. You know who he was. He's the one that tipped you people off."

"I remember." Hillman Randolph didn't know if that part of the story was true. He had never dared to ask who had tipped off the feds, because they thought that, as one of them, he already knew. "Go on."

"I reckon the fellow came to gloat. We had words, anyhow, and he wasn't nearly as good at taking insults as he was at delivering 'em. After one of mine he went for his pistol. And I went for mine."

"Just like the Wild West," said Hillman Randolph with a sneer in his voice. "A shoot-out at the O.K. Corral."

"Shoot-outs aren't quaint," said Jack Dolan. "They leave your heart pounding cold blood into what feels like a hollow cavity where your insides ought to be. It's a feeling you don't forget."

Randolph nodded. "Like burns," he said. "Did anybody see the fight?"

"Larry did. No. No, I reckon he didn't. Larry was outside, filling up the gas tank."

"Larry?"

"Larry Garrison. A fine young man. Like a son to me."

Hillman Randolph hesitated for a moment, but then he said, "So what did you do with the man you'd shot?"

"Put him in the backseat. We figured on dumping him in the woods somewhere between here and Richmond, and hoping he wouldn't be found until he was old bones."

"But instead you ran into a roadblock just outside Danville, and when you tried to drive through it—"

"Larry was driving. Poor soul."

"Your car crashed into the agents' cars, and both cars caught fire."

"Whiskey," said Jack Dolan sadly. "It does burn something fierce."

"You got away, and the corpse and the other man were burned up in the wreck."

"That's right. I was thrown clear and had a few broken bones and some gashes to show for it, but they were so busy with the wreck, they didn't notice me in the weeds, and I crawled away." He sighed. "Wish I could have saved Larry, though."

"Larry Garrison." After all these years the name sounded strange on his tongue.

"Finest man I ever knew, young as he was. I was going to make him a partner. Oh, you never saw the like of him. Brave. Smart. Son I always wanted." The old man's voice quavered. "I go to his grave every now and again just to talk."

"He's buried in Danville?"

"Paid for the stone myself," said Jack Dolan. "His family wasn't well off. But he deserved the best."

The lawman said nothing. Mr. Jack thought he saw him

wipe away a tear with the sleeve of his jacket. "Now, what was it you came about?" he asked after a moment's silence.

The man coughed. "Oh, just that," he said. "Just to hear what really happened. So it was self-defense, and I wondered about the other man with you. The one who died."

"Hasn't a day gone by that I haven't missed him," said Mr. Jack. "Not a day."

The stranger stood up. "Well, I'll be going now," he said. "I just heard you were still alive, and I wanted to know ..." There was a tremor in his voice, and he blundered out of the storage building without a backward glance.

After the door had closed behind the visitor, Jack Dolan sat in his lawn chair for a good ten more minutes, until he was certain that the man had driven away. That had been a close call. A close call indeed. He leaned back and let out a deep breath, feeling his heart pounding against his ribs.

Who would have thought that old Larry Garrison had been the one to survive that wreck instead of the lawman? He shook his head. Face like a jack-o'-lantern. Larry Garrison. That good for nothing so-and-so hadn't even had the sense to die. What a shock to find him back, stupid as ever, after all these years.

Mr. Jack struggled to his feet. Bound to be time for his afternoon snack, he thought. He must remind them to buy more sugar.

"I came back to save you," said A. P. Hill.

"Your timing was a little off, but thanks," said Bill. He was sitting at the desk in his new office, composing an account of his

----

statement for the Danville police on his word processor. "So you knew I was going to be kidnapped?"

"No. Well, I knew that P. J. Purdue was—"

"Purdue. From law school? Pit-bull Purdue?" Bill's eyes widened. "That's who she was. The one in the trunk. I thought she looked familiar. I guess that's why they didn't approach me together. She was afraid I'd recognize her."

"Yes. The other woman is a prisoner whom Purdue was representing. She helped the woman escape, and as fugitives the two of them have been robbing men and stealing their cars."

"Okay," said Bill. "But what does this have to do with me?"

"Nothing. You're my partner, though, and it had a lot to do with me."

"With you?" Bill swung his chair around to face her. "With you."

"Yes. The business about leaving guys naked and hand-cuffed . . . Well, Purdue and I did that once . . . back in college." She did not look at him once as she went through a wooden recitation of the facts concerning the abduction of Milo Gordon.

Bill said nothing. He appeared to be thinking things over. At last he said, "You think Purdue wanted you to join the gang, and when you wouldn't, you think she went after me in order to embarrass you?"

"Something like that."

Bill thought some more. "Can I sue her?"

"No. I'm going to defend her. Before I came in I spoke to her for just a second. She's out there in the police car, and I said I'd have to go in and talk to you, but that I'd be back to discuss her case." She sighed. "Purdue was a friend. I can't let her throw her life away."

Bill frowned. "Are you even going to comment on the new house?"

A. P. Hill barely glanced at her surroundings. "It's great, Bill," she said. "I'll just go talk to Purdue, and then you can give me the tour."

She walked out into the front hall and opened the door. A second later she was back at Bill's desk. "You'd better call the police," she said. "The police car is gone."

"They'll be at the station," said Bill. "Just go and interview her there."

"I don't think so," said A. P. Hill. "There's a uniformed policeman out there handcuffed to a tree."

Bill ran for the window. "Is that a gag in his mouth?"

A. P. Hill nodded sadly. "Pantyhose."

"We came to save you," said Elizabeth MacPherson. Her medication had worn off during the long drive north from Georgia, and now she was suffering from nothing more serious than bereavement and an overdose of Louis L'Amour.

"I have been saved, thank you," said Bill. "The two ladies are still at large, but they are believed to be headed for Canada."

"Ladies?" said Elizabeth. Geoffrey, who had escorted her into the house, was slumped in an armchair by the fireplace, too exhausted to speak. He kept closing his eyes, and his head jerked as he tried to force himself to stay awake. "What ladies?"

"Some outlaw friends of Powell's," said Bill. "Blondes with handcuffs. Sounds like a movie of the week, doesn't it? Never mind that. What exactly were you going to save me from?"

"One of the patients at Cherry Hill . . ."

"An escaped mental patient. Oh, good." Bill sighed.

His sister winced. Technically she was an escaped mental patient, but she wisely refrained from pointing this out. "He was pretending to be a federal agent. Well, a retired federal agent. But he knew Jack Dolan, who he claims was a murderer, and we think he came up here to kill him. He's about seventy with a badly scarred face."

Bill nodded. "Oh. Him. He was here."

"He was?"

"Hours ago."

Elizabeth opened her mouth and closed it again.

"He left," said Bill.

"Where's Jack Dolan then?"

"In the kitchen," said Edith from the open door. "He's stealing sugar."

"Stealing . . ."

"He thinks I don't know. I figure it'll keep him busy though. Every man should have a hobby. I think there's a still in the storage building."

"That's illegal!" said A. P. Hill.

"Not unless he tries to sell it," said Edith. "Let's leave him alone. I'll watch him. I think we ought to let him cater the Christmas party."

Bill turned back to Elizabeth. "You're supposed to be in Georgia," he said, with the air of one who has found one certainty in a haystack of ambiguities.

"Umm . . . yes."

"Did Cherry Hill release you?"

- -

"Not exactly. Geoffrey got permission to take me out to dinner . . . yesterday."

"Oh." Bill sighed. At this point he didn't think he could cope with any more. "What are you going to do?"

Elizabeth considered it. "I think I'm going to go back," she said. "I have some issues to work through. I'll let Geoffrey get a good night's sleep first, though. And this time I'll do the driving."

Chapter 15

"You're back," said Emma O., glancing up from her notebook. There was no surprise in her voice. Either Emma O. always knew everything, or else she was very good at pretending she did.

"Yes," said Elizabeth. "I'm back. I thought as long as I'm paying for this, I might as well finish out the month."

"So they didn't bring you back in a straitjacket?"

"No."

"Oh. We all thought you'd flipped out when you finally realized that your husband was really dead."

"No," said Elizabeth. "I think I knew it all along, really. It's just easier to cling to false hope than it is to pick yourself up and start over with nothing. Right now, the rest of my life looks like a long, empty tunnel, and I didn't want to face it."

Emma O. nodded. "Yeah. They tell me something always turns up, though, if you hang in there." She looked at her scarred wrists for a moment, and then she went back to writing in her notebook.

"Did anything happen while I was gone?"

Emma O. looked up with her customary smirk. "Anything happen? Well, let's see . . . Seraphin gained thirty pounds, and Rose lost thirty. Mrs. Nicholson became engaged to Prince Andrew, and I was voted Miss Congeniality in the Miss Georgia Pageant."

"So . . . nothing changed."

"Nothing ever changes." Shrugging, Emma went back to her notebook. "There's probably more drama in state mental hospitals, but we're an exclusive private place. Not much excitement. Besides, this isn't life. It's the green room. Sometimes people get out of here, but they don't get better."

"I'm going to get better," said Elizabeth. "Whatever it takes to stop feeling like this, I'll do it."

Emma O. nodded. "Whatever," she said, still scribbling.

"Are you writing another letter of apology?" asked Elizabeth.

"Nah. Dr. Shokie had a new brainstorm. Now I'm making a list of my friends," she announced. "Or trying to. It's hard to know if you have any, isn't it?"

"No, Emma," said Elizabeth, thinking of Geoffrey's long drive back to where he had just come from in Virginia. "It's easy. Try asking someone to do something extremely inconvenient for an insane reason, and if they do it, they're your friend. But, here's the tricky part: You have to be prepared to do the same thing for them whenever they ask. So most people's list of friends is pretty short. But even one is enough."

It was as good a reason to go on as any.

"I should have told you," said A. P. Hill. "I should have trusted you. I guess I did trust you, really. I was just afraid you'd laugh at me. I was too proud to tell you what an idiot I had been as an undergraduate."

"Well, I'm not giving you my blessing for your terrorist activities," said Bill. "But in Milo Gordon's case, you may have done some good. He wasn't nearly that much of a jerk by the time I roomed with him. In fact, my sister dated him, did I tell you?"

"I knew that. I was afraid you'd never forgive me for what we did to your friend."

"You're my friend," said Bill. "Try to remember that."

A. P. Hill nodded. Time to change the subject, she thought. "Where do you suppose Purdue and Larkin are now?"

"Canada, I hope. There must be some places where you can cross the border without an I.D."

"They may have I.D.s by now."

"True. Anybody who wears handcuff keys for earrings wouldn't let a little thing like an international border stop her."

"They didn't hurt anybody," said A. P. Hill.

"Aside from dignity," Bill pointed out. He realized that if he had been one of the PMS Outlaws' victims, he might be feeling less charitable toward them.

"I haven't even seen the new place yet," said A. P. Hill, looking around her at the old money elegance of Bill's office. "Will you give me that tour now?"

"The upstairs isn't finished yet," Bill told her as they walked out into the hall. "So if you want your apartment's color scheme to be pink, you just say so. . . ."

"Pink!"

Group therapy still took place in the sunny ground-floor conference room overlooking the flower garden. Hillman Randolph had not returned, and Lisa Lynn was gone, but otherwise the group seemed unchanged. Petress was the last person to arrive, and the men and women still sat in segregated bunches, as if they were schoolchildren.

"Now that you have accepted your loss," Warburton said to Elizabeth, "I think it is time for you to try an exercise that will help you get in touch with your feelings."

Elizabeth smiled. "I took pills to keep from getting in touch with my feelings."

"Yes, but now you have to face those feelings."

She looked uneasy. "What did you have in mind?"

Warburton smiled. "It's a role-playing exercise. I want you to choose someone from the group to be Cameron. You may select anyone, for any reason. But during the exercise you must react to that person as if he were Cameron. Do you understand?"

"I guess so. I don't see where you're going with this, though."

"Try it."

Elizabeth studied the faces of her fellow patients. She eliminated the women without a second glance. That left Petress, Matt Pennington, the amiable lawyer whose name escaped her, and Clifford Allen, the sullen burglar. Without giving herself any

----

time to analyze her choice, Elizabeth said, "Clifford. I choose Clifford."

As she said it, she noted a fleeting look of surprise on Warburton's face. The nurse must have been expecting Elizabeth to select the gentle, friendly Matt Pennington as her surrogate loved one, but as soon as she'd said Clifford's name, Elizabeth felt the rightness of her choice. "Clifford."

With his customary loud sigh of exasperation, Clifford Allen pushed himself out of his chair, pushed the tail of his shirt back into his jeans, and stepped into the center of the room to face Elizabeth.

The rest of the group watched in silence.

"Now," said Warburton. "Clifford, you know what to do."

He nodded. Looking less smug than usual.

"Elizabeth, you can talk to Cameron. He will not reply to you. He will not react. He will simply . . . be there to listen. You may begin."

Clifford stood still, hands at his sides, watching her with an impassive face. For once, there was no mockery in his eyes, only the calmness of waiting.

Elizabeth looked at his shirt, not at his face, as she tried to summon up an image of Cameron Dawson. "I miss you, Cameron," she began in a hesitant voice. "It's really lonely without you. And the worst part is not even knowing what happened."

Clifford said nothing.

"I stayed in Edinburgh as long as I could. I badgered the searchers until they were sick of the sight of me. I walked the beach. I wouldn't give up."

Opposite her, the figure stood motionless.

"I don't know what I'm going to do without you. It seems so disloyal to give up without any proof. Like abandoning you."

Through her tears, the man's shape blurred.

"But why shouldn't I abandon you? Why shouldn't I? Didn't you abandon me? Didn't you go out alone in that stupid boat even when I asked you not to? And I asked to go along and what did you say? 'Too much we-erk to do, dear. Can't stand any distractions.' I was a distraction. Oh, yes. The work came first, didn't it? I was an afterthought. If there weren't any seals to be tracked, or paperwork to catch up on, you might spend an evening with me."

The man was silent.

"When did my wishes ever matter to you? Did you ever think what would happen if you got yourself killed in a storm at sea? What would I do, widowed before I'm thirty? What am I supposed to do, now that you're gone forever, and past caring about me? What am I supposed to do? Find somebody else?"

He stood facing her. Impassive.

"Well, why shouldn't I? What else am I supposed to do? Kill myself? Am I supposed to spend the rest of my life building shrines to you? It's always you, isn't it? I hate you, Cameron! You were thoughtless, and selfish, and inconsiderate, and pig-headed. You were an arrogant fool who thought that he and his little boat could take on the great North Atlantic. Well, you were wrong! And you died for it, but so what? Your suffering was over in a couple of minutes. Two minutes? Five? I'm the one who has to hurt for years. I'm the one who's hurting after all this time. Damn you, Cameron! Damn you! Damn you!"

Elizabeth began to cry, and as she stepped forward to beat

---

her fist against the impassive figure of a man before her, Clifford took one step back. Out of her reach.

She stood alone in the circle and cried.

Emma O. was watching *Deep Space Nine* on the television in the patients' lounge. She was alone, but it would have surprised her to be told so. Half her friends were right there on the screen in their Star Fleet uniforms, and she valued their company above all others. They had made the top of her list of friends. When Elizabeth MacPherson, dressed in street clothes and carrying a purse, came in to say goodbye, Emma forced herself to glance away from the flickering screen.

"So you're getting out legally this time, huh?" she said.

"That's right," said Elizabeth. "That last session with Clifford finally did it. I let it all out. I think it's time to start moving forward now."

Emma nodded, her eyes straying back to the space station. She knew this episode. There were still a few more minutes before the good-looking Dr. Bashir appeared in the program, and then nothing could distract her from the screen. "Well, good luck," she said. "I hope things work out for you."

"You, too, Emma," said Elizabeth. She tried to think of something else to say, but even insincere pleasantries like "I'll miss you" or "I'll write" seemed wasted in the vastness of Emma's indifference.

At that moment a man poked his head into the lounge. "*Deep Space Nine?*" he said. "Wish I had time to watch it with you, Emma. Hope it's a good one. Bye now."

Emma O. waved toward the door without looking up, but the man was already gone.

Elizabeth was still standing there, though, staring first at the door and then back at the Trekkie on the sofa. At last she said, "Emma, could I ask you something?"

"Shoot."

"That man just now in the doorway? Was that kindly old Dr. Dunkenburger?"

"Yep."

"The shrink I've been talking to while I was here?"

"Yep."

"And is Dr. Dunkenburger about thirty-five years old . . . with wavy blond hair . . . Robert Redford's features . . . and the body of a quarterback?"

"Yep."

Elizabeth thought about it. "I'm getting well, aren't I?"

Emma O. grinned at her. "Yep," she said, and turned up the sound.

ABOUT THE AUTHOR

SHARYN MCCRUMB is a *New York Times* best-selling author whose work has been cited for "Outstanding Contribution to Appalachian Literature." She has received the Chaffin and Plattner Awards for Southern fiction, two Best Appalachian Novel awards, and many other honors. She launched her acclaimed Appalachian Ballad novel series with *If Ever I Return, Pretty Peggy-O.*

Sharyn McCrumb has been writer-in-residence at King College (Tennessee) and Shepherd College (West Virginia), and she has lectured on her work at universities and libraries throughout the United States and Europe. She lives and writes in the Virginia Blue Ridge Mountains.